To Norty:

A Daughter

To Norty:
A Daughter

Charlotte Bishop

Order this book online at www.trafford.com
or email orders@trafford.com

Most Trafford titles are also available at major online book retailers.

Printed in the United States of America.

ISBN: 978-1-4269-5704-8 (sc)
ISBN: 978-1-4269-5705-5 (hc)
ISBN: 978-1-4269-5706-2 (e)

Library of Congress Control Number: 2011902477

Trafford rev. 07/30/2011

 www.trafford.com

North America & international
toll-free: 1 888 232 4444 (USA & Canada)
phone: 250 383 6864 ♦ fax: 812 355 4082

To Norty, A Daughter

For one year Norty had carried her daughter within her, and the year had dragged slowly by. Now the time was here, her daughter was being born at last. She knew her child to be female; her mind was linked with her as it was with her sisters, and through the linking she knew where her sisters were and, to a point, their thoughts.

Throughout the year she had cursed the Gods elves must carry their unborn three months longer than other races, yet she realised it was a gift also; they were born the most intelligent of all the races.

Shunning the tradition of midwives attending the birth she preferred the company and help of her sisters. Her younger sister, Malinna, was there and would manage better than anyone. Through the linking she would feel her hopes and fears, and those of her unborn niece.

Her breathing was short and heavy but with little pain, only anticipation, and she began to wonder how her mother had coped with the birth of three children; one was enough for her at this moment.

Her breathing increased in rapidity as the moment of birth drew near, sending her mind wondering back to the days of her childhood in the tree top city of the wood elves, when they had discovered their minds were unlike others. Never had any minds been linked; they thought were as one, acted as one, and fought as one.

As her child moved downwards, eager for life outside of her, her mind raced through the years to the time they left the woods to enter training in their professions. The elves were astounded when each refused the path of their parents, choosing ways different to the druids to whom they were born. Never before had it happened in elfin memory, and their memory was long, measured in over five hundred years.

Now, as her daughter's head began to emerge, her mind reached the quest for which the Gods had given them their lives. She remembered the battle and how they had fought alongside their protectors, given to them at their birth by the Gods.

Finglas was her protector, and now husband. Xandorian of the gnomes had sworn in protection of Icee; the dwarf, Keitun, had sworn to Malinna.

She recalled how her sisters and herself had almost died before they realised the Gods had given form to the mystical thing called love, and it had fought back with the only power it knew; each time any had tried to harm and hurt her they had also harmed someone they loved. With realisation came surrender. They could not, should not and would not kill love, even though the Gods themselves had demanded it. They laid down their weapons and refused the fight; knowing the world would be destroyed because of their failure. Yet it was no failure, the Gods had sought to test the love of one for another, and in their surrender they won the battle, their world survived.

With her child cradled gently in her arms she wept for she knew love had indeed survived; there could be no more proof than the new life she smiled down on, "Welcome. Welcome, Nortee, to the land of the wood elves, the land of your father and your mother."

As she gazed at her child she saw bright green eyes matching her own, hair just as yellow, only shoulder length, while hers hung to the waist. Druid fashion was for their hair to be worn short, as it had been since the first druids were known in the lands. Her mother, Elesee, had fought hard against the council for hers to grow free and wild, now her daughter would also have the right choose how hers was to be worn.

Sitting beside her Malinna looked from daughter to mother, "A beautiful child she is, sister. She will follow the path of her mother, an enchantress she will be."

"We were born to druids and I joined in wedlock a druid. Ours is the first union of mixed professions in the history of elfin kind. I fear what she may not be."

"Your fears are groundless. Dismiss them and let her be what she will be."

"How may I dismiss them? It is my dread she may have none of the magic of Finglas or I. She would become an outcast, an Undesirable Elf."

"Look to her, she is as you, an enchantress, worry not."

"Worry will remain within me, I cannot deny my fears."

"I joined in wedlock to a druid yet a cleric I am. Soon I also will consent to be with child yet I will worry not over my child's profession."

"You know this has never happened, she is the first of her kind."

"You remember when we sat and thought of a child for you?"

"I remember well, yet I know not if we are blessed. New paths we travelled and our children will travel more."

"Then wish them well on their paths. We travelled ours and have been proud to do so, as I believe they will be proud of theirs."

"Three weeks I must wait to I see if she will carry a profession."

"She will carry your profession, sister, it is easy to see. Cease your worries."

The sound of footsteps pacing outside the room forced back the tears; she would not let him see them in her eyes at a time such as this, when happiness should reign supreme in her.

"I think my Finglas would see his daughter. He is not happy to wait."

Nodding Icee opened the door; he was at his wife's side in moments.

"All is well with you and Nortee?"

With Nortee wrapped in silks she offered her to him, "Your father wishes to show you the world to which you are born."

"Druid ways still run in your blood. You were shown the world on the day of your birth, now the time comes for our daughter to see it also."

He disappeared into the cool night holding her close to him for protection, "Trees, hear me. I hold before you my daughter Nortee. She is as one with you as you are one with her."

Giggling softly Icee sat with her sisters, "He is druid and must do his druid ways, yet it sounds strange to hear."

Malinna finished fussing over her sister, "As Flight will also show our child. I have rejected not the ways of the druids enough to deny him his rights."

For almost an hour he walked, his daughter held close, showing her all the wonders of the forest before resting, "River, hear me, I hold before you my daughter Nortee. She is as one with you as you are one with her."

With her still in his arms he smiled down at her once more. The year had also dragged by for him as much had done for his wife. He had thought this day would never arrive; she had refused to be with child when their love had first flourished. Now he walked with her in their forest and a deep contentment had settled on him. Yet he had to test her, to see if she would follow him and his ways.

He knew his wife would test her in three weeks time but he could not wait, he had to find out now. He should wait the three weeks, as his wife must, until he could test her to see if she would follow him and become a druid. He could not test her as it should be done, she was still far too young, but he had to find a way. As if in answer to his unvoiced prayer a wolf trotted into a clearing some fifty paces to his right. The test could begin, with baited breath he moved towards the wolf, kneeling down and calling softly to him. The wolf responded as he would to any druid who called to him.

Gently stroking him he whispered, "Wolf hear me, I hold before you my daughter Nortee. She is as one with you as you are one with her."

Sniffing the child he licked her face before turning and heading back into the forest.

He was elated, "You will be a druid, my daughter. The wolf loves you as he does all druids."

She gave a little giggle and seemed to smile at him, making him hold her closer, "You have the smile of your mother, little one, yet soon I would wish for you a brother but tell not your mother, I believe she will consent only to you. Come, we go to see your birthright, the city high in the trees and the home of your grandparents; Elesee and Juin have the Feast of Celebration prepared and will be eager to see you. No longer must I withhold from them the right to greet you."

Once more she giggled as the Goddess of Tranquillity closed her new eyes, and peaceful sleep found her.

"Your father rests, little one. Three weeks have passed and the time is here. They have taken so long, never are they this long when he is away from me, never this long whilst I carried you inside of me. Now we see if you follow your mother."

Placing her carefully in the chair she stepped back, arms reaching for her daughter, "Concentrate, little one, concentrate. Reach for me, please."

Almost instantly Nortee reached for her mother.

"Good, little one, yet the test has just begun. I pray you will pass."

Drawing a deep breath she raised her arms and, as they came down, she began her chant. Grey spheres of smoke covered her completely and, as the smoke cleared, a dwarf stood in her place.

The world became full of doubts for her, as moments seemed to turn to minutes and the minutes to hours. The wait was becoming unbearable for her and tension mounted. Her daughter was not reaching for her and her heart began to ache within her breast. To follow her she must see past the illusion she had cast, to see her mother.

Her daughter's head dropped to one side as she looked at the dwarf in front of her, and slowly a smile appeared on her face.

The heartaches ceased the instant her daughter reached for her and elation took hold. Screaming with pure joy she was still sobbing as he rushed into the room. Unable to control the feeling boiling within her she threw herself at him, "She sees her mother, she sees her!"

He realised what she had done, and thought of how slowly the weeks must have passed for her. With his wife so happy he could not speak of how the wolf had licked their daughter, "Would I could see her also."

Her hands rose once more, and as the grey spheres surrounding her vanished, she appeared to him as herself, "I am sorry, beloved, I was so happy for the moment I forgot myself."

Rushing to her daughter she picked her up, "Welcome to the world of the enchantress, little one; the world to which I welcome you."

He stroked his wife's face, "Now I think the worry stops, she follows her mother into the enchanters' guild."

"She sees through my illusion as only an enchanter may do. These weeks have been so hard to bear, yet I know you would have her follow you to the druids' guild."

Fishing beside the river he began to think once again of how Nortee was not to follow him but her mother. He had learned over the years how to hide his feelings from her, this time it had been easy. She was so excited with their daughter she had not noticed how he kept his body relaxed so she could not read it as easily as she did all she met.

'How could I have been so wrong, did not the wolf lick her face?'

His fist struck the ground to relieve the tension and frustration, as he continued to think of the events so newly in the past, 'It was me; it must have been me the wolf came to. It seems she will follow me not to the druids' guild, but to her mother's. Norty is pleased beyond which I have seen her before, and what must be must be.'

Malinna placed the wine glass back on the table, watching as Norty held hers almost to her lips, never drinking. She had asked her to visit in the new home Flight and she had set up, and her sister was impressed.

Her fingers snapped in front of her face, "Sister, return to me."

"I am sorry; Nortee would like other than milk and water."

"You feel the link so strong you know her tastes?"

"The link is strong with her, stronger than I feel my sisters, as strong as I feel Finglas."

"When my child is born I would wish the link to be as strong for me."

"I must go to her, her mind calls for me."

"Icee knows her needs; she will feed her the herbs and mashed roots."

"Icee would feed roots to all, it is her favourite of all foods, and she knows as I my little one's needs. Yet Nortee needs her mother also."

"I would have you come again; all has not yet been seen by you."

"I will return as asked, when Nortee is fed."

Sitting on the grass outside her home she watched as he played with their daughter, never was he as happy as when he was with her, "Speak your rhymes to her."

"She is too young to understand."

"I speak to her the words of the enchantress; she is not too young to hear the words of druids also."

"Her understanding would be limited."

"She understands more than you would know. Recite your rhymes for her; speak of the roots and leaves."

Without thinking he began the rhymes taught to him in the days before he had reached his first year, speaking of shining and dull leaves; of poisons and cures.

Satisfied she lay back and relaxed; her daughter was listening to him, head cocked slightly to one side, understanding the words, she could see it in her face as she watched her father intently. It had been almost two weeks since she had first spoken; exactly the same age as she was when her first words were uttered, but something gnawed at her mind, as yet too weak for her to know it was there.

With the passing of another month she found her daughter to be quick, the earlier gnawing at her mind still lay too deep beneath the surface to cause concern, "She grows so fast, soon her childhood will be over."

Elesee closed the book she was scribing into, "It is a gift our children grow so quickly to maturity yet also a curse, it gives us only half the time with them as the other races."

"I would speak with the Gods and ask such a gift be taken back; the time of childhood is precious."

"They have their ways; ours is to follow them."

"I question those ways, yet understand them."

Turning to her mother she looked at the closed the book on her lap, once in a while her mother would open the book to scribe into it, yet never for long.

"You scribe in the book once more, mother, and not once have you spoken to me of its contents. What do you place in its pages?"

"Words and drawing for another time."

"Will I be permitted to see the pages?"

"The answer is as before, it is not for now. Ask me no more."

Her attention returned once more to her husband and daughter as they played a chase game, watching as he taught her the ways to anticipate the moves of others, the ways in which the body alters slightly before it changes direction. For most of his moves she stayed close to him, yet she knew he was not trying to lose her. To do so at this early stage would discourage her, and she must learn fast, her very life would depend on his teachings. Pride flowed through her, she was learning so quickly.

Spinning round Finglas swept his arms down to pick her up and instantly Nortee dropped flat, but she was not quick enough, his arms went under her and threw her into the air, catching her as she dropped.

"Good, little one, yet you have a lot to learn."

"Again father, throw me again."

"Time for me to hide. Look to the east and count to five."

"Yes, father. One...."

Juin was watching Nortee as she raced to try to catch her father, "The Gods have their reasons, daughter. It is for them to decide and not for us."

Smiling as he leaned against a tree, seeming to disappear, to become one with it, she knew he was teasing their daughter, she was no druid, it would be hard at her age to see him and he knew it. Laughing softly as her daughter glanced round looking for her father her laughter stopped and she sat upright. Her daughter ran straight to him.

Now the gnawing voice in her mind was heard, and the worries began, "She cannot see him yet, mother."

"You are troubled, daughter?"

"Mother, she saw him, and almost instantly. She is enchantress not druid born. A druid of her age would find it hard to see him, yet she does."

"Her mind is linked to his; surely she would know his whereabouts?"

"The linking not yet so strong she would know exactly where he is. This game they have played often and never has she run to him as she does now. When she sees the anniversary of her first year I will take her to high elf city, Caspo Kwil will know the answers."

The city of the high elves was nothing like she has expected. The low murmur of noise was constant, replacing the sounds of the forest to which she was so used. Buildings of intricate lattice-worked wood and stone were abundant, yet built on the ground instead of high in the wide girth trees of her hometown. The shops fascinated her yet she never seemed to have enough time to investigate before her mother urged her onwards.

"Mother, it is not often you leave our city. Why do you do so now?"

Crouching down she held her at arm's length, "I leave often to attend training and to teach; now you have entered your second year this is your treat, to show you the land of the high elves were you will continue the training I have begun with you. Tomorrow you may spend all day looking in the shops and have you hearts desires. Today I have a friend or two I wish you to meet."

"There is more, mother, you hold back all I should know."

"So your father will remember and be on his travels once more."

"You wish him to leave us?"

"He must travel the lands as do all druids, it is within them. The call is in him once more yet he stays with us."

"He wishes to go yet he wishes to stay. It must be hard for him."

"I try to make the choice easier, if I remind him of the world outside of the forest he may choose to adventure again."

"But this will make you unhappy."

"His longing for travel is as much a part of his druid life as are the songs I greet the sun with some mornings. Always did he travel when I was a child as young as you, I missed him then and will miss him now."

"I will miss him also."

"You must say nothing to him, Nortee. He must be what he must be and he will return to us often, such will be our reward. While he is gone I will instruct you in song. I know the yearning is in you to greet the sun, it grows stronger in you with each passing month."

"I wish to greet the sun, to sing as sweet as you."

"Many sing so much the sweeter."

"I wish to learn all the ways you may teach."

"You have your life to learn, it must be taken slowly for there are other ways to learn also."

"I trust you to teach me all the ways."

"It is not for me to teach all, your father will instruct you also."

"Father cannot teach me the ways of an enchanter, mother."

"The ways of the elves must also be taught."

"Father teaches Lore to me."

"Lore is for guidance only, Nortee, our ways change yet you must learn the old ways; they will be with us for many years."

Bowing low she hugged him, "Nortee this is Caspo Kwil, my mentor and dearest friend."
"Sir, I am pleased to meet you. Mother has spoken often of your teaching and friendship."
"I have seen you not since three days after your birth, the time flies quicker as the year's progress."
"The years are not shown in your face, sir."
"Manners and charm of your mother, you are welcome here."
"Thank you, sir. I look forward to my days here when I am of age."
"Mentor, I come with reason. I wish an audience with you."
"Such is easy to see, I wondered when you would call on me. Sit and speak, Nortee will be well cared for."
His hand pulled a cord and they waited, the study door opening a few moments later as a dark elf entered.
Screaming she walked quickly to her, "Norty! May the Gods bless you."
"Pose! It has been months since last I saw you. I must visit more often."
Holding her in a warm embrace she looked down at the child next to her, "Your daughter has grown."
"Nortee this is Pose, a friend as dear as Caspo Kwil."
"Mother speaks highly of you."
"So, you nod in greeting."
"Mother instructs dark elves hate to bow and has tried to explain, yet many ways I do not understand. You are our mortal enemy and should be at war with mother yet are the closest of friends."
"I follow not the path once learned."
"Mother has spoken much of you and I have longed to meet you. I wish to know why is your skin is so blue, how did it come to be so, where is the city of your birth, may I see it? I have a hundred questions."
"Come, I have a class, after you may ask all you wish in my room."
With her mother's nod of permission she left with Pose, "I have heard you also mentor."
"This is a class who need special care."
"How so?"
"They are new to the ways of group instruction and left alone too long they will begin to play the games."
"Which games?"
Stopping at the end of the hall she motioned her to be quiet, "What do you hear from the training room of the first time students?"
"I hear nothing, Pose."
"Then they have begun against my instructions; time for the play to end."
"What games do they play?"
"Those forbidden for good reason; mind games may be dangerous if not supervised. Come."

Guiding her to a chair he insisted she sit, "No harm will befall her while she is with Pose, cease the worries. She is as powerful as my favourite student." Through worry still washing over her as they talked together she teased him, "And who may such a person be?"

"Worries crease your face."

"I am afraid for my little one, afraid of what she may be. She is enchantress born and sees through illusions as only we may do."

"Then an enchantress she will be."

"Yet she sees with the eyes of a druid, when Finglas hid she saw him with ease. The linking of her mind to his had no part in this."

"I see not why you worry. You have joined in wedlock to a druid and should expect her to be part of you both."

"She cannot be both! Never has this happened; it is impossible."

"She is the first child born of such a union; did you expect her to be of one profession only?"

Her mind drifted back to the days after the halfling war with the goblins, when she and her sisters sat and thought of how a child born of a union between druid and enchantress may be, "I planned my daughter and thought of what she may be, should I consent to be with child."

"You are the planner and your sisters' the guides."

"I thought her to be enchantress or druid, or a child with no profession, no way to obtain one. It was my deepest worry, a reason I would not consent. How may she be both, my friend? In my thoughts I had tried to imagine her to be part enchantress, part druid yet I dismissed them and my sisters agreed, such could not possibly be."

"I hear Malinna is soon to give birth, does she worry as to her child?"

"She does not."

"Your child is special, as are you and your sisters. You are the Chosen Ones, chosen by the Gods."

"To fight the quest."

"I do not believe they give you life for one purpose."

"I have given no thought to another quest, only to which we were born."

"Your mother is the first to give birth to more than two children, now it seems you also break the rules. Nortee is to be able to use the skills from both professions. Finglas must also teach her his ways."

"Yet we require time to fully understand our profession, how may she hope to learn those of both?"

"Worry not for she will cope as did you. Comfort and support her, give her the training she needs, if you do not she will be unable to be either. We must help others; it is in our blood. If you do not train her she will be unable to help others and be denied her rights. Ensure they are hers."

"Your words are wise, my friend. We begin the training in earnest on our return to wood elf city."

Feeling a little better she left him to find her daughter, the compass in her head pointing to her holding steadfast. No matter where her daughter was she knew the direction, as she knew the direction of her sisters and the protectors. The thought of them made her smile, they were never away from her daughter for long; it was as if Keitun and Xandorian had arranged for one of them to be with her most of the time. Her smile widened as she thought how Keitun chased her daughter around the forest and how he could never catch her. She had watched as she easily outran him and climbed the trees when he was not looking, dropping on him before rolling on the grass together, laughing and happy.

Xandorian loved Nortee almost as he did Icee, chasing her in the river and diving beneath the surface for minutes on end, always to surface behind her and pull her under, he was the only one who could outwit her in the water, the gnomes' ability to hold their breath for so long was famed.

The room occupied by Pose was the same one she had taken when she first arrived for training, and knew her way blindfolded. They were reserved for those with no homes close at hand, they were rarely used. As she approached she heard Nortee laughing and a smile creased her face. Opening the door she stopped, Pose had cast the illusion of a werewolf; her smile vanished, "Pose! Do you seek to scare her? Such forms are not for a child to see."

With hands above her head she brought them down, grey globes of smoke encircled her, as they faded so did the illusion.

"Our children see these forms from birth, this way they are not startled by the world when they enter it, or the creatures they see within."

"There is a difference in our cultures, we protect our children longer, yet there is sense in what you say."

"She is a bright child, Norty, encourage and let her grow."

"Two friends offer the same advice."

"Then should it not be taken?"

"I will think on this as we stay a few months while Nortee learns what I may not teach. Finglas will be happy to spend some time fishing with Yester Highleaf before he begins his journeys once more."

"Your return is well timed, sister, Malinna is to give birth."

"I felt her whilst in my guild. Strange the linking should take place; I may not feel her when she is greater than a day's journey from me."

"I too felt her needs. Come, the time is fast approaching."

Icee offered Malinna her child, wrapped in silks, "Your son, little sister."

"Welcome. Welcome Sha'Dal, to the land of the wood elves, the land of your father and your mother."

"Sha'Dal? Never have I heard such a name."

Throughout the year she had withheld his name from them, refusing all requests and pleadings, when they threatened her she had laughed at them, "In the old scrolls I saw it, the ancient elfin word for healer."

"So much time do you spend reading the scrolls; life passes little sister by and she knows it not."

"The scrolls are no longer understood by us, I wish to do so once more; so much has been lost to us over the years."

"Yet the dwarves miss you, return to them again."

"Soon, and I will take my child to show them."

Icee pulled silk sheet off his face, "With his mothers red hair a cleric he will be; brown druid eyes also, healing in his blood. You choose his name well, sister."

"It would seem all males are the same, his father paces outside wishing to show his son the world."

"Flight, your son is eager to see his father and the world."

Entering he kissed her, "You are well, and our son?"

"We are well. Take your son and show him our world, I know you wish it."

"Come, Sha'Dal. There is much for you to see."

"So, your husband knows his name whilst it is withheld it from us."

"I had a wish to tease."

"We know, and the teasing was good. I have a question if I may? You know he may be both cleric and druid, yet it worries you not?"

"In three weeks I will know if he follows both of us or the one. I worry not. You consented to be with child as I have done, as I have no worries none should be yours."

They caught the feeling from Icee, though she tried her best to hide it; Malinna moved to comfort her, "Fear not, sister, you will meet an elf and know him to be yours, as we knew ours. He will come, I feel it."

"Two sisters I have and both have born a child, yet still no elf for me."

"Cease your worries. The Gods will send him in their own time."

Her eyes looked towards the heavens, "Then I hope not to wait long. I have a need to be loved and the need is now."

"You worry without cause, sister. Nortee and I will stay a few days and ensure all is well. Finglas will return not for a week yet I have the need to return to high elf city."

"For what reason?"

"I saw the look in her eyes when we passed a shop I also like, and Nortee will also find it to her tastes."

"We return early, mother, I had thought you would have enjoyed more days with your sisters."

"This is for a treat which may not be found in wood elf city. You may have your hearts desires from the shops you have seen."

She knew instantly the shop she would go to, "Minlets, mother, they have such wonderful treats. May I see Pose also?"

"Norty, it is good to see you again. How do you fare?"

Bowing she smiled to Olva Minlets, "I am well, thank you. Nortee wishes for a treat, Pose and I will have a white wine if we may."

"Always the white wine and it is with Pose you drink it."

"Fresh supplies are sent to dark elf city for Mel D'elith?"

"Knowing Pose I find I hate them not as much as I had thought; I have done as you asked."

"Thank you. There is no rush, little one, choose your wish with care."

"So many choices, mother, I know not the one to have. How may I choose?"

A hand touched her shoulder, "May I be of help in the choosing?"

Turning she saw the young elf, her long blonde hair almost hiding her face, "So many sweet things, I know not the one to try."

"You are Nortee, born of Finglas and Norty."

"You have me at a disadvantage; I know not your name."

"I am named Aurorai, second born of Senas and Olva Minlets. Enchantress too young to be in guild; as seen by my clothes of silver grey."

"It is customary to speak the first born name first."

Changing the subject she left out the answer, "This looks sweet yet tastes sour. These sticks from the lands of man are sweet beyond imagination, yet a treat should not upset the stomach I feel. These should be chosen. River elf sweet berries rolled in red wine."

Opening the bag she peeked inside, "More than I would eat, mayhap you would help me with them?"

As they walked to a table Olva nodded to Norty, "Aurorai is shy and makes not friends easily. I feel one has started."

With her head slightly to one side she watched Pose talking with her daughter as they sat in her room, trying to be happy and explain why she and her mother were friends.

"Why wear a robe of red? Few enchantresses choose the colour of danger."

"Each chooses a colour suiting them. Red is for me as the green black your mother wears is hers."

"Do many of your people wear the red robe?"

"To us it is the Colour of Rejection. I have denied much so it is fitting."

"Colour of Rejection?"

"When an elf decides to leave the guild and travel it is said they reject the teachings."

"You do not reject them; you train here, and also teach."

"It is but a saying. I left my guild to travel before most would wish to. It is how I first met your mother."

"I have heard not the tale; mother speaks not of it, though I have asked."

"We met after the battle of the halflings and goblins; I challenged her to fight for your father."

"Why would you offer the challenge?"

"The Gods place all which is in our hearts, and love for him is within mine. Your mother refused the fight though I pleaded with her to release him."

"She could not do so; her love for father is strong."

"Love for him is still in me. Now I feel I know why it is there. I am to be as none before me. I will have no other love and, therefore, remain childless, the first of my people to choose to do so."

"There is an elf for each; you will find yours, this I know."

"I have found mine, yet his love is denied to me."

"What is it you do to your hair? I would seem not a white as once it was."

"Long ago my people stopped their ways with dyes. No matter how we tried always our hair would remain white."

Norty decided it was time to stop the course the talk had taken, "You worry, Pose. May I offer help?"

"Mother is ill and I worry for her. I must return home yet fear it."

"Why? It is the city of your birth."

"No longer is it my city. When you brought me here I made enemies. I fear I may not return should I go back, and I wish to return."

"I will accompany you. Nortee will stay with my sisters."

"No, mother. I am first born; my duty is to be beside you."

Her arm went around her daughter as she and remembered the time her own mother had asked why she was not playing with her sisters, Nortee had answered with almost the same words she had done so long ago, "First born, little one, what makes you believe another is to follow you?"

"You will have another child, mother, such is easy to see."

"The dark elves do not welcome us, you will remain."

Green eyes flashed back at her, "As you remained whilst your mother and father journeyed to the dungeon on the quest for your robe? No, I will not feel the pain you had to bare. I will not!"

"How is it you know of those days, I have spoken not of them?"

"Malinna and Icee have both spoken of them. I will not feel the pain, mother. My duties are clear, as first born I protect you as Lore demands."

Dark City

Her head shook in dismay as she looked at the city. Once it had been beautiful, standing in defiance of its very name. Now elves stared at them as if they were diseased; the city seemed hollow and without soul. Most of the lanterns in the streets were unlit; the only lights showing carried by those on their walks through the streets. Those brave enough to set forth argued amongst themselves and air of mistrust hung like a heavy odour over the city.

Pose touched her, "I heard it was like this yet never did I imagine..."

"Much is changed. How so?"

Hurriedly she led them through the streets, anxious to keep them hidden from as many eyes as possible, "When you came here to train with us you were the first white elf to do so. Some of my people wished to rejoin with you yet the faction was small."

"Mel D'elith spoke of them calling them the unionists. They believed our differences were not as large as the others thought."

Sidestepping into an ally she opened a door, "The old ways fought back saying the differences were so great they could not be reconciled."

"She called them the anti-unionists. Closely they watched us."

"The factions are equal now and war will enter the city, it seems many blame you and I. We must be careful and stay off the streets."

The thought made her hold Nortee tighter; how she had let her talk her into coming she did not know was scared for her safety.

Pose opened a passage way in the wall, "Through here and up the stairs."

Following the twisting stairs to the top of the building she entered a long a narrow corridor, "A dead end, Pose."

"All is not as it seems."

Reaching forward Pose pushed a stone, immediately the wall moved and a passageway showed beyond it, "The city is full of such hidden ways, I know a few yet there are hundreds of them I believe."

"Mel D'elith spoke nothing of them."

"It surprises me not, only we know of them. They were used once when the race of man invaded. From these passageways we fought back, each time they thought to have captured an area they found retreat cut of as many of us came from behind them. It was a slaughter, or so our teachings would have us believe."

"It would seem you do not believe the tales."

"I have learned much in my travels. I believe they hate us as we hate them, this I have seen for myself. The Book of the Family also describes it."

"What is the book and what of the battle?"

"The females of each family scribe in a book handed from mother to daughter their stories and thoughts. In each telling of the tale in classes I have heard changes; mother and father instructed me in the tales and each speaks differently of it. The victors, not the vanquished, write history."

Walking its length they glanced through thin slits acting as windows to the streets, they could almost see the tension between those walking below, hanging heavy, seemingly ready to snap at any moment.

"Mother lives near here. Come, her life is measured in days."

"How is it you know this?"

"I still have friends in the city; they send word her husband and sister have poisoned her. Mother wishes us to unite whilst they do not. Now brother fights brother, sister turns against sister. There is so much hatred war must surely come. "

Once more the passageway seemed to dead end and Pose placed a finger to her lips as she moved a small stone and peered though the gap.

"Mother is in her bed and no one is around. They let the poison take her and leave her alone to die."

"Then we can see her and talk as you wished."

"They disgust me! We must die in company or may not enter the Promised Kingdom."

Pressing a small stone the wall slid slowly out; before it had ceased movement Pose was at her mother's bedside, "Mother I am here, open your eyes to me and see."

As she rolled slowly over Norty gasped, she looked ancient but she knew it was the poison's effect. It seemed to be eating her very soul. She had seen her once before, when she had first entered the city, and knew her age was less than one hundred years, at the time she found it hard to tell if she was the mother of Pose or elder sister.

Her eyes flickered open and recognition coming slowly, "Pose, is it you?"

"Yes, mother, I am here. I come as bid."

"Listen well to me. The factions gather their forces for war. Stay from the city, promise you will not return unless the fight goes for the union."

"I promise, mother. Now dress and come with us, we take you from here."

"The poison is strong and my time is here. You can do nothing except to save yourself."

"I will leave not without you, it is why I came; you must come with us."

Reaching out she touched the hilt of her daughter's stiletto, "I cannot as well you know. I ask the Sacrifice of you."

"No! I cannot do it, mother. I will not do it."

"You must, I have no wish to die alone. I ask of you the Sacrifice."

Nortee pulled free of her mother's hand, "She wishes to die, for Pose to take her life. She must be taken to Malinna, she will help her."

"She cannot make the journey, Nortee. She is too weak to travel."

"You are the mother of Pose and yet you believe this will help her?"

"I will not place her at risk, child, I cannot do such to her."

"You place her at risk when you die. She speaks to me of you and her heart is full of love. If your heart be also full leave your bed and follow me."

Backing away she pulled Pose with her, arms outstretched to her, "Come, show your love for your daughter."

"I cannot."

"Show your love as only a mother may do. Come to her."

Slowly she struggled from the bed and stood, shaking and unsteady, "Pose, a book is under the bed, we cannot leave it behind."

They were at her side helping her towards the secret door, desperately wanting her to leave quickly but not daring to hurry her. Entering the passageway Nortee closed it behind her.

"Someone comes, mother, they will have elfin ears."

For minutes they remained motionless and quiet until the sounds faded before starting the journey back.

For hours they struggled to lead her to safety though the narrow streets as she steadily became weaker, ever watchful for danger, always ready but unwilling to fight. Whenever her strength failed Nortee encouraged her and she found the will to continue. By the time they had found a safe place near the cities south gate night had fallen once more, "Our eyes are poor in the night, Norty, we see not as you do. It is a blessing; they will wait until the sun rises to search for us."

"We must be far from here by then. The only ones seen on our way were the necromancers; three have followed yet it is odd they did nothing to challenge us. It is as if they guard us rather than look to us as the enemy. I will look for a wizard to teleport us from here. Nortee, stay with them."

"There is little need, mother, a necromancer points him to us."

Malinna stood as she finished her examination, "She is beyond my help, I am sorry. The poison used has been in her too long and is too strong for my magic to heal her."

"You tried, Malinna, I thank you. Leave us please, we wish to be alone."

"You may use the bedroom as your own. I will be near, call for any needs."

For two days they remained alone in the room calling only once for fresh water. When Pose emerged the strain was gone from her face, to be replaced with sadness.

"She is in the Promised Kingdom, Norty. She died in my arms and not alone. I could let her take no more pain. I performed the Sacrifice. This I vow before you; I will have my revenge, his life will be mine!"

Slipping her stiletto from its sheath she handed it to her, "Lore demands blood for blood and must wear the mark. Cut on my forehead the shape of an S and destroy it. All must see I have made the Sacrifice."

Taking Pose by the hand she pushed the sleeve of her robe and cut the mark on her forearm, "An enchantress must be perfect and such would scar you. I will do this not to a friend."

Pulling away she dried the tears, "To you and Nortee I owe so much, I would not have been with her when she died. May I embrace?"

As her daughter settled in bed Norty examined the stiletto Pose had left with her, she had not destroyed it as she should have done and it began to worry her a little. She did not fully understand the ritual of the Sacrifice but had heard of it, Mel D'elith instructing her in their Lore as they trained. She had a feeling it still had a part to play in the life of Pose. Carefully slipping it in the drawer she turned to her daughter, "Do you understand why Pose embraced you?"

"For friendship I believe, mother."

"We have spoken of oaths and their meaning."

"I try hard to be a good study for father and you."

"As we swear an oath they seal theirs with an embrace. To be embraced is for them to be pledged to you. She would willingly give her life for you."

"I wish not for her life, she is my friend and nothing more."

"Close your eyes, little one, think not of it."

As he entered her mind once more her head dropped to one side, a smile crossing her lips as she moved quickly to the draws containing her finest silk robes. As fastidious with her clothes as her mother before her, the silks were smoothed and flat in the draw, exactly as she had placed them. Choosing the blue robe she knew he loved she dressed and waited for him, she was in the mood for love.

'Nortee is right; we will have another child. I hope to follow in the footsteps of mother; and he to have his wish. With the Gods blessing I will also have more than two children.'

Their loving over she lay with him speaking of the last few days, as her tale unfolded she felt his body stiffen. He was upset; she could feel it in him.

"You were wrong to take her to the city. She may have been injured or worse. They are our mortal enemies, I am disappointed with you."

The harshness in his voice had not surprised her and she moved to calm him, "Lady Fortune smiled on us. Without Nortee she would never have left the city and have died alone."

"This I understand yet you could not have foreseen the help she would be. Take her not to dangerous places until she is trained."

Throughout she had tried to ease the tension in him, stroking his chest with her fingers, as he loved her to do. Yet still he would not relax and she needed to calm him. Her voice became sweet; "We cannot keep her safe and protected from all until then. The more she sees of our world the more she will be ready to greet it. Trust to me and the training I offer."

"Use not your ways with me, wife!"

She had felt his body stiffen and instantly regretted the voice she had used, her desire had been to calm him, "I apologise for my ways; it would seem they slip from me without my realising."

"Enough! You know well the ways you use!"

He had not accepted her apology and she realised why, it would seem as if she would use her charms to gain from him anything she wished, "I did not realise the ways I used my voice; I wished only to explain. I would use the ways of a wife and not those of an enchantress."

"Cease your explanations, they weary me! She has five hundred years in which to learn, there is no rush for her."

He was still not responding to her body movements and the love she placed in each gesture, her voice responded in kind, "She must be ready for the world and we must teach her!"

His voice rose in return, "I wish not for her to be rushed. Life is dangerous out of these woods. Here she is protected, looked after by our own kind."

Pulling away from him she sat up, "You remember not the dangers my sisters and I faced before we left the woods?"

"I remember only too clearly! As I remember my feeling when you were in danger, I will not have those feeling forced on her. Those dangers were brought by the Gods to test you. You will do as I say; there is an end to it."

The words 'there is an end to it' were used to end an argument, nothing could be said once they were used. Struggling against their Lore she pushed her words out of stiff lips, "There is not an end to it! You remember not the vow you gave at our wedlock?"

"Sometimes a vow must be broken!"

"Never must a vow be broken, this you teach Nortee, yet break your vow as you feel the need! Is this to be the way it will always be, *my lord*?"

The words took him aback; she used them before they let their love show; now she was using them once more. Was she angry or was her love fading?

The hurt was plain to see as it entered his face and saw his body action, felt the sting as her words entered his heart and was immediately sorry, but she could not back down on her stance to him. Her daughter must know all the ways to protect herself in their world as she travelled. She would ensure she taught her all she could of the land, peoples and travel. Nortee would be allowed to see all she could of the world. It still pained her Icee and Malinna had been forbidden to travel before they had reached the coming of age. They had only been allowed to see high elf city, no matter how much Xandorian and Keitun had tried to persuade their parents. Only she had been allowed and realised it was only because her mother wished her to follow in her footsteps to become the ambassador to the land of man.

"She *will* be trained in any way I see fit for her! It will be done *where* I choose to instruct her and *when* I chose to do so!"

"You will do as I say!"

"Still you go back on the words you gave at our wedlock. It is...."

"Mother!"

The tearful voice spun her around; in the argument she had forgotten they were linked, what they felt their daughter would feel also, the anger in both of them.

Regret was tearing at her as she approached her daughter, anxious to comfort and explain to her, "Little one, in my anger...."

Backing away from her, her arm stretched towards her mother, palms facing her in elfin denial, "No, mother!"

With her daughter's posture she could not move towards her, elfin ways prevented her from approaching, "Nortee......."

Feelings she had never known in her parents had flooded through her mind and woke her. Moving to the room she watched the argument as it grew, felt the feelings she knew they had no wish to be there. Yet neither would stop and apologise, even though the argument was over her, and it was upsetting to think she was the cause. She had to be firm, to control the argument and bring back the love now buried deep under their emotions,

"Stay your ground! You fight with my father over me and I like it not! I feel your hurt and pride yet you would let this come between you?"

With her hands still holding her mother from her she looked to her father, "And you would scar all for such foolishness as to my seeing the world? It is *my* world and I have the *right* to see it!"

His heart went out to her, but as approached, her left arm, palm still held upright, swung towards to him, right arm still holding her mother at bay. It was if an invisible barrier were before them, elfin roots were deep within them, no matter how much they refused to believe or reject them; neither could approach their daughter while her arms were stretched forth in such denial.

"I will see this argument end. Embrace and stop such foolery."

They looked at each other, unsure as if to embrace or not, neither willing to take the first step.

Once more their feeling of love stirred in her mind, knowing she needed to push them just a little more her voice became softer, "I ask you embrace, is this too much to ask of those in love?"

Still neither moved, still both wanted to.

Their love had returned, she could feel the need for each other as it built inside of them, but stubbornness still bared their way.

Her voice grew demanding, "*Embrace*! Do it *now*!"

They let the differences depart, sharing a long embrace, each thankful to be in the other's arms.

Nortee moved to them, arms stretching up, asking to share in their love.

Looking from wife to daughter he lifted her to him, "Little one, you have wisdom beyond your years. I will not argue with your mother, she has always known best. She will do as she sees is good for you."

It was impossible to hold back any longer, her mother had taught her the elfin ways only too well. She had upset not only her husband but her daughter, it was time to make emends. Her bow was low and her voice calm, "Husband, daughter, I have been foolish and you have the right to chastise me for my behaviour. I stand ready to receive any punishment you deem fitting. I apologise to both, please accept it in the way it is given."

Grinning at his daughter he winked, "Should we forgive her?"

"It would seem best, father. Mother is strong willed and as yet I have not been hugged as much as I would like."

"Then her punishment shall be to give more hugs to you and I."

She laughed, "A punishment you may ask of me anytime."

A Meeting of Minds

Motioning his daughter to him he crouched, "You wanted a rabbit. They will come to you should the druid self be strong within you."
As the rabbit hopped in front of her she called, "My friend, come to me."
Untold joy entered her heart as he came to her call. Stroking him she placed him back on the ground, watching as he hopped a short distance from her, no sense of fear for her within him.

He was proud of her; he had been almost four years old before he could call creatures to him from the woods, she could do it half way through her third year. He had even managed to teach her to hide once or twice, to become one with the trees, almost invisible to the untrained eye. A small smile crossed his face as he remembered her bright yellow hair standing out from the trees when she hid.

Norty whispered, "Let your mind leave your body and enter the rabbit. Do as I have instructed, be as one with him."

Her mind moved towards the rabbit at it nibbled on the sweet grass twenty paces from her, pulling it back as she saw so many minds around her, scared as she realised there were so many in the forest. Her mother had been much nearer when they practiced how to let her mind leave her body, and wondered why she stood so far from her now.

Her mind extended once more, feeling it's way slowly; exhilaration taking her as she became aware of how many minds lay open to her. So many creatures with so many thoughts were before her; she had only seen her mother's mind as she trained with her and decided the next time they trained in the glade she would ask.

Then a mind full of aggression overwhelmed her. This mind was stronger than the others, more complex yet singular in its thought to kill and eat; food high in its thoughts. Her mind felt the death of the rabbit as the claws of the eagle sank into his body.

Her mind snapped back, "He killed the rabbit mother, it was horrible."

"Death is a part of life, little one. You were distracted and found the one you wanted hard to see?"

"So many minds and so many purposes, as if a hundred elves spoke to me at once and I knew not on which to focus. As I found a mind a new one entered and took my attention."

"You will learn to focus on the one you want. It takes practice and it is what we do for the next few years. You train in the ways of the druid and of the enchantress. You have twice to learn as do all others."

"Except for Sha'Dal. He will train as druid and cleric."

"Find a new mind and try once more."

"My mind hurts, so many have I seen."

"The mind is like your muscles and must be exercised a little past its limit or it will never become strong. Try once more."

Her mind found another and she called it to her, firmly and quietly but the mind rejected her and it was soon lost amongst so many others.

"I called a squirrel to me, mother, yet it would not listen."

"It will take time; your mind is still weak to the one you wish to speak. You see other minds yet should not do so for many years to come."

Her arms reached for her father, "I wish to go now, I hunger."

"Truly your mother's daughter, always she is hungry."

"Take us to see the gnomes, father, their food is nice."

"I feel her appetite for roots has waned since you treated her to the delights in high elf city."

"Minlets was wonderful; so many sweet things to try yet the gnomes' meats are so tasty. I wish to try more of them."

"Meat is not the food of elves, little one."

"You have eaten meat, mother, as has father. Xandorian brings them when he visits."

"I ate meat out of necessity, not for the wish to kill."

"I have no wish to kill for food yet if it is there and I hunger why should I not eat it?"

"Nortee is right, we go to the gnomes, Xandorian will be back and we have seen little of him for a good few months."

Pointing to the hill she bent beside her daughter, "The city on the hill was once the home of the gnomes. Now it is but ruins, none venture there."

"Xandorian refuses to speak of those days."

"The city is from times long ago when the lands were so much the younger. Now they have moved to the secret valley they live in. The tale is for another day; darkness comes and I long for the comforts of his home."

"I fear not the land during darkness, mother. I am druid also, none will harm me here."

"You are also enchantress, tonight you sleep in the city."

Xandorian welcomed them, taking his time with their embraces, "Come in, sit and be at home."

Stooping to enter his house they took the seats offered, Nortee clinging to his neck, her way of greeting him she knew he adored.

"Xandorian, you come not as often as you should, I miss you."

His clenched fist gently touched her chin, "As I miss you, and it is nice to hold an elf more my size."

He had no need to ask the reason for their visit, he knew Nortee would have instigated the move, and it pleased him as he steered her towards the back room, "I know why you come, it is to try more of my meats is it not?"

"May I?"

"Take no notice of your mother, in my house you eat as you please."

"An elf with an appetite for meat; what I am to do? What keeps you away so long my friend?"

Placing small cubes meats on a plate he offered them to Nortee knowing the ways of the elves only too well, she would never dream of taking one until the offer was made, , "I watch for when the dark elves wage war."

"Easy for you, gnomes are tolerated there. We would be dead ten days from the city gate."

"Not easy for those not of dark bearing these days, all are viewed with suspicion by both sides. It is hard to say which would win this war."

Nortee finished the meat, "The ones for union will win; it is easy to see."

"You see through the eyes of want, Nortee. The ones for keeping separate are the more powerful."

"This meat is the nicer. They are at a disadvantage, Xandorian."

"How so?"

"They have the numbers yet not the will to fight, or know how to fight a long battle. The unionists will win."

"How do you know this? You spent so little time there."

"It is easy to see. The unionists have fought long in secret; the others know not how to do such. They wish to show how strong they are yet are scared for they believe they may lose the fight."

"You believe war may come?"

"Not for many years, none wish such though they show they do."

"How may war be delayed?"

Nortee pointed to the plate, "May I have some more of these please? Mother, even here you seek to train me, may I not rest?"

"Your thoughts must flow, your mind searching, ever alert for danger."

"By giving them a common enemy; yet it is only one of several ways."

"How many ways do you see, little one?"

Her head dropped to one side as she thought, "I see five ways."

"I must ensure I look to your planning more, I see eight ways."

"Then you include Messenger in a plan. Never is it good when you rely on hope, so many times have you told me this. Your count should be seven."

"You fail to see two ways. Messenger has come before when I called to him. For such reasons as this he will come again."

"It is only your hope, mother, and plans based on hope may fail. You wish to avert war and believe he will help you. The Gods may wish this war. It is one way to keep the dark ones constantly uneasy; they have desires to fight others, as does the race of man. Whichever faction wins the losers will be forced to meet in secret as the unionists now do. In this way they compete only with each other and not against other races."

"Your thoughts run true. Try once more to find the ways you overlooked."

With her appetite sated she pushed the plate away, "You are lucky, Xandorian, to have such fine foods. Mother sets the table with naught but elfin foods."

Her eyes widened as she felt the sting in her mother. Running to her she knelt, "Mother, I am sorry I have no mind for my words to sound so cruel. I would only wish we had different foods once in a while."

"I have been as my mother and father before me. They too thought not of others needs."

With her daughter settled down she continued her thoughts of the dark elves, "I had thought to call the Messenger to avert this war yet Nortee is correct, it is a hope and nothing more. He may not answer my call."

Finglas nodded, "Yet he was the one who helped when you went to kill Agroth and Fenny."

"Hindering us also; he delayed us so the fight was almost lost to us."

"He had reasons; you now know the power of the staff you carry."

Almost without realising her hand reached down from the arm of the chair and touched the staff, a faint tingling sensation greeted her and, even though it was made of gold, it felt warm to the touch and light to hold, "I like not to use its power."

Placing three glasses of wine down Xandorian sat next to her, "It helped save our lives in the battle for halfling land."

"Yet it was its secondary power and still brought naught but death. My staff shall not be used if I may avoid it."

Xandorian offered her a glass, "And averting a war is not such a time?"

"The Gods may easily avert a war should they choose to act."

"They should not act. It is for all to stop a war and we must strive to ensure it is so. If we demand of the Gods for all we do not like there would be little left in this world for us to do. Little left to live for and less to die for."

"Yet I think this war is not meant to be, as if someone else would have it rage, and relish in the killings."

"You suspect a God has a hand in this?"

"I am unsure."

"Why would the Gods wish such a war?"

"There have always been Gods and wars. I know not why."

"Malinna may know."

"Should she know she would have spoken of this."

"As your guide she knows their ways."

"Xandorian, entertain us with tales of your deeds these last months."

"I have been to lands not yet visited by my people. Seen wonders I thought never to see. Only a few days ago I was at risk of life. The river flowed gently as I dove for fish."

"I have seen you do so many times, never have you failed to catch any, even from the salty lake of the lowlands. There would be little danger."

"You heap praise on me once more, my friend, yet never have I seen what lay so temptingly before me."

He smiled as they leaned forwards; caught in his story, "A shadow in the grey depths I saw, huge, yet the shape was unmistakable. I could not reach it this time, the breath almost gone from my body I surfaced for air. My lungs happy once more I started down to the gloomy depths to see if the shape was but a trick of the light, yet still it was there. I approached with caution and excitement. A sunken ship, mayhap a pirate ship, lay half buried in the mud of the river. As I swam round a mast I realised it was not old, the rigging and sails still in good condition. One thought ran through my head, to sink so low in the mud could mean it was laden with treasure."

"Was any found?"

"I know not. As I searched I saw the crew, hideous, most cut in half where they lay. Then a hand was on my shoulder and I swam as never before."

He laughed, "Xandorian, you are a tease, yet a good tale."

"Who is to say I tease?"

"Surely you do so?"

"One day I may return to Black River where it flows into the salt lakes and see if the ship is still there."

"No ship is ever seen on the salt lakes or the river."

"Then the mystery deepens."

In the glade she asked the question she had kept to herself, "When we looked for the rabbit you moved from me, mother. Why so?"

"Your mind needed be free to do as it must."

"It was free, mother, there is another reason."

She smiled; her daughter's reasoning was becoming sharp, "So my mind may not influence yours, it must seek another's on its own."

"When first you taught me to let my mind leave my body I saw no other minds. Did you block them from me?"

"I guided your mind towards mine, in essence I gave it a path on which to tread. You followed the path carefully and concentrated on your way, seeing no others on your journey."

"I could not let my mind leave my body yet I tried so hard, then I could. Did you pull my mind from me?"

"The enchantress's most difficult task is for her mind to leave her body. The first time for me was when Caspo Kwil guided it; he spoke he had never seen a mind so willing to leave. I have taught the ways to many yet with you I had only to tease a little and it followed, as easily as did mine, yet you may do it at less than half the age I was."

"You spoke of practicing on the small creatures in the forest before you left for training."

"I was young and foolish and had not an enchantress to show me how it should be done. I tried to control them with mere thought and it is not the way, as I found out. For years I had doubts as to my profession."

"Yet the Gods had decided what you should be."

"Doubts there were and the price I paid for them was high."

"You must explain them to me, mother."

"Later, tonight we speak and train. Your mind must enter the one you wish to control; you cannot wish it to be controlled."

"Is this not for those of greater proficiency than I?"

"All enchanters teach their young the ways before entering the guild. It would seem my mind might teach others easier than most. Many ask I teach their child the way."

"You have the gift to make learning fun. My mind needs exercise, mother."

"Centre your thoughts; let your mind fly as straight as an arrow to the one you seek. A bird sits in the tree, look to it and imagine your mind is an arrow. Let it fly straight and true to the bird, remember to call not shout."

Her mind almost shot from her and she felt the birds mind easily with her own, 'Come to me, friend, come to me.'

Spreading his wing he flew, screeching as he went.

"Mother?"

"You shocked him, little one; you entered the mind too fast. You must be gentle and feel your way in. As you did it just now was to attack, a way we use when others fail. The bird will be fine in a few minutes."

"I will be more careful."

"There is time to try more before we must return home."

"You wish for father's comfort, what ails you?"

"My dreams have been troubled as late."

"Speak of them."

"I do not fully understand them."

"Explain which you remember."

"I see a man and a woman in a strange white room."

"You know them?"

"I do not, yet believe I should. They are speaking together."

"Of what do they speak?"

"Their language is strange and not understood by me."

"Yet you know all languages."

"Not all are known to me. This one is stranger than any I have heard."

"What do they do in this room?"

"They speak of she who sleeps on a metal bed; it seems they worry for her."

"Who is on the bed?"

"I know not."

"The time for training is ended. Come, we go home and speak with father."

26

The forest was alive with thoughts and she was getting better at sensing them, able to cut them out almost entirely. Now she must find another mind on which to focus and it leapt forward in its search, swinging right and left until it touched a mind, complex and strong, with death directed at her. Her mind recoiled in panic.

"Down, Nortee!"

At her mother's command her training took control, instinctively dropping flat to the ground as the arrow hurled just a little over her.

Dropping and rolling on top of his daughter Finglas protected her from more attacks as Norty threw her mind at the attacker, hurling him backwards to the ground with violent force. She did not care she had hurt him; he had attacked her daughter and would pay the price.

"Now, Finglas!"

Standing he cast, the fiery ball of mana hitting the attacker in the chest as he tried to shoot once more. Casting with all the fury he could muster he saw his second spell engulf the man as his wife's hit him also, he died in agony.

At her side she helped her daughter to stand, "All is well, little one."

"He wished to kill me, mother, I liked not his mind."

"It is normal to see any who attack; it is part of an enchantress."

"I saw him not, he was hidden from me; I saw only his mind."

Puzzlement took her; her daughter should not see a mind until she saw the person to whom it belonged, no enchantress could, except herself; her mind was a gift from the Gods. Several trains of thought were rejected almost as quickly as they entered her mind, leaving her with just the one. Nortee had inherited her mind as she had inherited her looks and enchantress ways. She was happy her daughter could do it, it may save her life in the future, but her training would have to be amended to take it into account. "Man has a liking for elves; mother has taken me to their cities many times in her duties."

"I hurt him not, mother, why would he wish to harm me?"

"We will find out, little one, *by the Gods we will find out.*"

Finglas handed Norty the ring taken from the man, "The ring of the assassins. He was a rogue hired to kill her."

"I will have the truth. Whoever ordered the attack will die in pain unknown. An oath I swear now, the one who planned this shall die."

"No, mother, you do not kill, so many times you speak we kill only when all other ways fail. I would have you kill not for me, not now, not ever."

"I have sworn, Nortee, and my oath will stand. Any who may harm an innocent have no right in this world. I will send him on his way to the next world for the Gods to judge."

"The Gods decree who is to live and who is to die. It is not for you to decide, mother."

"He hired someone to do it by stealth; it is the act of a coward. He will die in such agony as I may give."

Finglas watched his wife as she sat at home with her eyes closed; she was planning, "Never have I seen you so determined."

"Our daughter has been threatened, and I fear it will not be the last such attack. An oath I have sworn."

"I have seen you in temper, never in anger. You have the power to do as you say?"

"The enchantress controls the mind and by doing so the thoughts flowing through it. I may make a mind scream in terror, or drift into peace. He will beg me for death; and I will torture him so much more."

"You speak of the training gained from the dark elves. It is not our ways."

"We teach how to use our minds for attack and defence as well as charm. The dark ones teach how to see thoughts in the minds of others."

"I knew not such was possible."

"I have seen how to take thoughts and read them. She is our daughter and someone would harm her. She may fight many battles in the years to come yet this is a battle no child should have to fight. For once I am pleased mother insisted I accompany her in her duties. I know of the rogues and the city in which they are to be found. You like a drink, husband. You like malt and ale do you not?"

"I have been known to sample a wine or two."

"Icee is not fond of ale or mead and looks to it as if it has no place in this world. Only rarely have I seen her drink wine."

"There are those to whom its taste holds more than just a passing fancy."

"Then show me how to drink ale and not be drunk, I have a need to learn."

The Assassins

Kessin was an area of Seaporth few people would choose to visit, and those living there did not take kindly to strangers. The dregs of all races made it their home, but it was unique for it possessed something found nowhere else in all the lands. There was no interracial friction; ogre and gnome lived side by side; elves would speak to trolls and goblins befriend halfling.

The docks spread across the narrow beaches offering moorings to over one hundred ships, and all races traded with Seaporth. It was this difference, which had lead over a startlingly short period, to interracial harmony. It was soon discovered where trading exists the practice of war and hatred cannot prosper. They had begun not only to trade but also to be friends, and the friendships had become firm with the passing of those few short years. Families settled, and the area around the docks had blossomed.

Yet its original citizens had drawn further inland, wishing little to do with those inhabiting the docklands. The dock folk had been only too pleased, it left them in peace and they named their new home Kessin, from the troll word Kez, meaning mine, and the halfling cin, for water.

The houses were often three levels high, a mixture of architectures from all the races, leading to some very strange designs as races settled where they could find the smallest of places. Often built close together due to the scarcity of available land near the waterfront, it made the streets dark and foreboding. The only lights came from the occasional lantern behind the shuttered windows of the shops and houses. There had never been street lighting, lit streets were the reserve of other sections of towns, and most villages had it in abundance. It was a form of protection from marauding bandits, robbers and some four footed creatures.

Yet Kessin boasted another unique feature, all villages and towns had ale houses for travellers yet Kessin had more than any other city in the known lands, and it was into one such hostelry a bedraggled old woman limped as she held her left leg. Choosing a stool at the bar she sat with difficulty, banging a coin on the table she called for ale.

The barman nodded to her as he spoke quietly to his customers, joining in their laugher. He had seen her type so often, and they were not the customers he wanted, they would buy a few drinks and collapse on the floor, to be dragged out after they had been searched for any valuables of course. His idea of a customer were men and trolls, they would get drunk and return the next night for more. Those he knew he would normally let sleep it off in the back room.

Dropping the coin for him she eagerly upturned the offered pot to her mouth, draining it before banging it back down on the bar, "More. I have money, lots of money. I want more."

Reluctantly he refilled the pot, taking the coin still lying in the ale she had spilt. She would get drunk, and probably rowdy, before coming on to the men in the bar and propositioning them. His stomach felt sick, any drunk enough to take her up would end up regretting it the next morning when they woke next to her.

Knarred fingers slowly released a handful of gold coin, letting them spill on the bar; instantly bringing him to her. Each time the pot was drained he was there, refilling it before she asked, a smile always playing on his face. After the seventh mug had been drained she dropped more gold in the spilt ale, almost falling as she let go of the bar.

Years of watching customers, knowing when they were susceptible, came easy to him. It was time to ask questions, and in her present state she would not get suspicious, if he looked as if he were asking in a casual manner, "Nice to see someone pay; where's a nice old dear like you get the money?"

"Wouldn't you like to know, eh? I finds it, lots of it, and all mine now."

"Where is it, my dear?"

Slavering she tapped the bag on her hip, "In here. Mine now, all mine."

His smile lit up his face, "Let me look after you, my dear."

Her words slurred as she tried to control her body, "Yes, looks after me. I want a room. And bath. A hot bath."

Reaching for the pile of keys he sorted through them to find the one he needed, the room furthest from anyone else.

Carefully he placed the keys in her outstretched hands, "Finest in the house. Top of the stairs; it's the last door on the left."

He watched her slow, unsteady progress as she stumbled from chair to table, table to stairs; she was half way up before he gave a sharp nod towards two men watching from a dark alcove.

The knock at the door was answered by a croaky voice, "Go away!"

"Hot water."

Waiting on the landing they heard the key fumbling in the lock, eventually the door opened an inch, enough for one eye to watch them.

"What!"

The two men stood there before her; in each hand they held a pail of hot water, "Your bath water."

Opening the door wide for them she hobbled towards the next room; "Spills any and I don't pay."

"You won't have to worry about it." One replied, winking at his partner.

With the pails they carried left on the floor next to the bath they headed towards the room the woman had entered, daggers drawn and ready for use. Gold would be their today, and from the bulge of the purse it was to be a rich haul. Their training in stealth was about to pay them back dividends; they knew no one could have heard them as they approached, least of all a deaf old woman. They would surprise her as they threw back the curtain separating the two rooms and slip a knife into her before she even realised they were there.

As they drew back the curtain the surprise was complete. In front of them was a beautiful elf in a green black robe with a smile to enchant the heart of any man. Her long yellow hair pulled to the back of her head to pass through an amulet to hang in a golden cascade to her waist. Her movements were pure grace as she stepped past them into the room they had just left, and he knew his friend was going to kill her.

He would not let anything happen to his mistress, she must be protected even with his own life. He knew the plans of his friend to kill and rob her, but she must not be harmed. With a grin he slid his knife into his friend's ribcage, and found the heart. He was pleased, her enemy was dead and she was smiling at him in gratitude of his work.

"Come to me."

Happiness flooded through his very being; he would do her bidding no matter what it was or how small and insignificant it may be to her, it would be a command to him. He would do anything she asked, her every whim would be granted, she was his mistress and must be obeyed.

Her hand on his chest pushed him gently into a chair, "Speak of the men who would send your kind to wood elf city. Where do the assassins meet?"

His mind became turmoil, he must tell her all she wished to know, she had asked and he must speak, yet his mind would not let him and his brain began to hurt as he struggled between two loyalties. With arms covering his head he cradled it as he swayed from side to side, "Tell. Don't tell." "Tell your mistress, speak of what I ask."

Her voice was soft and sweet, begging him to tell her all he knew, and he wanted desperately to tell her anything, but the oaths and comradeship of many years fought to stop him. He began to moan and hug his head harder, wondering why could he not tell her, what was stopping him. She was his mistress and must be told, she must be obeyed.

Her hands soothed his head as she coaxed him to talk to her, "Tell your mistress of these men. Tell me where they are, I have a wish to meet them." As he tried to stand he felt hands slip to his shoulders and he remained seated. 'Tell her, she is your mistress, you must obey, she commands it.'

"Speak! I grow weary of the wait."

"By the docks in an old warehouse. A man…"

Old loyalties took over once more. He tried but the words would not come. Smiling she placed more pressure on his mind, just a fraction of the power she was capable of applying. Bringing forth her training with the dark elves she felt no compassion for the brain she was torturing. These men had tried to hurt Nortee; they had forfeited the right to live, "Which warehouse? Tell me all, I command it."

"No, I cannot. I must tell."

"Tell me and the pain will go away. I am your mistress. Speak!"

"Mistress, I am sworn in loyalty."

"To whom do your loyalties belong, to others or you're Mistress?"

"I am yours to command, Mistress."

"I ask and you do speak not, is it you think so little of me?"

"Mistress, you are all to me."

Boredom had begun to set in, she had had enough of torturing him; he was too easy to control. Placing the right amount of pressure here, a twist of his thoughts there she had found it a pleasure for a time, but now her pleasure had come to an end; she removed all thoughts from his head.

Her voice was like the tinkling of a tiny bell in a quiet room, demanding to be heard in the sweetest possible way.

He heard the bell and he focused on it, "Yes, tell all. They meet in the warehouse at, Old Jim's place. Each new moon they meet in the secret passage..."

His voice trailed off as the bell stopped its tinkling, and his mind stopped its thinking.

Looking down at his body she sighed, "Not much did you tell me, yet it is a start. May the Gods welcome you to your afterlife."

Her arms rose above her head and came slowly down, bringing with them spheres of swirling grey smoke, as they cleared they revealed her illusion of the old woman, smiling.

An Old Friend

Slowly he shook his head, "Ack, so many times I try to teach you the druid ways, never do you learn."

Placing one last branch on the fire he had started in the woods she dropped her head to one side, asking an unvoiced question.

"The fire is too big and bright; it will frighten away the animals yet may cause others to investigate. It should be built in a beehive of stones to warm them, none of which you have placed near the fire, they will provide heat long after the fire dies. And so much smoke, you place too much greenwood on the fire. Others will see and come to such a beacon."

"The very reason I make the fire bright with so much smoke."

"You are too secretive these days. Why do we come to the Woods of Faith and whom do you wish to see?"

"When she arrives you will hear her."

"Through the crackling of flames? I think not."

"She is no elf. I heard her when first we met. Sit and wait."

For almost three hours they sat and talked as she rose several times to place more wood on the fire, to ensure it was kept bright and enhance the smoke, always returning to his side. His tales of other lands enthralled her, listening to him and asking for details of those he had met, the friendly and the not so friendly. She loved to travel with him, to go to strange lands and talk with others. She had been to many lands but sat and listened to him and her mind drew pictures of those he described, made notes of how they moved, their strengths and their weaknesses. At times such as these she knew the sorrow of not being a druid, unable to cast spells to take her to distant towns and places in the wink of an eye. He enjoyed a life of freedom but at the price of never being able to settle down for long in one place. The land called to him too quickly it seemed to her, each time he was home for a few days she could feel the call enter him, see the listless way he moved as he yearned for travel once more. One day they would travel together once more, they still had almost five hundred years to see their lands.

Nortee was her concern at the moment, she needed guidance and teaching, the time for travel would come soon enough.

"I have a need to speak of the dream I have."

"You have spoken several times of your dream."

"The dream scares me, Finglas. They are of the race of man yet different."

"In which way are they different?"

"The language they speak and the way in which they hold themselves. The room is strange and I am unable describe what I do not know. Do you know of others who look as man?"

"They are far and wide in this land; I have seen them wherever I travel."

"The room is so bright yet outside darkness prevails. How can this be?"
"Mayhap there are torches aplenty to light the room?"
"There are none I remember, the light comes from above yet I know not how. Do you know of any who sleep on a bed of metal?"
"Why would one choose such a place to lie?"
"I know not and fear for she who lies on the bed."
The arrow found its mark a foot from his feet, he was up instantly assuming a defensive posture in front of her for protection, eyes alert and checking for movement.
"Damn the fire, Norty, I see naught through it."
With a laugh she rose, "Your movements are quick yet without cause. The arrow announces her, she has found us."
"I like not to be shot at! The arrow could have killed."
"If she had wished to kill you then would be dead. Mother taught her to shoot the bow, she learned well those lessons."
"We come here to see Kyna?"
"Friend Kyna, step forth. 'Tis too long since last we met."
Stepping into the area lit by the fire, her arms outstretched in welcome, she called to her, "My arms are empty, how long since you were in them?"
Needing no second invitation she embraced her, "It has been too long."
"I shouldn't see anyone; I'm in prayer for thirty days and nights."
Eventually he managed to get a hug from her, "You reach for the Gods, to be accepted into the high priesthood?"
"We shall see. It's plain Norty has need of me."
"I am truly sorry to break your meditation. I have need of your services; I cannot wait until the days pass."

She listened in total silence as Norty recited of the events leading them to the wood to find her, "Is it really so long since last we met? You need a rogue, not the services of a humble paladin."
"Rogues would trust an envoy of the Gods."
"Some envoy I'd make. Come the morning we return to the city. I know the very person you need but don't place your trust in him."
"You are troubled, speak of it."
"Perhaps another time. Your sisters, are they well?"
"Malinna is so happy with Sha'Dal...."
"She has a child?"
"Never will you see another who spoils a child as does she."
"She is one to care, I'm not surprised."
"You must return to us more and see him."
"And Icee, has she a child?"
"Icee has yet to find her elf. She hides it well yet worries it will never be."
"I pity her elf when she does. Blyth named her well; I like her choice of name. Icee has fire burning in her; he had best be the same."

It had taken several hours for Kyna to find the man she was searching for, but he was reluctant to speak in the presence of elves. The room hired from a local innkeeper was secluded and well away from the main hub of the town but he was nervous, and it showed.

"It's against all I believe. They're brothers you ask me to betray."

"Not betray, no. To assist in finding the passage is all I ask."

Norty rose, all of the ways Kyna had used were too subtle for her liking. He was half a head taller than her, but his size did not intimidate her, she had fought bigger and better men than him, and was alive to tell of it, "Kyna is too careful with her words. Betrayal it is and betrayal I would have. You may do so for coin or any reason you may justify to yourself, or I will rip the knowledge from your mind. I give you the choice, yet make it quickly."

He glanced towards Kyna unsure of what to do.

"She can do it easily; she is Norty, enchantress of the Chosen Ones."

He had noticed the feather in her hair the moment he entered the room, his training in observation had saved him from trouble many times. But he had seen others wearing a feather and claiming they were one of the Chosen, some had lived to be embarrassed later. This time he had a feeling, and had learned to trust them, he was a rogue and for him to live to his fifties was because he had learned to listen to those feelings.

He thought it was the way she stood, proud with no hint of fear in her eyes. He had rarely seen people without fear, yet she stood there and those eyes seemed to pierce him, to look right through him to his very soul. Or perhaps it was the way she spoke; sure he was incapable of touching her, let alone harming her. Whatever it was he knew there was only one way to find the truth. Trying to take the feather in her hair he could not feel it in his hand and started to sweat a little.

"None may touch my feather. Does it convince you who I am?"

For long moments he stared at his empty hand, the tails he had heard were true after all. It was said none could touch the feathers of the Chosen Ones.

"You're who you say. I'll show you what you need to see, but I won't be caught with the money on me."

"Why so?"

Taking the money he had been offered he placed two coins back in his bag and handed the rest to Kyna, as an envoy of the church he knew he could trust her, "I will betray for money if there is enough, if all this is found on me I will be assumed guilty. I'll claim to be enchanted if caught."

"Claim what you will. Take us to the Old Jim's place and find the passage."

He nodded in agreement.

Kyna stood, "If you want your money you'll find me in the prayer rooms, for today only."

"I'll be there in a few hours."

Turning she hugged Norty, "Don't make it so long till the next time we meet, and I want to see Sha'Dal soon. Is there anything else I may do?"

Leading her away from the rogue she whispered, "I have thought to speak with you. I have need to know your people and look to you as tutor."

"I'd be happy to teach you."

"I know not why yet I must learn; dreams trouble me."

"I want to speak with you also. Remember our time as we hunted the birds? You spoke of faith; I would speak of mine to you."

"In the woods it was obvious your mind is troubled."

"I must speak to you; doubts enter my mind, as they did yours."

"Then I will return."

"Go and make sure Nortee is safe. You know where to find me."

"Thank you, Kyna; I feel the chase draws close."

Returning to him she nodded, "We are prepared, lead on."

"I risk all by taking you to Old Jims place."

"Nothing will happen to you if you do as I have the need."

The tone of her voice and the look in her eyes convinced him. He had heard tell of the Chosen Ones and from those tales, probably mostly exaggerated; he had no wish to bring their displeasure on himself.

Listening at the door of the warehouse for minutes he decided it was safe to enter. Removing a set of picklocks from his pocket he set to work.

"None are inside."

"I don't trust you or her; I do the job the way I know."

The lock was almost too easy, too simple, as if deliberately left in such a way, within seconds the door was open and they were inside.

His voice was quiet even though it was obvious no one else was present, "You have any idea where the passage is supposed to be?"

Her glance told him enough and he set to work on his task. His fingers moved around the wall, he may have to feel every inch of them and it was painfully slow work. Yet his mind was racing, why the simple lock and easy entrance? His comrades in the assassins guild had spoken often of Old Jim and his warehouse but he had never been here, never received an invitation. It was as if they did not want him near, or could not trust him. But he was a rogue and he knew he could not be trusted, now he had a way to ingratiate himself with the assassins. He was getting too old for picking pockets and cutting purse strings, his fingers were not as nimble as they once had been; several times he had almost been caught.

A few kills while the victims slept would be more his line of work, and the pay would be much better than the few gold pieces he would normally get for his services. He would seek them out after finding the tunnel.

Leaning forward she whispered, "He seeks to delay us, perhaps to wait for friends to arrive and attack."

"No, he works fast for such as he and has no wish to be here a moment longer than he needs. His fingers feel for hidden catches and pressure points. Wait and let him work."

For half an hour they sat while he searched one wall, as he started the second she moved towards him, his look made her sit down, "Stay still, I don't need distractions, let me to do my work."

"If you enchant him he may work faster for us."

"His mind would lose some of the ability to work in its desire to help. He may well miss what he would find otherwise."

Ten minutes later they heard the faint click and were instantly at his side. Turning on his heels he called. "I want nothing more to do with you!"

As she moved to the passage his hand stopped her, "This is for me."

The open panel revealed a set of steps leading down twenty feet to a large circular room, a passageway heading towards the town centre. As they climbed down the air was heavy and cold, cobwebs were forming around the pillars holding up the roof and the smell irritated their noses.

From the beginning of the passage their eyes searched every inch for signs of danger, ears alert and straining for the faintest sound. At his nod they followed the passage for almost seventy paces, the single torchlight he held the only light to guide their way, "We are too late."

"No, they must be here. He could not lie, he was under enchantment."

The disappointment in her voice was obvious, his hand stroked her face; "This passage has not been used for a while."

"They could still be here, in hiding."

"They are not. We would have heard them or your mind seen theirs. The footprints are covered with dust. No new ones for seven days."

"I had such hopes yet now we must start again. Time for me to return to Kessin to see what I may find."

"No, we return home and to Nortee. Pose will comfort her but she will worry even so."

"I know my daughter; Pose will be hard pressed to help in her training."

"I think you would welcome the rest from her training."

"It is good she has others to teach her the ways, yet I feel Pose will be tormented to the limit to teach her ways she should not yet know."

"I know not the ways, to what do you refer?"

"Pose will be asked to teach the ways to alter thoughts in the mind."

"She is far too young, you have explained to her so often."

"Yet she will try her best. I hope Pose will relent and teach her a little."

"You confuse me."

"When she enters the guild she will need to know how to play the mind games others will try on her. They are a test of the enchanter's prowess. The mind is used to push another, to force them back. Yet it is just one of many dangerous ones they play."

"Then why are they left to do this if it is so dangerous?"

"I hear the druids have games also, are they not dangerous?"

Scuffling noises from above made his turn, "Time for us to leave."

"Take us not far, husband, Kyna has a need to speak. I must see her before she leave come the night."

"You will see her soon, worry not."

As he cast his spell to take them away from danger they saw the men advancing; the rogue with them. Kyna was right, they could not trust him.

"I am grown, mother, now five summers in age, I wish to see our land as you promised when I was a child."

With difficulty she fought down a smile, "There are those who still wish you harm. We stay here where it is safe and friends may watch you."

"They attacked but once and in my home city where I should be the safest. If we were visiting other cities it would be harder to find us."

"We may visit the very city where those who would harm you dwell. No, there is an end to it."

She had hoped to talk her mother into visiting the places her heart desired but it seemed as if she would have to force the issue. Yet to turn and argue with her mother was not to her liking, and she had said the words there is an end to it. Spoken normally to bring to a close an argument it was hard for any elf to speak further once they had been spoken, yet she was determined, "There is not an end to it, mother. Your promise to me has been broken. In all my teaching it is spoken it is not the way of elves."

Finglas chuckled, "She is correct, your promise is not yet fulfilled."

"I said not when, just we will visit."

With her father clearly on her side she took advantage, "Mother, your words were 'When we are finished in the city of the elves we will journey to other places.' We are finished, the time is now."

"I would seem I am outnumbered and your arguments make sense. We travel on the morrow, should your father be willing take us."

"I am yours to command. Speak of the place foremost in your thought."

It was hard to decide which city should be first; the lands of man had always fascinated her yet of all the races she knew from her studies the river elves were the ones she most wanted to see. Only once had she seen them, when she was three summers in age. Some had visited wood elf city and spoke to any who would listen of a quest they were tasked with, to find a sword of pure silver stolen from their people.

They fascinated her; their build elf-like yet thicker set due to the mating with man, and their magic was limited, once again she surmised, due to the same reason. Yet their voices had been soft and their movements flowed, as with any elf. Her mother had let her listen to the tale for almost half an hour before urging her onwards to a friend who would teleport them to Gronich, and Xandorian.

He had promised to take care of her while her mother was away for a few days with her grandmother, and she was pleased. Xandorian was her favourite gnome, and she knew quite a few of them now. He was always ready to please her and would play with her in his rough way, teaching her how to dive deeper in the river than she had ever done before, as long as she promised never to mention it to her mother.

He would, on occasion, let her read in the Chamber of Wisdom, if she were quiet and always return the books to their original position on the shelves. He would be in serious trouble if any were to be found out of place; the Chamber was their pride, containing all knowledge not within spell books.

Icee had found her more than once in the Chambers and asked why she was so interested. 'To ensure I know all I may of my friends the gnomes.'

Yet her browsing always took her back to the same shelves and books. When her mother had pointed to the ruined city, it had sparked her interest and she wanted to know all about it, and of those times. It held a purpose, somehow she knew it, and she wished to discover what it was. For now she had an idea of where she wanted to go but it was time for her to tease, just a little.

Yawning she excused herself, "I will think of this, father, you will know come the morrow."

When sleep had eventually taken her in its arms there was a smile on her face of almost pure pleasure as she thought of her visits to other lands.

With her goodbyes said she waited impatiently for her father to come take them to Seaporth, one of the cities in the lands of man. Shaking her head she smiled as she remembered obtaining the promise she could accompany them on the anniversary of her eighth year. Thoughts of man had troubled her since her father had first instructed her in their ways, wondering why they were the most warlike of all the races, fighting for any reason. In her teachings she had found they were friends of the elves, although they had fought against them on occasions.

Her mind turned to the dark elves and why her people hated them above all others. They were elves in all but colour of skin and hair; she could see no reason why they could not live in peace with other elves. In her talks with Pose she had discovered the hatred was returned, they would leave an elf to die if they saw one being attacked, or join the fight against them. Yet nowhere could she discover the reason for the hatred, she bore none towards them. Pose loved her father, the first time a dark elf had ever loved another race, and was the first of her kind to train with elves. Initially none had dared to attack her, possibly fearing the wrath of her mother and sisters, none wished to attack a friend of the Chosen Ones whilst the Gods protected them. Her head nodded a little as she realised the fear of dark elves was waning amongst those who knew Pose. She was well respected by most the enchanters and few would wish to harm her, many considering her a friend. Pose was free to wander around the lands of the elves as she would in her own, the rangers even stopping and escorting her to wood elf city on several occasions.

Pulling a chair she sat and thought for a moment. The only cities she had seen were those of the gnomes and dwarves, this was to be her first time in any other city and would be allowed to walk its streets, to take in the sights. She began to puzzle over what it may be like, how the buildings may differ from the ones she knew so well, on what type of land it was built, whether fertile ground or rock to afford protection. She began to see a flaw in her teachings; she should be instructed in all aspects of other races, not just their languages and, sometimes, their customs.

Standing she glanced towards the door, wanting her father to come and relieve the impatience she found herself in. Her head shook once more; her mother would be displeased if she could see her this way.

'Mother, why is it you alone go with grandmother to their lands? I am your daughter and would follow the path you chose to ignore.'

It was getting difficult to hide her impatience but she knew her father delayed for just such a reason, speaking impatience would be her downfall. She resolved to be calm; he would not be allowed to see it in her. When they came she would feign indifference to the time and say she still had clothes to pack.

Taking the seat once more her eyes closed as she let her mind look around for others nearby, she would calm herself by practicing her mother's teachings. Malinna was closest, in the room to her left, easily within her mind's ability to search; Icee was sat in meditation outside. Her mother and father were nowhere to be seen by her mind, though as yet she could only find a mind within thirty paces of herself.

A new mind became clear to her, an elf passing close by; she inspected the mind as closely as she could, druid; anxiety uppermost within her limited ability to see. Then the mind was gone once more, passing out of range, and she searched yet again. No other minds were near the house her mother had so carefully, if somewhat sparsely, furnished on the forest floor, most preferring the upper trees. When she had inquired as to why her mother had replied, 'Here I see less minds so I may relax all the more.'

Then the mind was back again, the anxiety replaced by determination, 'So, her mind is set on the task she must accomplish.'

The sharp sting on the back of her neck made her instinctively feel for the spot, her fingers finding a small wooden dart. Dizziness washed over her as she tried to pull it out, nausea causing her stomach to heave uncontrollably. Fighting to retain consciousness she stood to call for help, yet words would not come from a mouth too dry to speak. Her hands grasped the table for support as the walls of the room span round ever more quickly. After a few moments of futile attempts to use the table to steady her she knocked it over as she crumpled to the floor.

Her hand slapped her neck as she felt the pain of her daughter, felt the way her mind closed and went blank, she was up and running instantly, her daughter's name screaming from her lips, "Nortee!"

Running with his wife towards their home he knew his daughter must be in serious trouble, Norty was running! She was an enchantress; it was unbecoming to rush anywhere, only once had he seen her do so. As she swung left and headed away from their home he wondered why, but only for a moment. With both her sisters close these last few days he knew Nortee must be already safe. His wife would never have been taken a different route had she the slightest doubt.

Malinna rushed into the room as the figure slipped soundlessly from the window knowing exactly what she had to do. Nortee was her first concern but her sister would want the elf with all her being. Dropping beside her niece her mind formed a picture of the elf and the direction she had taken, a vision strong enough for her sister to recognise her instantly. She had no need to examine Nortee to know where to look; she had felt the sting, but not the darkness, which had swept across the mind of her niece. She must be treated immediately or she would die, already she was losing the link as Nortee began to fade from life, "No, Nortee, no! I forbid you to leave whilst I am here, I forbid it. Listen to me, listen."

With the fleeting figure of the elf just a hundred yards away she found the extra speed needed in the chase, the life of her daughter had been threatened once again, it was all she needed to coax the effort from within her. She would not have this elf outwit her, a chance to find the one attacking her daughter had once more been presented; it would not slip by her. With her daughter's mind returning to consciousness, albeit very slowly, determination took hold, the elf would tell her all she knew. But a smile also crossed her lips as her daughter's mind fought in vain against the spell Icee used to put her to sleep.

Glancing round she saw she was being followed, and did not have to ask who would be chasing her; the warnings about the mother still fresh in her mind. It was exactly the reason why she had brought a spare dart, hoping she might get a chance to use it. This was the first time they had trusted a kill to her without someone watching her every move, and she wanted to impress them. If she could kill the mother it would prove to the assassins she had a place amongst them. The thickening forest to right would offer safety, this was her home and she knew every tree, each blade of grass. Reaching the trees easily ahead of her pursuer she smiled, she would have a little fun with this elf, but not for too long; someone else was close at hand.

Finglas grabbed her, "No, a druid will not be easy to find."

"I see as do all elves, she may hide not from me."

"I will find her."

"The offer is not needed."

Letting her mind leave her body to enter the woods she sought her with all her will, ignoring the hundreds of lesser minds within the area; they held no meaning to her. She wanted just the one mind and would find it, no matter what. With her mind swinging left and right in its search she sought out her quarry remorselessly, until she found the only complex mind in the area, the mind of a druid. Entering the mind she demanded she come to her.

Suddenly she lost all interest in hiding and killing the one following her, all she wanted was to be at the side of her mistress, she had called and must be obeyed in all; it was her duty to serve. Her arms let go of the tree and she ceased to be one with it and ran to her, pleased her mistress had taken the time to wait. Now she would be there to do her bidding, listen to all she said and ensure her mistress was cared for.

With the wood elf standing before her she managed to hold herself back from tearing her mind to shreds. Within her the torment seemed to have reached its limits, but it would only sate the anger within and not get the information she needed, it would be pointless to lay ravage to her mind.

"Return home with me."

"Have no fears, sister; the rogues snake fang poison was used yet had little time to take effect. The poison is well known to me, it has a smell unlike any other."

"Thank you, sisters, she needs to regain strength."

Icee laughed, "She is strong, she tried hard to resist my spell; she is safe and you need to speak with the girl."

"Beloved, best you leave."

"I stay."

Icee took his arm, "Do as she asks."

"I have seen her anger before."

"As is your wish."

The determined look on his face left little room for argument; she turned back to the elf, "Who hired you to kill my daughter?"

She smiled, her mistress had spoken to her and she was pleased.

Sat crossed legged on a chair Icee giggled, "She does not succumb to your charms, sister; you must be more persuasive."

Gently she applied more pressure, unwilling to destroy her mind; it was too fragile, ready to slip into the abyss of insanity. Something, long ago, had driven her far from the teaching she knew as a young elf and into realms fraught with danger and mistrust. All this she could see in her mind, yet her thoughts were on matters more urgent; "Who sent you to harm my daughter?"

Opening her mouth she grunted the reply.

Finglas was at her side, his hand forcing open her mouth, "Her tongue has been removed, normal for one training in assassin ways."

"She is druid, a worshiper of the Mother of Life. Her God gives all to her children and she must be true to her. How may she kill when the Mother says all life is sacred?"

His head shook, "It is the way the Mothers words are interpreted by some."

"Then she must see the words for what she says, not those who would place others on her lips. It is time for her to answer, and to return to the ways of the druids. For a while the Mother of Life must leave her."

The idea of his God leaving him made him feel sick, and in a small way he felt sorry for what she was to suffer. He did not know what Norty had in mind but he knew she would do all within her power to find the one responsible for the attacks on their daughter.

In their discussions he had tried to understand the ways her mind could implant a thought in someone else, to see what was in their mind and to control the feelings within, yet try as hard as he could understanding always eluded him.

With worry for her daughter still high in her she was finding it hard to concentrate on holding the elf within her charm while lost in thought as to the way she could obtain the secrets held in her mind. They were there, along with all elfin secrets, yet she needed just the one. She was a druid, and would love the forest and all within it. With hers sisters to guide her plans formed in her mind and a smile danced on her lips as her plans began to gel. Gently she entered the mind of the elf once more.

Suddenly she found herself on the riverbank of a lush perfect forest, the trees rich with leaves, animals roaming where none may harm them. Watching them she walked through the beautiful land, yet never straying far from the river, occasionally stopping to stroke an animal or offer one food she knew it would love. The thought came to her as she sat beside the river, only the Mother could create such a beautiful forest, to be here would mean she was in the afterlife. Her mind tried to recall when it was she had died, but with no memories of the event she settled to enjoy her newfound happiness.

As her mind watched the elf sitting in the forest her thoughts returned to Finglas and how he would like to see the forest; how it should be and be cared for. She loved the forest also, but could not match his love for it. He was a druid and the forest was his life. To her it was a wonderful place to live; to him it was the meaning of life. She would lay with him for hours as he described in detail each tree, each glade and how the river flowed through the forest to water the trees. His vision of how the forest should be she planted in the mind of the elf, and from the smile on her face she knew the same thoughts were in the girl's mind. She needed to keep the vision in her mind for a while; the longer it was there the more devastated she would be when it was removed. But she could not leave it there too long, her timing needed to be perfect.

Dipping her hand in the river, gently moving it in the water, peace and tranquillity flowing through her as she remembered songs taught to her as a child. All was good in her life; the forest was growing and rich with leaves, the animals within content. There could be no better place in any land, the Mother had planted the forest herself and she knew she had been chosen to help, to tend the forest and animals within it. She had an idea why the Mother had chosen her; long ago she had abandoned the druid ways and the forest when he had first asked her to join the fight against his enemy. Yet her childhood teaching seemed to be true, the Mother was all forgiving and had brought her back to the land she once loved. Her happiness knew no bounds as she closed her eyes in thanks.

The crack from behind startled her for a moment but chose to ignore it; it could be of little consequence in this perfect land. Nothing could harm the forest while the Mother cared for it. The noise started again, gathering speed and changing direction as she turned to find the cause of the sound. Her eyes widened in horror as she watched the fire a little way off to her left, somehow mesmerised as the flames took hold on the grass, devouring it, growing ever larger, eager for more.

For a moment panic seized her, she had to kill the fire before it harmed anything else in the forest; she must destroy the enemy of all life! Running to the flames she stamped on them, trying to put them out before they consumed anything else. Yet the flames ignored her as they sought out other grass to burn. Worry swept over her as she wondered what the Mother would say to her for letting the flames enter the forest. There was only one way to stop the fire; dipping her boots in the water she carried them back to the fire, it was her enemy and the enemy of all, to her it only consumed and destroyed, to leave devastation in its wake. Water had been the enemy of fire since time began, and she would let it fight its enemy again, and this time she would help it. Tipping her boots she let the water splash down on their enemy, but the fire roared even hotter as it consumed the water, as if feeding on it. She ran to get more, surely it was a mistake, water hated fire, they were enemies who fought whenever they met, they must fight again now, they must!

Water must fight to save the forest, it loved life, gave life to all, without water there could be no life. Pouring more on the flames she watched as they grew ever bigger and hotter the more she fed to it. Then the trees began to burn, those closest to the fire at first, followed by the ones behind as they began to twist into grotesque shapes as the fire found them. They screamed in agony as the flames began to dance up their trunks and round the branches, hissing at the fire, warning it to come no closer, yet the flames ignored their protests.

As she watched the elf it pained her to know what was happening to the forest. Though she knew it to be a seed planted in the girl's mind it was strong enough to bring feelings out of her. With difficulty she ignored them as she began to push the ending of the scene. To leave it any longer the girl's mind may turn in on itself and she would never get the information she so desperately wanted. And the girl never able to return to the path she was born to follow.

Her eyes scanned the devastation around her, soon the forest would be destroyed as the flames consumed all in their path. She looked round for help, someone must help but she was alone. All races used the rivers and mayhap a traveller would pass by in a boat, anyone who could help her. As she watched the river it seemed it had grown ashamed of its part in helping the fire, shrinking to a trickle. Where the great river had majestically flowed only dry cracks marked its passing. Slowly she dropped to her knees and forced her eyes away from the river and back to the forest, to the destruction she knew to be behind her. She had no wish to face the truth, but to hide from it, to curl up somewhere until it was all over. When her eyes opened there was not a flower, tree, or a blade of grass to be seen. In place of the forest was total devastation, burned and smouldering ruins of once proud trees. It was too much for her, she could feel it overwhelming her, tearing at the wood elf still within. The ache in her chest could no longer be denied, with tears streaming down her face she gazed on the horror she was witnessing. She had failed in the task set by the Mother and she had no way to explain to her what had happened and why she could not prevent it.

Finglas saw the agony on the face of the girl and a small part of him felt for her, she was a druid and, therefore, a friend, but he could give her no sympathy; his daughter had almost lost her life to her. He began to wonder how she, a druid, could turn from their ways. What could have entered her mind to reject the Mothers teachings of respect for all life, no matter what its form?

Looking up at the sound of footsteps hope entered her life once more. Help was here and she would beg of them, offer anything they would ask, if only they could help restore the forest. Relief flooded through her as she saw the owner of the footsteps, standing as the Mother of Life seemed to be calling to her. Pointing to the forest she looked for help from her God, but the Mother seemed to blame her for this devastation, it was all her fault, her God had spoken. She shook her head, desperate to tell her she had tried her best to fight the fire, she did not know from where it came or how it appeared in the forest. She pleaded with her God to return the forest to its former splendour but the Mother would not listen, not even look at her.

She had done nothing to cause this and wanted to scream to her God, to beg her to listen. As her God turned to face her she held her arms outstretched to welcome to her and the girl ran to them, happiness coursing through her.

The Mother of Life turned her hands palm up to face her and the girl stopped; shocked she should be barred from her Gods embrace. Disappointment and doubt fought for a place within her as she fell to her knees in front of her.

A new thought entered her mind from her God, 'tell me who wanted to harm the elf child; they caused the fire and the damage. Speak and you will be welcomed in my arms and all will be as before.'

A picture formed in her mind of an old dark elf as he handed her a scroll. Reading it she studied the drawing on the bottom.

Norty grinned. At last she had found the one who may lead her to those trying to kill her daughter, the image on the scroll confirming her fears. She had the information she needed and it was time to return the elf to the druids, and ensure she was instructed once more in those ways. If the elf thought her world had come to an end she was mistaken.

Once again she saw her God beckon her to her arms, she had told her who had ordered her to kill the child and was forgiven; she would be welcomed in her arms once more. Swiftly she ran to her for the comfort they offered, for the sanctuary within them. As she drew near her God stopped her once more, and she was confused.

'You have turned from my ways; from the forests I gave you, those you once loved. Return to them and I will welcome you in my arms.'

Sinking to her knees, her forehead touched the earth before her in elfin shame, as she waited for the Mother to forgive her.

'You are forgiven, child. Stand and look back on your past no longer for it is gone. Never must you return to them for you will raise in me a terrible anger against you and your kin.'

Blinking, she found herself in the home of the elf she had tried to kill just a few short minutes ago, the mother of the child standing before her. Fear took control as she knelt before her, ready to accept she was about to die.

"Release your fears, I offer no harm for your action against my daughter, only a path back to the ways the Mother asks of you."

Standing she stepped back, her head shaking in disbelief, unable to understand why they had not killed her.

"The Mother forgives you, as do I. Now you must return to the ways of the druids, as the Mother commands. Finglas will ensure the guild welcomes you if you go with him on the morrow."

Unable to believe how they knew of her vision she knelt once more, the expression on her face asking the question her tongue could not.

Icee took her by the arm, steering her towards the door, "My sister knows, there is no need to ask further of her. Come, this night you sleep in peace once more."

As she watched Icee lead the elf away she turned to Finglas, "I have a new lead, a dark elf hired her and it would seem to make sense, yet in other ways it does not."

"The elves against the union would wish to kill you not our daughter. I see what you mean."

"In harming Nortee they would drive me harder to fight for the union. It makes little sense at all, yet I will find the reason."

"It will be hard to tell Nortee she cannot travel to other towns; she slept little last night thinking of them."

"She will go to those towns, we start in dark elf city yet we must wait."

"Why so?"

"The dark ones enjoy the Festival of Enrok. I know not the purpose yet know even the trolls go not near the city at this time."

"They are accepted there I hear."

"The festival is wild; wine and ale are consumed in great quantities."

He shook his head, "It is at times like these I am sorry my skin is not blue."

"It seems the necromancers leave the city at this time. I blame them not."

"They are loved not even amongst their own people. To leave the city when drink flows so freely is wise."

"We visit with Mel D'elith with the passing of the full moon; the end of the festival. Till then I must return to my guild; word reaches me Caspo Kwil has need to speak with me."

"Is it safe to trust her?"

"We are firm friends. I had a mind to visit with her when I took Nortee to their city yet it was not to be. If all goes for the disunion I will ask Pose to help in the training of their ways."

"You cannot! Nortee is not dark elf."

"As I am not, yet I trained with them and learned, as she must learn."

"So she may enter and place thoughts in the minds of others also?"

"All the ways of the enchantress must be known to her, our ways and those of the dark elves. I would have her know all the ways to survive our lands."

"You know what is best for her."

"Those are to include the ways of the druids, they too are important to her, yet at this time she does not realise how much."

A Mothers Words

The door to her sleeping quarters opening brought a smile to her face but her mother's posture left a heavy feeling in her heart, "Greeting, mother, the day has yet to begin; you rise early to be here."

Elesee took a seat and beckoned her daughter to her, "I would speak before the enchanters' bell summons you to study."

Ensuring the rest of the silks were smoothed she closed the draw; "There is little time; Caspo Kwil speaks I may instruct those who attend first class as mentor. I admit to feeling both proud and nervous."

"It of duties to the young I would speak with you."

The feeling in her heart lifted, "I know little of the ways I must use; advise from you would be most appreciated. Caspo Kwil will observe as I instruct; I wish not for him to be disappointed."

"You avoid the truth. I speak not of the enchanters as well you know."

The feelings in her heart returned as she realised the trap into which she had walked. Here in her room she could not escape; her mother had timed her arrival to perfection. The bell, the only way she could escape, would not be rung for another thirty minutes but she would not succumb to the discussion her mother wished. She has watched as her mother used her ways on man as she spoke to them in her duties as ambassador, to have them realise they had greater needs than the ones so obvious to them. In discussions with others she found her mother, and others, could easily match her ability to turn the subject from the one they wished not to speak. Her mother had always been a challenge and she had enjoyed the battle of wits. Juin and Caspo Kwil were two who could also divert others; it was often with a smile she had watched as they did so.

Though her mother's obvious stance she tried her best to deflect her once more, "I have tried to be as you, mother, yet I cannot be an ambassador to …. them. Nortee shows an interest yet I find it unbefitting she should do so."

"Since the birth of my granddaughter I have held my tongue; now I find I must give voice to my fears."

"I cannot take the role of ambassador, this I tell you so often."

"My daughters are not as others, this I freely admit. I found it difficult to remain silent as you grew; indeed there are times I have fought for your right to be unlike others."

"I have heard how you defied the council and insisted my hair was my concern and not theirs."

"You know so little of those days or of how your father fought so hard against them not you have you banished as Undesirables."

"I knew not father had defied them also."

"He is the strength on which I lean. Do you believe he would stand to one side and fight not for his daughters?"

"To my shame I admit I have thought not of this. I must speak to him."

"You will hold your tongue; he wishes not your gratitude. Though it was my voice the council heard on these occasions he was at my side. It was he who offered the challenge to any council member who dared to object when I spoke my daughters were not to learn the bow. How oft is it we visited with Yester Highleaf?"

"I count over one hundred before our coming of age."

"On each occasion one subject was oft spoken; do you remember?"

"He would speak of our paths. As if ...."

"You begin to see?"

"I believed him to be concerned, nothing more."

"He has the ear of the council; his voice is well respected. Knowing the councils thoughts he was able to help me guide you in life. A guide must not lead but show the way to go. It was through his teachings I became ambassador to man."

"I believed your mother to be ambassador also; daughter follows mother."

"You follow not my path."

"I have other paths to follow, this you know."

"If Blyth had spoken not to all in the forest on your birth would you have followed my path?"

Her head slowly shook, "No, mother."

The slight smile her daughter wore did not go unnoticed, "Enough of your ways!"

"Your voice is not often raised, mother."

"It is not in anger but against the ways you use. An excellent ambassador you would have made. I will speak my thoughts and you will cease your ways to distract me."

"I feel I know the thoughts in your head and wish not to hear them."

"If the words cause heartaches they must be faced and defeated."

She stood, "Another day mayhap. I must be about my business."

"You will sit and hear me."

"I am no longer a child, mother."

"It is of a child I would speak."

"Nortee is my child and her upbringing my concern!"

"As my mother was taught so did she teach me; as I taught you. Nortee is my grandchild and I may not sit and watch as her instruction is forgone and she ceases to be elfin."

She spun round at the door, "Think not to speak she is not elfin! Anger would erupt within her; an anger she has yet to know is there."

"It is of this spark in her I would speak."

Walking quickly back she breathed heavily, "Our ways change! I teach not ways which bind us to the past; ways which will have us fade from this land!"

"Our people were the first created, still we are here."

"Others change their ways and prosper; we change not and suffer!"

"Our people grow; never have we been so many in numbers."

Suddenly she realised, "Mother, the foxes teach you their sly ways."

"My teachings have taken not from you the spark within. Indeed have you just shown it still to be there?"

"It is still there."

"We fade not from this land. Our people grow and prosper once more."

"We are threatened by so many and wars will reduce our numbers. There must be another way, mother, there must."

"Blyth herself guides you. If there be a way she will show it to you."

"The ways of the fox shows in you once more, mother. I will give thought to your words. Nortee will also be once with herself yet it is I who will decide where and in what she is instructed."

"Instruct her soon afore it is too late. If I may be of help...."

"There is a way in which your help would be most appreciated. It seems so long since last I was held and comforted in your arms."

Return To A Dark City

Slipping out of the shadows Pose opened a door before signalling the others, "Best we come at night, our eyes are not as yours, we see little with the fading of the light."

Finglas squeezed her shoulder, "The least time spent here the better."

He had touched her, only in friendship, yet it had sent a little shiver up her spine. She could not help the thought as it entered her mind, 'if not for Norty you would belong to me'.

Dropping the thought instantly she led the way through the hall and down the stairs to a fireplace. Casting a quick look round she pulled a brick, almost silently the fire and hearth slid to one side, "Yet more of the secrets of our city, this known only to the enchanters. It will take us to Mel D'elith; she will be in the Great Hall."

Entering the passage last Norty turned to her, "I see the way you react to his touch, I blame you not for your feelings. He is a good and those feeling are mine also."

"I cannot help what the Gods place in me."

"If anything befalls me I can think of no other I would have my Finglas be with."

She smiled back, she had been given permission for him to be hers should Norty die, but she would give her own life before she would let anything happen to her friend.

Almost racing along the torch-lit passage she called back, "She finds the night suits her and enters the hall to study with the ending of each day."

"Always did she like the night, we would spend hours in the restaurant of an evening, speaking on many subjects."

The door to the hall opened, freezing them in their tracks.

"Who is there? Speak or suffer my wrath!"

"It is I, mentor, with friends."

"Pose, Norty?"

"Yes, mentor."

"You return at a bad time. The festival brings only anger these dark days."

"I came a while ago, a short visit of necessity. I had little time and could not visit with you."

"The enchanters are blamed for the thoughts of reunion and a watch is kept on us. It would have placed all in great danger."

"I seek your help, my friend."

"You have but to ask."

She stopped, her hand gesturing, "I ask you forgive my inattentiveness, I have not introduced to you my husband Finglas."

"I have heard much of the love of Norty; I am a friend to you, Finglas."

He had to try hard to refrain from bowing, "Mel D'elith, from what I hear I would rather be a friend than an enemy."

With a brief smile to him she turned back, "As much an elf as you say."

Once more her hand gestured, "And the pride in our lives, our daughter, Nortee."

"Welcome, young Nortee. Your mother and I are good friends as I hope you will be a friend also."

Nortee gave a nod, "I have heard much of you, Mel D'elith. I wish for you to train me as you did mother."

"We shall see, Nortee."

"You speak out of turn, child."

"You are correct, mother. I speak without thought and apologise."

"Scold her not, she expects her mother to ensure her training is fulfilled, from wherever it may come."

"I understand, Mel D'elith."

"It is dangerous here, why do you come?"

"I seek the one who hired a druid to harm our daughter."

"You know the enchanter and his name?"

"I do not, yet I would see the face and recognise it."

"Many are away; after a festival many return to their journeys."

"I ask to see them all in training on the morrow, if I may?"

"There are many classes and many attend. I will ensure it is possible."

"Thank you, I owe you much."

"A friend seeks not payment. We start with those around their mid levels and their mentors. Come, once we have spoken Pose will show you to where you will be safe."

Entering the hall behind Mel D'elith, she took her by the shoulders, "There is much sorrow in you. Speak to me of it."

"I found long ago how you read the body. You remember the time of your training here? I spoke of the one who was to be mine."

"I remember, yet you say was."

Her face saddened as she nodded, "He was killed on his task to find others to help us the day after you left."

Her hands slipped round her shoulders as she pulled her tight to her, "I grieve for you, Mel D'elith. I know how you must feel."

As she sobbed quietly on her shoulder she held her in an embrace until she was able to face others once more.

Rising early he found his wife sat in the corner of the room, eyes closed in mediation. He had dropped to sleep before she came to lay with him, and it was unusual, they would normally speak of the day before finally sleeping.

"You have not slept?"

"I have not. Much is on my mind."

"You have sung not your morning song."

"I have not as I have instructed Nortee she must not do so."

"The other enchanters would hear and know you are near?"

"I know she would sing her songs, the pull in her heart is strong now."

"Each time I speak of the reason for your songs you do not answer."

"The reason for my song is the same as the reason you must travel."

"Travel is a lust in me which may not be helped, yet it is there."

She rose and woke Nortee, "The reason for my song is the same. I must sing of my fears and hopes. It has the same pull on me as the wanderlust within your soul. Caspo Kwil once spoke the sun brings light to our dark minds."

"I had heard such from others."

"Yet still you choose to ask?"

"I had a mind to hear it from the lips of my wife; Jenay spoke of you."

"Ah Jenay. The mentor of the first class I attended. Mayhap you would not have been so quick to speak with her had you known her a few years ago."

"How so?"

"It is for another time. The enchanters' bell sounds and I must heed it. While Pose and I are in guild this morning you are not to leave this room, it will be far too dangerous. Understand my concern, both."

With Pose at her side they entered the training hall at first light to be there when the one she sought arrived, if he arrived. Yet she was unsure if she would be able hold back her feelings and attack him on sight. She must bide her time, her plans had been made throughout the night and she would carry them through, without the mercy she had shown to the elf who had tried to kill her daughter. First would be the classes of mid levels, the elders trained them and he would be most likely to be at one of those classes. If he were not in the first she would visit each of the other levels, until they all had been searched, and he had been found.

The students entered in groups, each giving a nod to their mentor before taking a seat, anxious to know why an elf was in the room. Yet none spoke; their customs demanding they wait until permission had been given.

Benjin Di'Vere rose, "Greetings. Today Mel D'elith would speak to all."

Slowly she walked round the seated students and, as they stood, spoke their name aloud, returning to her desk before facing them once more, "I have introduced all to those you see before you. I have now the pleasure to introduce you to them"

Standing between them she placed a hand on Pose, "Many of you already know Pose, some have trained with her."

Pose nodded, she knew most of from training, and a few by reputation. Only the newest of them to reach the proficiency demanded by this class were unknown to her.

She placed her other hand on Norty, "Only one has trained with this elf."

Mel D'elith smiled inwardly as a gasp of astonishment ran round the room, "She has trained here with us. She is named Norty, enchantress of the Chosen Ones."

Stepping forward she gave the customary nod to all in the room.

"She has powers above all other enchanters, what you may have heard of her is probably true."

Mel D'elith smiled at her, noting her cheek colour had turned a slightly darker shade of pink, "She is here to see how far we have trained in their ways. She is a friend to me and to this guild! Think not to fool her, as did I when first we met; she reads the body as you read the scrolls. I would have one stand and offer the challenge."

With deep satisfaction she noted each of the students stood, "Those of less than understanding thirty may be seated. I thank you all for the courage you show, and your support for your guild."

Most of the guild sat reluctantly, each knowing the chance for honour had passed by. To battle an elf was deemed an act of good faith, to fight the legend of the elves would ensure fame for the opponent.

"Jesit is the one I choose."

"I thank you for the honour of being chosen."

"In a few moments you may not believe it such an honour."

"It will be so to lose against her, yet I have no intensions of so doing."

"Take your place, the...."

She stopped suddenly as the door burst open, a young enchanter entered; as he stood before her he nodded,

"You know our ways; we are not to be disturbed when in training. If it be not of great importance I will speak with your mentor."

"Jol E'ath is found in his study, a knife in his heart."

"Come, Norty, make haste."

They found him as the student had done, lying on his left hand side; his stiletto visible under him, it had entered the heart. Slowly Mel D'elith turned him over and gently closed his eyes with her fingers, and heard Norty gasp. "What is it Norty?"

"The enchanter I sought; it is he."

"Dead, yet who could have killed him? He was old yet his powers were greater than my own. None could have passed to do this. He was my teacher... my friend... my mentor."

"There is an answer easy to see, he would have been off guard if his killer were known to him."

Mel D'elith was in distress and she could see it, waving the onlookers from the room she closed the door behind them, then turning to her she held her as she cried for her loss.

Finglas held her tight, "You did not find him; I see it in your face."

"I found him in his study, a knife through his heart. Come, this place saddens me. Take us to another town, any town, take us from here."

"What of Pose?"

"She is to remain a few days under the protection of Mel D'elith. Word has been sent to her family, they would dare not to harm her."

"It is good to know she is safe."

"It is good to know my husband cares for her."

For days they visited new towns, showing Nortee sights few of her age would see, and should not see until she was at least of age. Yet every place visited was carefully chosen, no city where they would not get a warm welcome was visited, and the fact did not go unnoticed.

In the room hired for two-nights she decided it was time for questions to be answered, "Father you take us to wonderful places and for this I thank you. Some of the people in them are nice, others strange, yet I know you hold back from me."

"There are those who love elves and those who do not. We visit where we will be welcomed, nowhere else until you are older. Then I will take you where ever you wish."

"Father, seek not to protect me, I am able protect myself from harm."

"You are so sure?"

Breathing deep she stood as erect as she could, "I am enchantress and druid born. My powers are from you both and protect me well."

"How would you protect yourself from an assailant, little one?"

"With my enchantress or druid ways. It is my choice which I use."

Rising from her sitting position in their room Norty moved towards her daughter, "I thought not to do this for many years. Think of me as someone who wishes to harm you."

Almost instantly she felt a mind trying to enter hers and realised her daughter was fast, the way she had tried to stop her was clever, but she threw her mind to one side.

Her arms wrapped around her, "One...two.... three. You are dead."

"Unfair, mother, your mind is so much more powerful than my own. You deflected it with ease."

"You think others have not powerful minds also? Yet there are other ways to attack. Husband, attack our daughter, yet do it slowly for her."

He saw the reasoning behind her method and approved, she was beginning to think she could win over any situation. His wife was correct; she needed to be taught a lesson.

As he moved towards his daughter he felt her mind try to enter his and the time spent with his wife was put to use, he had learned how to deflect a mind entering his, as long as the mind was not too powerful.

Sidestepping she tried to roll away but he easily caught her, his arms wrapping around her, "One... two... three. You are dead."

"Father, you are too fast and my mind did not stop you. How is it you could do this?"

"You believe I would not know how an enchantress uses her powers? Others know also, little one. You wear your hair in the way of an enchantress while your clothes are of one not yet of guild so your powers are still weak. Any will know the ways you would use to fight them. Many may stay your mind for it is too weak to harm, too weak to enchant. Twice now you have died, how many lives do you wish?"

She hung her head, "I am chastised. I think myself above my station."

He smiled, "You learn well, daughter. There is yet time and so much for you to learn, your journey in this world has just begun. Take your steps one at a time."

"You are right, father."

"One more thing, daughter."

"Yes, father?"

His voice became a hard, "You are elfin kind! When someone speaks of your wrongs lower not your head in shame."

"Yes, father."

He opened his arms for her daughter to come to him, "It is your heritage, daughter, always remember."

The Robe

Once more back home he stroked her hair as she sat with her head on his knees; he liked it there. She had removed the amulet from the back of her head and had let her hair cascade down her back in the fashion when she was young, before she had left for training.

Content with his hand as he gently stroked her she sighed, "She guides him well and will be there as long as he needs her. Yet it is not the cause for which I worry."

"Sha'Dal looks to Nortee for guidance. For what cause do you worry?"

"She approaches the time when my sisters received the gift of mana."

"It worries you, yet why should it?"

"I worry she may have the pain I had to bear."

As his mind returned to the day and remembered her pain a shudder ran through him at the thought of how near he had come to losing her. Death himself had called her to him and she had almost followed, but won the fight against him. For her victory over him Death had given her a gift, the gift of charm. He knew all enchantresses were trained to charm, but knew the attempt could be resisted, or broken. Many an enchanter paid with their lives when it happened. Any who broke an enchanters charm felt pure hatred for them crash into their mind. They wished to kill them above all, letting nothing bar their way. Yet Death had given her the gift of never failing charm.

His hand sought hers and found it, "I have no wish to think of the day our love was almost over before it began."

"I wish not for her to bear the pain as did I, but I wish for her to have the pleasure of mana as did my sisters."

"I remember my gift, it entered me at the moment I started the walk down the druids' hall. Its timing was perfect."

"You have spoken often of it, yet I love to hear you tell the tale, it was a happy time for you."

"A warmth spreading through my whole being, I remember it filled more than just my heart, my very soul was given the gift."

Removing her head from his shoulder she tried to hide the sting of tears, "My sisters spoke of those feelings yet when I had the gift I was filled with pain, I have no pleasant memories to ponder on."

Although she tried hard the tears would not hold back, they trickled down her cheek leaving a track for him to see. He knew he could never match her smile, yet all his love was placed in one for her now, "Brush the tears to one side. Those days are best forgotten."

Nortee felt her mother's sadness and turned to look at her but did not move, knowing it was for her father to comfort her. Her turn would come later when they would walk to the glade; it was a ritual for them now.

Her arms went around her mother's neck as soon as they sat in the glade, "You must have no fears for me, mother. I will welcome my gift, even the pain you had to bear."

"You should not have to see Death as did I, little one. Nor have to bear the pain. Mana is as it says a gift from the Gods. Never has anyone been in pain when it is given."

"I will be happy to follow in your stead, mother, pain or no."

"You have but a few years left to choose which profession to take first. Has your choice been made?"

"You know my choice; I choose the path of my mother, the path of the enchantress."

"Your father knows also, yet I feel he will be saddened when he is told."

"I wish to tell him, mother, I will do my duty."

Her arms held her shoulders, "Then you must do it soon. He grows impatient and should know."

"It will be done on the morrow, when you have helped with my hair. It is time for me to wear is as you do, yet I am different to you, and my hair should show the difference."

They walked to him side-by-side, mother and daughter in harmony, bowing low as he stood to greet them.

"Father, I have important news for you and would have you sit and listen."

He started to speak but her hand rose and he remained silent.

"I have made my decision, father. I know of your feelings yet I must follow my heart and my mother. I choose to first follow the ways of the enchantress, and later the ways of my father and the druids."

"It comes as no surprise to me. I am happy you follow your heart and your mother. I am proud of you."

He saw her smile was natural and childlike in its ways, she was growing too fast for his liking, but to him she would always be a little elf.

Her head slowly turned for him to see, "I have thought long on my hair father; how does it suit me?"

She had it fashioned much the same as her mothers, pulled back and passed through a small amulet, but where her mother's was straight back she had a twist as passed over her ears, hiding the tops of them. The amulet she wore on her neck was thin and curved to follow the flow of her neck, pure silver in colour and made from mithril, it shone bright in the sunlight.

As she turned a second time a lump found its way to his throat, she was turning into an elf every bit as beautiful as her mother, "I believe I have seen your robe before."

"Mother stitched it when she was the same age as I to impress you. I wear it now."

Opening his arms he hugged her, "I am as impressed with you as I was with your mother, well I remember the day."

"I made no adjustments to the robe; it fits her as well as it did me."

"The robe seems made for her."

"It will suffice for now."

The thought struck him and he turned, fear had showing on his face.

"No, I do not have such thoughts in my head. I have no cause to return to Leffing dungeon to obtain a robe as mine. She will have a robe before she begins to train, no danger will be involved."

"I remember your feelings as Elesee and Juin left for the dungeon. I have no wish to see Nortee in such pain and misery."

"I have my robe, mother. I care not for another."

"I care, little one. I plan another robe and another you shall have. White is not the colour of an enchantress."

"You wear your green black robe and it is not the colour of an enchantress. Pose wears red to show she rejects the ways she knew. I too wish to be different; I wear my robe with pride."

"You have the courage of your mother and the pride of your father."

Turning they saw a wood elf stood close to the corner, a large grin on his face, in the clothing of druid but his stature taller than any elf before him.

At first she was overjoyed to see him, before a cold hand suddenly clutched her heart, "No, Messenger! Tell the Gods I refuse them. No quest was she born for; no quest shall she be asked to do. I forbid it!"

As he walked towards her daughter she stood in his path, "No! The Gods may not have her as a plaything as once they had of my sisters and I."

With a smile he disappeared, to reappear behind them in the wink of an eye, "The choice of a quest for her is not for you to decide, and mortal spells may not harm me."

"I may harm you, Messenger, as well you know."

"Nothing in your world may harm me."

Her staff came up to threaten him, "This you made for me and it is not of our world but of your own. I think you may be harmed by its power."

"It has the power to harm me."

"Then leave without my daughter, she is not for you or the Gods to toy with. I have done their bidding. They may ask no more of my family."

"They ask nothing yet of your daughter."

At last Finglas relaxed, "Then why are you here?"

"You know not of this? The wife of Finglas invited me."

"Untrue! I did not call for you."

"You wished a robe for Nortee and thought to call me to help, I answer your call."

"I had thought of calling."

"My promise was to come when you called and your need great."

"I have not called or asked help of you."

"Then ask of help from me."

"What is the price you would ask?"

"The price is paid."

"Who paid the price?"

"The Chosen Ones and their protectors all have paid the price."

"You speak of our quest?"

"Much is asked of you. The debt for the robe is paid, as is for the armour of Sha'Dal and the robe of the unborn child of Icee."

"Icee is to find her elf at last?"

"Icee has been tasked."

"Then we also; my sister fights not alone."

"Danger there is for her, yet a danger she asked for and she alone will face. The Gods heard her voice and granted her wish."

"We are as one, what one sister fights the others fight. It has always been so. We fight as one!"

"She will thank you not to fight by her side."

"We fight as one!"

"Enough! It is not for you to decide. I have need to take Nortee to the land of my birth."

"I would go with him, mother, you have spoken often of Messenger and never has he harmed you."

He bowed to her, "Come, Nortee, daughter of Finglas and Norty."

As she took his outstretched hand they were gone.

"Messenger seems to remain a part of your life."

"I had thought to ask for him to help Nortee, yet I have no wish for the Gods to quest her. Only a robe to protect her; nothing more do I ask."

"Your robe is a gift the Gods blessed you with yet they owe nothing to Nortee. How may we ask more of them?"

"I ask Messenger as a friend, he has the powers to grant my wish."

"What is the task set for Icee? I knew not what he meant."

"Nor I, she asked no quest. I must think of this."

Sitting she retraced her life as she had done once before, when Messenger had hinted at the answer to the quest for which they were born, knowing it must be after the quest was won she started there. It took her only moments before she grabbed her husband, "I know her task, I know."

"Then we may help her."

"Messenger is correct she would not wish it; she would surely not."

He had not seen her lose control since she saw the pendent around his neck after he had killed the giant; soon after her training in high elf city begun, "Tell me, do not leave me waiting."

"I cannot, she would know your happiness for her and be ready. She would leave this instant if she were here. I may hide the happiness as she is not close enough to link; my thoughts will remain lost to her."

"Yet when you see her next you will remember and she will know."

"The thoughts and pleasure in my heart I will conceal. She will not know."

"Who will not know, mother?"

Turning she rushed to her anxious to know all was well, nothing amiss. Her eyes fastened on Messenger, "You say there is no cost to the robe?"

"Her robe is as yours."

"In what way?"

"In the power to protect."

"I thank you, Messenger."

"Goodbye Nortee. You will have need of me in the years to come, when the time arrives call my name and I will answer."

He vanished from the spot, his voice remaining "The Gods have yet no quest set for her."

"Mother it was so strange, there was nothing to see except the anvil and the furnace. He spoke I would see only what I understood."

"He took you to his anvil?"

"The noise was pain to my ears as he hammered the robe and gave it me back. It feels the same yet softer."

Hope raged through her heart as she touched the bottom of the robe with thumb and forefinger as her stiletto was drawn from its sheath at her waist. Messenger had struck her robe on the anvil as he had done to her daughters. Anxiously she stabbed at the robe, her eyes closed in silent prayer before examining it. The blade had left no mark she could see as, once more, she stabbed the robe but with more force, yet still no mark was visible where the blade had touched.

"He has made it as mine. The robe is as armour yet is still soft to the touch."

"I disliked Messenger," Said Finglas, "yet now I would thank him."

Removing her amulet she handed it to her mother, "He took this also."

Examining it with great care she saw no difference, "Did he place it in the furnace?"

"No, mother, I saw not what he did. The work was on the anvil and I am not tall enough to see the top. I saw nothing, only hearing a wolf as he howled close by."

"You were gone but moments yet so much has he done."

"I have been away for most of the day. I returned on the back of a dragon."

"No, little one, you were gone but moments."

Her head dropped to one side as she put the amulet carefully back in her hair, "How can this be?"

"I know not the ways of Messenger. When first I saw him I was far from this land and not linked with my sisters, yet they were but two hours behind me. He has ways strange to time and place."

"As it would seem, mother, yet I rode home on the back of a dragon."

"I have met him as the dragon. The power of the amulet will show itself when the time is right, little one."

Stepping back she bowed, "I have a request."

"Ask."

"I have ridden on the back of a dragon, visited the land of Messenger before I become of age. I have a name you have chosen to use only at times; I would ask you not to use the words little one as you speak to me."

Finglas laughed to his wife, "Not yet of age and has a wish."

"And I worry for her."

"There is no call for worry, mother."

As she remembered the words her mother once spoke to Icee her arms wrapped around her daughter, "My daughter you were born and my daughter you will forever be. It is my right to worry about you and I will exercise the right whenever I feel the need. Your wish is granted; no longer will I use the words you dislike."

"I have never disliked them; it is now inappropriate to use them."

They lay together once more talking over the day, completely relaxed as she lay by his side, "You took Nortee to the glade to train once more."

"We like the evening, our training and talks."

"You are still undecided as to the power of her amulet?"

"I pray she will never have need of it."

"She would be in the greatest of danger to use it?"

"The Gods give nothing free. Always a payment is expected."

"The Gods did not intervene; this was the work of Messenger."

"I hope you are right. Enough talk, I have a need to be loved."

"A task I undertake with pleasure."

"You still wish for a second child?"

"I wish for another child, if it is your wish also."

"I have no wish for another child."

She could feel the disappointment as it ran through his body. She let it happen; she wanted to tease for just a moment longer.

He nodded.

"Nortee is my pride and we have much to teach her."

"She has much to learn and little time left before she leaves."

"Have you thought of what we will be when she leaves?"

"I have not."

"We will be alone much of the time. A time when you may resume your travels around our lands."

"It is of little consequence. I wish for our daughter to be with us."

"There are also two other choices."

"Which are they?"

"You could stay with me."

"I will always be with you when you need me. What is the other choice?"

"We could adventure together, take me to the places you visit, I would see them with you once more."

"A choice I like."

"You remember where you took me on the day of our wedlock?"

"The special place I found?"

"I would visit it again, too long has it been since last we were there."

"On the day our daughter walks the isle of the enchanters you will spend the night in our place once more."

First Steps

Stroking the rabbit in his arms he reassured him with each movement of his hand, keeping him calm for the test to follow. His wife and daughter needed the rabbit for training yet he did not like the thought of any creature being used. Carefully he placed him on the table.

He felt no fear as his friend had bent to pick him up in the forest, he knew he would not be harmed, and was pleased when he felt his fur stroked. Then he was carried him into a strange burrow, one so large he wondered why it needed to be so big; if it were smaller it would offer more comfort.

He saw her the moment he entered, the colour of the grass but he knew she was no friend to him. The one in whose arms he had been wore the colours of a friend, those of the trees and the grass. Panic seized him; he must run to the one who would protect him. Confusion took him, there was another in the burrow, one who looked as the snow in winter, she would not harm him; he knew it. Yet why was she as winter when it was still so far away?

"Now is the time, your mind has grown strong enough to enter the rabbit. Feel him with your mind; let him know who is mistress and who is the one instructed. Let your thoughts enter his head, yet with care, Nortee."

Her mind reached out easily now, the years of training at her mother's side had made it fun. As her mind bridged the gap to the rabbit to feel its thoughts she found fear his main instinct; the one in the colour of grass was no friend, and she realised how he saw her mother.

High in his mind was friendship to the one who had held him in his arms; her father was looked on as a friend to the rabbits. She began to wonder how he saw her and probed a little deeper. There she found, to her amazement, how she fitted into the minds of the animals around her. He saw her as a friend clothed in winter's colours. She was happy; her druid self needed to know the animals were to her as they were to her father, friends. She was pleased beyond anything she had thought she would ever be, the thought choking her a little. Her druid half showing itself to be just as important as her enchantress half.

Mentally she shook her head to clear it of the thoughts, for now she must be an enchantress, and an enchantress she would be. It was time to delve deeper into the rabbit's mind, to see what he wanted at this moment.

After fear the need to feed was in his mind; she wanted to feel each of his thoughts yet they were hard to focus on. Although her mother's training had been strict yet informative she still found it difficult to single out an individual thought. Her mind probed deeper into his but his fear grew as she entered. She felt his fear, not just sensed it, as it coursed through her, almost seeming to have form, somehow touchable and acting as a barrier to prevent her from moving deeper.

She wanted to get past, to break it down and see the rest of his thoughts, but she resisted. It would be easy to smash her way through, to take his thoughts, but it was wrong and she knew it.

He felt fear, he was hunted; something wanted him in a way he had never known before. He had survived attacks from those who would eat him as he would eat grass, yet he could see no danger. The one in the colour of grass was too far away and he knew he could outrun her as easy as he could the foxes and wolves. The one in winters clothing was a friend and would not harm him. He wanted to know where the danger was so he could run away, or stay here with his friend for protection.

She could see the rabbit's reasoning, something wanted him and only the burrow or the one who held him could give him protection. She smiled, the druids were friends to the animals, it had always been so, and she saw in what way they thought of their friendship. Sadness took her as she realised the fear she was causing within him and withdrew a little, instantly he began to relax and, as he did so, she began to see his fear more clearly. The way to enter his mind suddenly became so obvious to her. She began to sooth his fear, as she would stroke a friendly animal, pleased as it abated and he lay down to snuggle deep into her father's arms. Keeping a thought on its fear, soothing and caressing it, the rest of her mind journeyed into his thoughts. She found, as long as she kept a thought on keeping him calm, the rest of his mind was like a spell book she could wander around and turn the pages as she could the scrolls she loved. Her mind read each page, each line until she knew it by heart. Now she could return to tell her mother of the wonders she had found, of how it felt to explore a mind, to tell her father of how the rabbit saw him.
She tried to withdraw, to follow the path back to her parents, but found herself lost in the pages of his mind, no longer knowing which was forwards or which was back, and fear found her. Desperately she searched to find which page she had read first, yet the harder she searched the more lost she became. It was as if she was trapped in a maze with no way out, the more she moved the more confused she became.
'Think, Nortee, think. Mother has trained you so much better than to panic in this way. There is a way out; all you need is to think.'
In her mind she drew a breath, she had only to think of how she entered his mind and she would find the way home to safety. Each avenue she tried she found new thoughts in the mind of the rabbit, at each turn she discovered its mind was more complex then she had expected. Thoughts were in its head she had not seen as she had wondered around.
'Mother, where are you when your daughter needs you so?'
An image of her mother stood before her and instinctively she stopped her search, she had come for her to show her the way home, and followed with a sweet relief, from the mind of the rabbit.

"She is so white, will she be well?"

As Norty stroked her daughter's hair her eyes flickered open, "You were lost but safe home now. Lay a while and recover."

She no idea why she had found herself on the floor, her mother's arms under her shoulders, supporting her with ease, "What happened, mother?"

"You became lost as you explored the rabbits mind, forgetting to memorise your path as I had instructed. As you do in the forest you must make a note of where you tread, which direction you take."

"I was so happy to feel his mind, mother. Never has there been such a feeling. It was wonderful; so many new paths were open to me."

"Like the paths you will tread in the world you much watch the direction they lead. Had the rabbit had a more complex mind you would have been lost a long time."

"I see why you chose a rabbit. I saw you there, how did you know I was lost and to come for me?"

"I was with you as you entered his mind; you were so interested in what you found you saw me not. I followed you as I was followed when first I looked into a mind."

"Did you also get lost?"

"The Gods gave me my gift. To me there is no mind where I may be lost."

"Not even in the mind of father?"

"I have never been there. I have no wish to go."

"I am feeling well now; may I rise?"

"Go and lie down, think on the rabbit and the pages you saw. Think of how to make your tracks across his mind visible so the next time you will know your way home."

"How should I mark my way?"

"The way is obvious, should you think on the training I have given."

"She looked so ill. Are you sure it is safe for her to do this?"

"It is a path all must take; yet she began to worry and then to panic. She stopped to think yet still the way out did not slip easily into her thoughts. An enchantress must know instinctively the way around the minds of all. Had she thought as I had instructed she would have found her way back with ease."

"How?"

"She should have looked for the first feeling in the rabbits mind; fear. She had only to look for his fear to find her way out. She stroked his fear as she should be done, to keep his mind from panic, which would ensue had she not done. Yet when she found her way out not obvious she forgot to keep him calm. In releasing his fears there were more thoughts within his head and she lost the way home because of them."

"I cannot understand what she saw and have no way of knowing. If you were to see a mind would you know to whom it belonged?"

"If I had seen the mind before I would know it again as easily as you see a face and know to whom it belongs. We see the shape of the mind and not the thoughts within."

"I follow you not."

"Many believe an enchantress may read the thoughts of others, at times we use it to our advantage, yet we see only the mind as a whole, not the thoughts until we concentrate on them."

"You have entered the minds of others?"

She wondered where this was leading, and hoped she was wrong, "Yes. Many when I train."

"When you charm someone do they know you and feel you in their mind?"

"They know. Where do you lead me with this?"

"You teach Nortee to enter the minds of others."

"I have tried to teach how to mark her passage in the mind of another She has not yet leaned; there is more for me to do with her."

"When you lose contact with their mind they hate you?"

"Yes, none likes to have their mind turned to another's will."

"I wish you to enter my mind."

"NO! The mind is not to play with. Never will I enter yours."

"I have wondered long on your powers. It would give me an idea."

"NO! I will not enter your mind. I have no wish for you to hate me."

"You entered the minds of others and they do not hate you."

"They were enchanters and control their minds. If we were to use our full power to charm the other then hatred would be the result. There would be too much hatred for each; and the guild would fight amongst themselves and there would be no enchanters."

"Lore says if a guild were to fail then all elves would perish."

"I have thought on this and agree. If any guild were to cease then blame and fighting would ensue."

"Yet I have a strong mind and I would resist you."

"You could not. I destroyed a mind in the city of man with ease using only a little of my power. I will not do it."

"Enter only so I may feel you in my mind."

"NO!"

"I ask of you, I wish this to be done."

"No."

"I would know your powers. Touch my mind gently and cause no hatred."

"I must think on this."

Eventually she knelt at his side, chin resting on his knees, "I will do it, the merest of touches."

"Will there be pain?"

"I may cause pain, terrible pain in the mind, to have you to believe your body was hurting, yet, not physically. I do not wish to do such to you."

"Then why has your mind changed?"

"I like not a lie in any form. It may be done and mayhap teach you how to more strongly resist an enchanter. I will touch your mind as you ask."

With infinitely more care than she had ever used before she let her mind slowly leave her body and go in search of his, all the time careful to keep her face neutral, knowing the smile of any enchantress was part of the way to charm. Then his mind was there before her, eager and open, and she withdrew until only one part of it was visible to her, the rest shrouded in a grey veil. Gently she reached out, keeping the rest of the veil drawn across his mind, and touched it.

She let him feel her, all the time stroking his mind with calming words, and in response his mind sought hers, seeming to grab her, to hold her, embrace her. Gently she let their minds melt and mix together, to enjoy the touch. It was a form of loving neither had felt before, too intimate for words, too wonderful to reject.

For minutes they enjoyed the thoughts of each other, to know feelings neither knew, and their love grew with each moment. As she started to pull away his mind tried desperately to keep her there, she stopped it and withdrew completely.

He looked down at her, "Never have I seen you in such a way. You mind is so clear, so beautiful. I envy the enchanters their powers."

"You have a mind I like, it embraces my touch. You could never be an enchanter, you could deal not with the feeling after, never know the hurt we bear or how we deal with it. It is a reason why we use pets as a first defence and then spells, charm only a last resort or for special purposes."

"I have seen the link and feel those linked to you."

"What are your thoughts on the linking?"

"I would like not to be linked."

"I had thought it would be such. I have been linked all my life and would not like to be otherwise. It must be as disconcerting to you to see the links in me as it is to me to be unlinked. Whom did you see in my linking?"

"I saw Malinna with Sha'Dal and I saw Nortee. I knew who they were and the direction they were, yet I could not see their faces."

"I see the faces as well as knowing who the link is with. It happened only after Nortee was born. Now I feel her stronger than I fell you."

"I would join with you once more, when you grant our wish for a second child, to understand it more."

"During love my mind flows with thoughts. It may be too much for you."

"Our love will protect me as it did now."

"We will join again, yet not at such a time. We must keep the secret of how we consent."

"Ah the female. Were I blind I would say you were of the race of man."

"Why so?"

"Their females are ones for secrets, and they hold so many."

"When did you discover this?"

"I have spent time in their company."

"When was your last visit to them?"

"I have asked Elesee to instruct me in their ways and to be with her during her ambassador duties. I begin to see the way they think, their beliefs."

"You scheme, Finglas, I would know why."

"There is a feeling within me, starting when Nortee was but three in age. You have spoken of your dreams and the danger in them. I try to be prepared."

"Man loves the elves."

"Those in your dreams are different, not the man we know."

"They are so different, only this I know."

"In which way?"

"I cannot say. I am here and I am safe. Yet if you were to forbid me from journeying to their lands...."

"I swore on our wedlock never to forbid your hearts desires. I will not do so now."

Chance Meeting

His voice echoed along the narrow mountain pass, but for all the softness there was still a threat to be observed, "None may travel this pass. Turn and be gone lest I kill you now."

Icee stopped her steady run as her hands went to her hips, changing her posture to one of defiance,

"I tread the path the Gods set for me and alter for none who would offer a threat, least of all to a voice with no owner."

A dark elf stepped into view some thirty paces ahead of her, dressed in the robe of a wizard he presented a formidable sight, his skin shining bluer in the cold of the mountain pass, his hair reflecting the hue as the moonlight cast harsh shadows across his face, as if to offer no second chance were his commands ignored.

"Return I say; I give no warning but this. Leave or die."

"I leave or turn for none but follow the path set for me, yet you may dissuade me with words, the power is within you."

"Be gone!"

She laughed, "The power of words is strong yet you fail to use them. Have you the power to enforce your demands?"

"I have all the power needed to best an elf. Be gone and you will live."

"Use the words within you or stand aside."

His answer came as a ball of flame hurtling towards her, "Taste the power of action. Words are not for me."

Walls of ice surrounded the ball, shrinking it until there was just a flicker left to see. Then both were gone with her gesture.

"Robes of a high wizard and you cast but a fireball. Ha! You are not what you seem."

"I give but a warning. Be gone!"

"Use the words you know you should."

Casting once more he summoned a hoard of creatures from the air around her, enough to cause fear deep within his victim and send them screaming in terror.

"Your antics amuse me yet I have delayed long enough. Step aside."

"Be gone! I give no more warnings but this."

"I grow weary of your last warnings, I hear too many of them."

"Then taste the power of the true dark wizards!"

Summoning his strength he cast once more, the ground began to shake beneath her feet as flames soared into the air.

Instantly she cast and rose in the air leaving the ground heaving beneath her, "I delay no longer, the words to use have spoken not."

The ground in front of him exploded in fragments at her gesture, shards of rock engulfing him as he tried to step away. He fell, wounded.

Slowly drifting down to his side she wondered why his reactions to her spell were slow; he should have countered them with ease. Her arms went under his unconscious body, she must teleport them to Malinna and ensure he was healed, "I tried to warn you. I asked you use words you knew you must speak yet you would not listen to me. Oh why did you not speak them? Now I must take care of you for the rest of our lives, and I thank the Gods."

Bird songs woke him and his eyes flickered open, someone was sat at his side and the surroundings were different. Gone were the mountains and the cold, instead was the smell of a forest and warmth.
Malinna moved quickly to stop him from sitting, "Lay back you are to rest."
"What have you done with me and who guards the pass in my absence? Where have you taken me?"
"Icee did as she should and brought you to be healed. My sister and her husband stood guard and none have passed. You are in the land of the wood elves, the land of my sisters and I."
"I must return to my guard duties. I am disgraced."
"There is no disgrace when you do your best before an opponent."
"Few compare to me."
"Icee spoke you cast as a fifth lesson student, easily could she resist those spells."
Relaxing at her smile he let himself be pushed back to the bed, "I had no desire to harm her, only to heed her passage."
"Why would you wish such?"
"I cannot answer."
"You cannot or will not answer?"
"I will not."
"You should have killed her yet you did not, something in you does not like the killing."
"I kill and am proud to do so!"
"The killer is not in you or you would have given no warning. There is more to you."
"I kill when I have the need, she was not such."
Her head dropped a little to one side as she thought of her sisters, "We shall see, we shall see."

Malinna rose as they entered the room, "Sisters, he thinks to withhold from us his reasons."
"Sisters, these are your sisters?"
Standing between them Icee gestured, palm up, in the direction of Norty, "Elder sister by thirty minutes Norty is the enchantress of our trio."
Her hand moved to her other sister, "Malinna, little sister by thirty minutes, and the cleric we need for guidance. The day of our birth Blyth gave to us our names, mine she decreed to be Icee."

"You are the Chosen Ones?"

"By such we are called. You have been introduced, was your upbringing in such poor taste as to withhold from us your name?"

"I am Kare E'Thelt."

"At last I know your name and it pleases me."

"How so?"

"I have a liking for you, Kare E'Thelt; you have melted the heart of Icee."

Icee sighed, lost in thoughts of him, "I love him, sister, I know not why yet I love him so much."

"I feel your love for him. Messenger was right; you had no need of your sisters on this task."

"Messenger spoke of him?"

"His words were of a task set for you and we were not to help. I had thought it would be for you to find the love you asked for so long ago."

"He will be mine, sister, I swear it. I will have him unto wedlock."

"It is easy to see, sister, yet there is something in the way he moves, it disturbs me a little."

"What is it in him, what do you see?"

"I know not, I saw him realise something and resolve take him. I know no more."

"Have no fear, sister; you saw his realisation of our love and his resolve to be a part of me."

"Mayhap it was, sister, mayhap it was."

As she watched Icee leave her home her thoughts were troubled; she had seen the way he looked at her but could not determine in which way it was. But she knew she would soon find out.

Malinna opened her hands, "The last of the shards from the rocks as my sister's spell struck them. You sought to stop Icee with fire."

He looked at her, puzzled.

"I joke, Kare E'Thelt."

"I have heard wood elves have a strange sense of humour."

"Yet we laugh, sir."

"She is powerful, what understanding is she?"

"She felt the tingle of eighteen but days ago."

"She cannot be so low. She stopped my spells with ease and with one cast won the fight. My understanding is of the thirtieth level."

"She is Icee, born by the Gods demand and gifted above all wizards, as were her sisters also gifted."

"Norty has trained in our ways with Mel D'elith?"

"You seem not to approve."

"I do not approve! Never should she have been allowed near our city. Were I there she would have been killed for such effrontery. She and she alone caused the fighting taking place now. Some of my people would join with you again; I do not think those ways."

"Your mind will change. Icee wants you, best you surrender now."

"She is nothing to me. I would duel this Norty. Send for her. Now!"

The door opening so suddenly caught him unawares and he knew why she was here, but did not know how she knew so quickly. Malinna was still beside him and had not left the bedroom even for a minute. The look on her face was enough to warn him, never had he seen any in such a furious mood, but he had to continue with his plan, there could be no backing out.

"Kare E'Thelt, is this how you repay a kindness? Challenge me to the duel and not my sister for it was I who brought you here!"

"Be grateful you are not the challenged! She causes this war to come and she will pay with her life."

"She would win your challenge with ease! Yet she did not cause this war, Kare E'Thelt, you did."

"How can you say such?"

"You and your ways cause this war! You see not the light but only the darkness you were born into!"

It had worked and he was thankful. If she kept her anger it would serve to play into his plans, "Pretty words yet words all the same. I challenged your sister and the challenge stands. Or is she afraid of me?"

"My sister fears none!"

"Lead me to your arena."

"Fool! You choose to die this day!"

"I have no intensions of dying."

Sat in the challenge arena her mind recalled the last time she was here, death had been the result and she was challenged once more. Not by an enemy but by the elf her sister loved. With eyes turned towards the heavens she began to have thoughts on love. Elves fell in love instantly, a blessing from the Gods many thousands of years ago. Now it seemed it was a curse, if elves were to fall in love slowly Icee would not love him and she would not be going through the torment she was now.

Sat in the balcony watching her sister in the arena below Icee could not keep still. Her sister and her love were to fight a duel to the death and it was tearing her apart. If he won she would kill him, her love for him over as her sister died; he would be dead an instant after she lost the link with her. If Norty were to win she would have killed the elf she loved. The only honourable way would be for her to leave the forest, never to return. Yet how could she leave her sisters, and how could she stay with them when Norty had killed him?

Standing she cast her pet spell before turning to look at her sister in the balcony, knowing her thoughts. She had tried to plan, to find a way around the predicament in which she found herself, but none came to mind. Always she had plans for each eventuality and now she was at a loss as to the outcome. It was easy to surrender to him, to hope he would spare her life, but it would place Icee in a position impossible to live with. She would have to accept he had defeated her sister and reject him and his love, or to go with him to his city and probably be killed before she entered the gates.

The time for planning had passed, she watched Malinna escort him into the arena as she had been asked, and from the look on her face she knew she had the same thoughts as her sisters.

"Here me! Kare E'Thelt challenges Norty to a duel. The bell has rung for ten minutes as Lore demands. I ask they fight but fear to do so. I ask they bow and reject the challenge, yet I know they will not. I should wish each to fight with skill and courage, yet I will not ask such of either. In this there may be no winner only a loss for both. The challenge commences!"

"Ready, foul elf?"

"I am never ready to fight."

With his hands circling he cast a fireball, but as her shield of living glass formed around her it bounced harmlessly off.

Puzzled she wondered if she was reading him correctly so early in the challenge.

"So you think your shield will save the likes of you?"

Casting again his second spell was halfway to her when her spell hit the fireball and it exploded in the air. A smile started, at last she realised why she had seen his body move the way it had; she knew his plan and her part within it. Happy now she cast again and liquid poison dripped from the air above him. She watched as he rolled out of harm's way.

"A poor cast for an enchantress!"

Once more his fireball hurled at her, her living glass shield protecting her from harm before her spell exploded on his chest, sending him backwards and down to the ground.

"You win, I surrender. Spare my life; it is yours to do with as you will."

Careful to keep the smile to herself she beckoned him to approach her, "Assume the position of surrender, yet it will come at a cost to you."

He dropped to one knee, head bowed; "I pay any price asked of me."

Her voice rose so all may hear, "This is my will. You will stay here with my sister Icee to tend to her biddings and teachings. You have the protection of the Chosen Ones during the time you remain here. With the passing of three new moons your life will once more become your own."

"The price you ask is high."

"You refuse to accept my terms?"

"I pay the price you ask."

"You may stand. Icee wishes the teachings to begin."

Standing he winked to her, his voice almost too soft to hear, "Thank you."

Icee was close to begging, "Sister I am at a loss, explain to me."

Sitting her down she offered a glass of wine; "You beat him in a fight, Icee, a disgrace to him for he was the guard."

"You know my thoughts of wine."

"This time you will drink, sister. He had three choices, to run and hide from others and live his life in fear of being found. Or to face those he had let down whilst guarding them."

"To be beaten when you gave all is no shame."

"It is their way, not ours."

"You spoke of three ways, the challenge was the third?"

"He could have challenged you but it was not the way he wished for it would not work to his advantage. He asked if I were the one trained by the dark elves, so finding a way to issue the challenge."

"I would not hurt him unless he harmed you, why did he not issue the challenge me?"

"You know not their Lore. He was hoping I knew of those ways. Remember I spoke of his body movements when first we met?"

"I remember well."

"When he cast his spell I clearly saw he had no wish to fight and I understood why he challenged me. He cast only a low spell, one my shield would not feel or be powerful enough to destroy; they were for show only. Honour must be met. I also had to act the part; I cast a poor spell from which any may dodge."

"As I watched I thought it foolish of you to cast such a spell."

"He relied on my knowing their Lore and not fighting back, to accept his surrender and to make the punishment suit his needs."

"He *wanted* to stay with me?"

"His body screams for you, sister, I saw as you should have done. Often I have offered to instruct you the way the body speaks, as does the voice, had you accepted my offer you would have seen the words also."

"I must go to him. I have not the time to learn, sister."

"When your drink is finished you may leave, do not seem to be in a rush."

Finishing the drink in one swallow she turned to the door, "The wine is finished so I may leave."

"Your sister makes my punishment hard. Three new moons is a long time to wait. I will be happy when I am free of this place."

"I will ensure the time passes slowly for you. You have much to learn and I am to be the teacher."

His plan had worked beyond his expectations. Norty was versed in dark elf Lore and had seen the way he wanted her sister. She was a Chosen One, a wood elf turned wizard of good intentions. All were against his teaching but he cared little for them at the moment. He knew he wanted her no matter what her beliefs, or his own, may be. He had been granted three moons to win her, yet it seemed she might put up a fight. Her words were soft showing no feelings for him. He wondered if the fight was to be hard or easy, he would prefer the latter. Icee stirred him as no other had done. His life knew love and she must be his, no matter what.

"Is it wine I smell on you so early in the evening?"

"Sister believes it fitting I drink before returning here. I disagree with her yet she is the elder."

"You are of age; you need not accept all she says."

Yawning she excused herself, "Never has she acted without reason. The wine serves a purpose yet I am unsure of what it is."

"You do not drink?"

"Drink serves only to dull the senses. So many times I have watched as those who partake in drink act in silly or futile ways. It is not for me."

"Yet this time you drink her wine?"

Sitting down she felt tiredness taking her body, "It is for a reason; elder sister would not...."

Catching Icee as she fell asleep he lowered her gently to the bed before covering her with a silk sheet, "She is full of ways to ensure her sister is loved and comforted. I believe I may enjoy the task she sets me, and watch you all as I learn."

Dragon Kind

Placing a plate of food on the table she sat beside him, "You have no cause to worry, he wished me no harm."

"Yet you entered the arena again and I was not here to protect you."

"You could not have protected me, it is against our Lore."

"This I know, yet it is in me to protect you. I swore the oath on the day of your birth yet I would do so even without."

His words caught her heart, and she liked the way they tugged. Standing she began massaging his shoulder, when he was tense it relaxed him so much, "He hoped I would see his feeling for Icee, nothing more. He may return to his people with head high, and take a wife with him."

"At least some good comes from all of this. I am thankful Nortee was with Keitun; she would have been distraught to see you in battle. What does she do with him? When I call they are in the forest, I find them sat together talking, yet I know something happens."

"She will speak nothing of it to me."

"The link is also a curse, she knows when I arrive and has time to prepare."

As her mind filled with strange thoughts she did not remember when she had stopped massaging his shoulders, until his voice seemed to call from a distance, quietly asking to be heard.

"I am sorry. Thoughts enter my mind to distract me."

"Are they of your dreams of man?"

Her arms went under his shoulders, her forehead touching his, "Malinna and I are needed in the land of dragons."

Pushing her away he held her at arm's length, "No. It is too dangerous."

"It is not dangerous for us. They expect us and all will be safe."

"How so?"

"Their thoughts enter my mind, I know their needs."

"Of what use could they have for you or Malinna? They are so much more powerful than any."

"They have an ancient one, a white dragon, too ill for their magic to mend. They ask we take Malinna with us to heal him."

"I worry over this."

"There is little call to worry; you are to be with us."

"None know the way to their land; it has been hidden for centuries."

"You are to teleport us to the druid circle near the Mountains of the Two Sisters there they will come for us."

"Of this you are sure?"

"Come, I must speak to Malinna, she must be ready soon."

"Time is so precious?"

"Without Malinna to help he has not long for this world."

The Mountains of the Two Sisters were well named; from where they stood they rose majestically in the northeast, to take the shape of twin females looking out across the plains before them. Yet it was a barren land the sisters gazed upon, little grew except hardy weeds and moss, the grass hard and sparse, clinging desperately to life between gaps in the rocks. The plains were vast, stretching for over five hundred miles. Giants claimed the plains as their own and many a visitor was chased down and killed by them. Few would like to choose between the slow deaths offered by the giants, the sadistic ways of the ogres to the north, or ripping of limb from limb the trolls in the south would grant.

Most of the races had tried to find a way past those who inhabited the shadows cast by the sister as rumours of other lands beyond the mountains abounded. No passage into the mountains had been discovered, yet still they searched, still they failed, there seemed no way to go but over the mountains. Raging, boiling seas guarded the shore where the mountains finished; many a sea born expedition had been lost, the fate of the crews unknown in those seas. It was if the Gods themselves guarded the secrets beyond the mountains.

Looking around Finglas shook his head, "I hope the wait will not be long, we have no business here and the way the Sisters look disturbs me."

"We were asked to be here as few frequent this land, the dragon's promise was to come within minutes. I pray they do."

Malinna picked up an arrowhead, "Some share not our dislike for this place."

Examining it Finglas looked puzzled, "Only the cave dwellers use arrow tips of stone, yet they are three hundred days to the south. This is here less than two days, blood still shows on its tip."

"Mayhap they have just left?"

Malinna pointed to the sky, "The puzzle will wait; the dragons come."

As he slipped the arrowhead in his pocket he could see them in the distance, four dragons heading towards them, their great wings beating slowly as they drew near, circling overhead before descending, landing feet from them.

They bowed low, eyes towards the ground, unable to look at them until they had been bid to stand. It was deep rooted within them and they knew not why; they could not look to the dragons without permission.

"Rise, those days are long past."

They saw the dragons clearly now, three yellow and a red, one hundred feet long with wings of fifty feet. Their heads enormous compared to the elves, and somewhat frightening, their front teeth almost as long as the elves were tall. Scales covered them as they would fish, and their claws gleamed pure white in the early evening sun.

"Choose a mount and hurry, time is as precious."

The ride was exhilarating to Norty; the wind sweeping her face as they sped at an unbelievable speed towards the setting sun. Desperately she tried to hide her feelings; it was unbefitting of an enchantress, yet the wood elf in her thrilled as the land below swept so swiftly by. It was her most deeply hidden secret. She loved to travel fast, to ride the swiftest of horses; they set her heart beating as nothing had done before. Yet it did not remain as closely guarded as she had hoped. Elesee also knew of her weakness.

For five minutes the hurled along parallel to the mountains and she thought she caught glimpses of land beyond them. Her head shook; there was no land beyond the mountains, if it existed she knew the druids would have found it long ago. As they continued her eyes strained, searching once more; unable to believe the sights were just figments of her imagination. A bright flash from below one of the sisters caught her eyes, as if a golden mirror had winked at her.

At last the red turned to Malinna, "Has grows weaker with each passing day. You must save the ancient one; he has yet to choose his successor. If he were to die before he does we would be leaderless and fighting would be renewed between my brethren."

"You fought a war amongst yourselves?"

"You believe us to be different; do not all the races wage war amongst themselves?"

"It saddens me to admit they do; wars bring naught but pain."

"In the days before the coming of other races, when the world was large and had room for all dragon kind, we were happy. First came the elves and we treated them as pets for six thousand years. With the coming of the gnomes you saw the freedom they enjoyed and wished for freedom also, eventually it was gained."

"I have never heard of this."

"It was many, many thousands of years ago and the consciousness of those days has passed down to you."

"How so, I have not heard of us as your pets?"

"Did you not lower your heads and kneel when first you saw us? This is the consciousness of which I speak. In your stories you tell terrible tales of us, each of them portraying us as evil, we are not, such is the legacy left behind of us. Then came the other races, one at a time. Troll, ogre, dwarf, giant and then, worst of all, man."

"Why is man the worst?"

"They wanted all the lands, not just the ones the Gods have given them. They are aggressive beyond all others."

She nodded; she had seen the ways of man when first she had visited their lands yet still she liked them. As the younger of the sisters she was unhappy it had fallen on Norty to follow their mother on her ambassador duties, Norty held no love for the race of man.

She wished to follow her mother as ambassador to them yet it fell to the elder daughter to follow in the footsteps of the mother, as eldest son followed the father. Only she held a love for all races, Norty seemed to dislike any not of elfin kind while Icee looked on others with indifference. So often she had tried to speak to Norty, to convince her there was good in man, yet always she would argue. No amount of persuasion could change her thoughts. Yet never once did she mention her wish to be the ambassador; the role was for Norty alone.

"Slowly we were forced back into ever-smaller parts of the world as the races grew and demanded more space. We fought them all, the elves included, only some of the gnomes refused to fight against us, riding on our backs to carry the fight to some of our enemies. A few believed there was hope, if some gnomes refused the fight then so might others. It was then we made our mistake and split our forces. Most wanted nothing to do with any not of dragon kind and we began to fight amongst ourselves; it almost sealed our fate, so few of us survived. Realising our mistake we fought to hold back the races whilst those of us remaining pooled our magic and found a new land, the land we take you to now."
"Why have none found your land, surely the druids would have done so?"
"Many lands are unknown to even the druids. Ours cannot be reached with any magic known to others. You are the first to see the lands. Watch."
His wings beat faster as he flew a little way a head of the others to let forth a long roar. A blue point appeared in the skies before them, glowing like the first of the evening stars. It began to grow in size, swirling like a whirlpool to hypnotise them. Then they were in the middle of the pool and saw its beauty, and before they could begin to enjoy it, it faded.
"Welcome to the land of dragons."
The red began a steep decent, two yellows following his path while the mount of Finglas veered right and flew on.
"What is the meaning of this? We came in faith and you betray us."
"He has no call here and would distract you from your task. He will be returned to his home, whether or not you help the ancient one. Malinna will heal as you help her."
"Malinna has no equal in the realm of healing."

The cliff top was several hundred feet above a sea so vivid a blue it looked unreal while the rocks were as none they had seen before, grey for the most part with specks of colour glittering in the strong sunlight.
"To the north are forests so green and rich you would think yourself in the afterlife. Deserts lay to the west and in spring they bloom with flowers not yet seen by elfin eyes, filled with powers of magic as yet unknown to you. South lays the great sea full of fish for our needs, while east the mountains rise high and we may sore on the winds. The land has, above all, a peace we wish to retain."

"Peace would die with the death of the ancient one?"

"The reason we called to you. The cave to your left is his home but I have a warning for you. As you are he will kill you, cast the illusion of a baby dragon for he thinks himself a young one. His mind is gone and he wishes to play as he did a thousand years ago at the time of his birth. Keep the illusion or both will die."

"Malinna may cast not the illusion, she will be killed."

"He will think her your pet, whilst you keep the illusion she will be safe."

"I have not the power to cast the illusion of a dragon, never has an enchanter been able to do so. In our Lore dragons see through illusions, he would attack me."

"You think us stupid to forget such? I have a scroll for you. Read and cast the spell."

Taking the scroll she shook her head, "I cannot read dragon."

"You are a Chosen One! Read the words and cast your spell!"

Once more she looked at the page, studying for long moments before she realised, "I do not need to understand the words, only to speak them as they are."

Speaking the words aloud her hands rose above her head, as they came down her palms twisted inwards for the spell to be cast on herself. As grey bubbles of smoke dissipated they saw her illusion, a baby white dragon standing before them.

"Now enter the cave but be careful. Be a dragon, do not act as one."

Finglas watched the other dragons descend and land on the cliff edge, "What is the meaning of this?"

"Fear not, the Chosen Ones have duties to attend and you may distract them. I take you to the forests of Nor'checith where you may relax and explore during your time here."

"My wife will be safe and no harm will come to her?"

"I cannot give such a promise. She must be what she must and try to help her sister when the time to heal is at hand. Their task is dangerous in the extreme, yet it is a task in which I hope they will be successful."

"How can you know of her, of Malinna?"

"We watch your lands as we have done for countless centuries."

"Why would you watch and not show yourselves?"

"The time of the dragon is past for your lands. You are a young race and have far to travel. The Chosen Ones are to be the guides on the journey for the race of elves, and of others also."

"Ack, you speak as does my wife, in riddles."

"Even a riddle has its place in the world. They are not there to confuse, but to help once it is understood."

The Ancient One

With trepidation she entered the cave, Malinna close by her, slowly walking the one hundred paces of the passageway. They saw him at the end of a gigantic cave, spinning in circles and laughing; happy at the game he played. He stopped as they entered, growling at them.

"You I have not seen, or this pet. Who are you?"

Thoughts of compassion entered her head but swept them to one side as she returned the growl, "Ha! You forget your friend and her pet so soon? You are not worthy of me."

"Friend, forgive me. My head hurts and makes me forget."

"Some friend I would be if I knew it not."

He started to spin again, "Chase your tail. Catch it."

Now she would have to play her part as it opened out before her, and was worried. There was always a plan when she had to fight, several plans, but this was not a fight, "I come to sleep, the day ends and I grow weary."

His eyelids dropped as a scowl took over his face, "Sleep? We do not sleep but every hundred years."

Realisation came in a flash, the tales of the dragons told in her childhood were wrong; in them dragons slept at the end of a day just as any other. They were wrong this time and she began wondering how many other misunderstandings they had towards them. She had made a mistake and needed to correct it, quickly, "It is one hundred years since I slept, as it is with you."

The scowl remained, "I have no need to sleep; my years are not yet passed."

Imitating his scowl she let sarcasm enter her voice, "Ha! You think not? Why do you tire so easy? You have been awake too long."

"We sleep. Your pet will guard."

Her claw pointed to a corner of the cave, "Sleep there. Call if any enter."

As he circled the spot he had chosen to sleep she copied his ways, she could not afford any other mistake. The last one was easy to overcome; the next one may be their downfall, even their death.

With her eyes just slits she watched for signs of him sleeping, although she was tired she must wait until he slept to begin her hastily thought out plans. But she did not realise how tired she was, it had been a long and eventful day, only her strong will managed to keep her from sleep.

They waited for almost three hours before long heavy breathing and a slight whistle as he exhaled confirmed their hopes. Time was passing and she was getting worried; to keep the illusion of a dragon was draining her of strength, and she could not keep up the pretence much longer.

All illusions drained strength when cast and needed strength to maintain, this seemed to take more than any other. The illusion she had cast of a troll to enter their city had drained her the most. Her strength almost gone before she had left, thankful a passing wizard had seen her shortly afterwards and offered a teleportation home. Without his help she knew she would be found and killed without mercy. This illusion taxed her to the limit; the troll was easy in comparison.

At her beckoning Malinna crept from the corner, her fingers gently running over his enormous head, waiting for her sense of touch to find the cause of his illness. With all her being she willed her sister on, she was almost too tired to keep the illusion and was afraid if it dropped the ancient one would know, and kill them the instant he woke.

Malinna worked as quickly as she dared, it would take time and she needed Norty to ensure she had all she needed. She could feel her sister's strength draining but needed her mind to help in her search for the cause of his illness. If she could see the dragon's mind she may be able to tell her where the pain was, and so quicken her search.

Norty was at a loss; the dragon's mind was too active, she wondered how he could sleep with so many thoughts running through his head. They served to slow her down as she tried to find a way into his mind, but the path was difficult and hard to tread. Never had she seen a mind so closed to her, she shook her head at her sister.

The time dragged by as Malinna ran her fingers over his head, before they began the tingle she knew so well. It had started when the dwarf, Graforge, was brought to her care, his arm broken in training; she had felt the pain of the break and healed his bone and muscles.

Now he almost worshiped her, and most of the dwarves were her friends, she had spent as long with them as she had with her own race. For a moment she paused to smile and nod at her sister, the dragon would soon be well again and she could drop the illusion causing her so much distress. As Malinna cast the spell he snapped instantly awake.

Desperately she fought to find a way to keep his mind from thoughts of harming Malinna. Every path to the dragons mind she explored quickly, dismissing most of them as traps, others as false leads. Then her mind entered a strange world, visions of ages long since passed flooded through her of a land still young, when only dragons inhabited them. The scenes were almost mesmerising as she wondered how he would know of times before his days. Then she saw the reason, his dynasty lived within him, all the memories of his forbears were as clear to him as if he had lived them himself, and she knew why his mind had been so active, his ancestors' thoughts flowed freely while he slept.

Then her mind was thrown from his as easily as she would throw a student in their first class from hers. He had turned his attention from Malinna to her, and she was happy, her sister could now heal him while she took his full attention, if she lived long enough for Malinna to complete her spell.

His mind entered hers, powerful, irresistibly exploding into her thoughts, pushing her mind to one side as it examined her, probing her as she could an animal. She fought back, desperate to get his mind out of her head, but she was powerless to stop him, it was not just the ancient one in her head but also his ancestors. Never had she found such a powerful mind, he was toying with her, using only a fraction of his mind, showing her his power was unstoppable.

As he pushed harder scenes of her death assaulted her mind. Giant claws ripped her to pieces; teeth gouged huge chunks from her battered body and chewed on her flesh. Nausea swept over her as she saw what was to happen, but with all her will she fought back with her mind, sending thoughts of sleep and calmness to him, but still he advanced on her.

"Fool! You think your puny mind a match for me? Stand and fight!"

His head lowered as a slight trickle of smoke began to rise from his nostrils; he would burn this so-called friend and rip her to pieces with his claws, smash her body as his teeth ripped at her. She had betrayed him, called him friend yet was his enemy, and for such she would die.

Slowly she backed away while all her being screamed for her to run, but there was nowhere to run and she could not leave her sister to the fate she had seen in her mind. His flames would follow her if she ran along the passage and in there she would die, there would be no escape from his fiery breathe. Her only hope was to circle him, to keep him from breathing his flames while Malinna finished casting her spell.

He was almost upon her, his great jaws wide and ready to breathe fire when he stopped, eyes blinking as a puzzled look took hold of his face.

"Elf, you are elf? You were dragon yet now elf."

Her thoughts reached out once more and touched his mind but they were thrown away with such power she staggered, collapsing to the ground.

His thoughts pushed at her mind and she could not resist the onslaught, her mind was brushed aside so easily. She wanted him out of her head but he ran free amongst her mind, and she hated him with venom.

Focusing on his thoughts she pushed at his mind, but she knew she might as well have been a baby trying to fend off a predator. His right claw swung round in an arc and scooped her up before bringing her towards his great jaws.

As pain and darkness formed around her she called, "Goodbye, Finglas."

She awoke to find Malinna tending her and the ancient one looking down on them. She tried to stand, to run, but Malinna held her down.

"Stay, sister, he has no thoughts of harm to you."

"I hurt you, elf, I did not realise how soft are your bodies and I squeezed too hard. I damaged you but your sister is a mighty healer both you and I are as we should be."

Slowly she sank back to the floor and breathed a sigh of relief, but she could not help the hatred she felt for him. She wanted to reach into his mind and treat him as he had treated her, but most of all she wanted to kill him.

"He is well again, sister. He had a growth under his head, I removed it and he became himself once more."

As his great paw was offered to her she fought back the feeling of hatred, to reach for her stiletto and give him pain, any pain. She did not want him near her as, for the first time I her life, she knew how others felt when an enchantress left their minds, and it sickened her.

Finglas laughed as the bear's lunge towards him took it over the small drop and into the lake, "Too slow, my friend. Thrice I have fooled you."

The bear's head rose from the water and let out a growl.

Laughing once more he dived in the lake and swam toward him, "You are strong, friend bear, yet you must look to the path ahead of you."

Once more he growled as he tried to catch Finglas with his right paw.

"No, my friend, I will not be caught so easily. Come, I hunger and I know where we may both enjoy a meal."

Dropping lightly from the tree he held out his hand while the bear licked it. "Honey is a food we both enjoy, friend."

With the bear settled beneath the tree he was content to lay and relax with him. The sound of wings made him realise his time here was over in this perfect forest, "Seems our friendship must now end."

As the dragons set them down in the barren lands they dismounted somewhat reluctantly.

"You have done well, Malinna and Norty. We thank you."

"I am only too pleased to heal him, why were you unable to do so?"

"Our magic is not of healing, we have no such ways. Our bodies heal quickly; we rely only on our own natural abilities. A debt is owed, the ancient one will live and be well; there is mayhap another hundred years for him in which to think of a successor. Think of us in your hour of need, your call will be answered."

A New Friend

"Mother we come to the glade to speak and train, not to sit in silence."

"I am sorry; my mind wanders many paths this night. We will train."

"After you speak your mind. You told the tale of the dragons to father yet I feel you miss out so much. We will speak of them first."

"I leave out what I ponder on, nothing of importance to you both."

"Is this not the same as a lie?"

Her head snapped round to face her, "I have lied not to your father. You will still your tongue!"

"Withholding the truth is the same as a lie, whichever way you choose to look at it."

Her eyes flashed, "I do not lie! I wish not to worry him with my thoughts."

"You withhold them from me. I feel heaviness in your heart. Speak of it."

"Is there nothing I may hide from you? Think of your chosen profession, would you not be better with the choice of druid, as is your father?"

"There is more to this, mother, you speak so much and say so little. Think not to hide thoughts from me."

The half smile she wore began to spread slowly over her face. Three smiles she held in reserve for special people, Nortee, Finglas and her sisters, her smile was returned and they hugged.

"It seems my training of you in the way the body speaks has been well received."

"I love those lessons. Now speak your mind to me."

"I think of the words spoken by mother on the day I left to train, 'The enchantress can control the mind of any living thing, but it also makes them the most feared and hated of all the professions.' This I have always known, yet her words I have never truly understood until now. Think hard on your choice, you and Sha'Dal alone have the choice. Think hard, daughter, think hard."

"You do not tell all. How may I decide when I know not all the facts?"

Her eyes closed and opened slowly, "I will explain. I *knew* I would be hated by any mind I tried to control; yet I did not understand why. When the ancient one entered my mind he threw my thoughts aside as easily as I would those of a student in their first class. I resented his mind entering mine yet I could do nothing to stop it. I started to hate him with a passion I have never known in my life. I had thoughts of killing him and now I *understand* how others feel when we leave their mind. I wish not for you to be hated."

"I am proud of you and of your profession. I may no more change mine than you change yours."

Her hand moved to place a finger on her mother's lips, "There is an end to it. We come here to speak and to train. You must now tell all to father. We will train now and you will speak with us later."

She nodded and Nortee removed her finger, "Train me, mother, there is one who may be better than you as an enchantress."

"And who would be so?"

"I will be better than you. I have you as a mother and to train me, how can I not be better?"

Leaning back in the chair he thought, "Still you hate him?"

"I still hate him with every fibre of my being, yet I try to push the feelings from my mind."

"Then why cannot others do so when you leave their mind?"

"They are not trained as we, nor are their minds as strong as ours, I struggle even now, and it is a struggle I think I may lose."

"You are strong willed. I have no doubts you will win."

"Yet doubts still remain with me."

"Nortee is outside and is not often she relaxes and enjoys a day such as this. Come, we watch her."

With the sun high they sat and watched their daughter practicing chasing with Sha'Dal, dodging his attempts to tag her a few times before he touched her. Instantly she spun round, her hand reaching for him, missing by inches as he dropped and rolled left, standing with barely a pause in movement to continue his flight.

Finglas laughed, "I know not who is better."

"Sha'Dal is more of a druid than Nortee and his senses help him dodge easily, yet Nortee is the more agile."

As she sat between his legs facing their daughter she felt him lift her hair letting it fall across his legs, stroking it gently as it lay there, "My hair has always been a favourite with you."

"Since your birth I have loved it."

He had dreamt of her hair for many years, when she was younger he had been fascinated by her long hair and hoped she would never have it cut short in the druid fashion. Elesee had told him of her fights with the council, of how she had defied them and let her daughter grow her hair ever longer. When they had threatened her family with being outcast from the forest as Undesirable Elves she had remained steadfast in her denial, walking from the meeting without a word or backward glance.

Smoothing her hair he broached the subject of the dragons once more, "I understand why you spoke not all the tale."

"I am remiss; I knew yet withheld much from you."

"There were reasons, think not of it."

"Sha'Dal is called away."

"Ack, the linking is still a puzzle for me."

"Study time is here, Nortee must learn more of our Lore."
Standing slowly her hand reached for his, pulling him up, her eyes never leaving her daughter, "Watch."
His eyes turned to his daughter standing seventy paces in front of them; her arm outstretched and steady as a small hawk landed gently on it.
Pulling her arm to her chest she made soft noises to the bird, stroking his chest with the back of her finger.
"He is her first charm?"
"No, she has not charmed him, this is different. How it comes I am unsure."
"Then how do you know she has not charmed him?"
"I see his mind; it is not altered so it is not charmed."
As the hawk flew off she called to him, "Bye, little friend."
Her head dropped to one side and she called again, "Coming, mother."
"Explain how you controlled the bird, Nortee."
"I did not control him, mother. I saw his mind and asked to be his friend."
"How did you ask? There was no charm or control in his head."
"I saw loneliness in his mind I wished to fill. I called to him with an offer of friendship and he accepted, I had no wish to bend his will to mine."
"From where did you see his mind?"
"As he flew close by I felt his loneliness first, he has lost his mate."
"We train now. Tomorrow we speak of this."
"Mother I am no longer a child. I would speak of my future with you now."
"As you say, you are no longer the child I think you are. Sit and speak."
"I ask you speak with Caspo Kwil and see if I may join the guild."
"Tomorrow we speak with Caspo Kwil, some are accepted to the guild early, yet remember it is a privilege not a right."
"I fear to be a failure to you."
"If such a fear were in me I would not speak with him."

Their loving over he turned to her, "She is yet too young to train."
"I have trained her since her birth, before her third week, as all teach their children. She exceeds my powers when I first went to studies."
"Yet you worry for her?"
"Do my worries show so easily?"
"I see them where others may not."
"I have noted how your interest grows when we speak of the body's language."
"It may one day be useful to know such things."
"You may join us if such is your wish."
"I see all I need to know. What are your worries for Nortee?"
"She will be powerful, and with her druid half believe herself unstoppable. This is the worry to me; the reason I consented to speak with Caspo Kwil before the time most would be accepted into the guild. He will understand my concerns and why I must ask his permission to approach Pose."

My Friend The Enemy

Pose sat in front of her students, "You are all here for the first time as enchanters and the first lesson is one of vast importance, yet you may not think such. Today we learn the importance of dress, why it is so and why we dress in certain ways."

Standing she slowly walked around her students checking each in turn, giving advice here and prompting posture there, "Each wears a robe of bright colours as individual as each of us, and for a purpose."

Pulling the shoulders back on one of her students she continued, "Posture, as well as colour, is pleasing to the eye. They help us to win over the ones we wish to do our bidding."

She stopped at a familiar face, "Your hair is a worn in a way which does not enhance our looks, Aurorai Minlets, and every part of you must be perfect. When you are dismissed we will speak of the way it should be worn."

"Yes, Pose."

"You are past the coming of age, why is it you wait to join this class?"

"Nortee also starts training this day; I have delayed my training in order to be with her. I believe training may be more easily understood if enjoyed with a friend."

"I understand, yet training should not to be left until you wish to start it. Training alone will be your guide throughout life, and without it your life may be short."

"Yes, Pose."

Turning her hand gestured to Nortee, "I have spoken of looks and colour. This is *not* the way to dress as an enchantress."

Clutching the robe by the shoulder she pulled Nortee to her feet, "White? Really! It soils so easily and it has no charm of its own. It presents little in the way of looks, and this one is particularly poor on looks."

"How dare you!"

"I dare for I am the mentor. This robe is a disgrace to our profession and I instruct not one so poorly attired. You will change it immediately!"

"I will not! Mother stitched this and I am proud to wear it!"

"Ha! A mother's stitching, and it is in such poor taste. Tacky, poorly made, and reeking of sloppy workmanship; an ogre with her club as a needle would work better. Remove it immediately."

Anger flared up in her, "Take back your words!"

"Words given by me are rarely taken back. You are as much a disgrace to your profession as is your mother."

"I hear enough. Defend yourself!"

Her mind sought her tormenter but was blocked in an instant as Pose grinned at her.

"A poor attempt from a poorly trained enchantress. If such is all you may offer then any here may best you on their first day."

She had been pushed past her past her limit. For years she had seen Pose as a friend, teasing her into teaching her some of the mind games the enchantress's play in training when their mentor was not present. Managing to glean a little knowledge of thought control in the teachings. Now she knew she had shown herself for what she really was, "I have tried to be a friend to you, Pose, yet you make an enemy of me."

Her mind sped forward towards Pose and met a solid wall of force. She stopped, unsure of what had happened. Her mind was powerful, too powerful for any to stop her, and wondered how it was possible. Slowly she calmed herself, 'Anger does this. So many times mother warns anger is the enemy of clear thought.'

Her voice became softer as she calmed, "You cannot stop me. I am more than your match."

"You are trained poorly, never will you be an equal to any here; you are part enchantress and will always remain so. Never will you be my equal in your five hundred years. Return to the woods from whence you came, lowly druid, this profession is not for the likes of wood elves."

Furrowing her brows she sent her all in a force she never realised she had at her mocking tutor. Pose caught the thought with her mind and returned it to her, hurling her backwards to the wall; she slumped to the floor, unconscious.

When she awoke her mother and Pose were smiling down at her as she lay on her bed, as she saw Pose standing beside her anger flared up inside once more, "Beware, mother, she is no friend."

"She is a friend, Nortee."

"She insults you and my robe and attacks me. No, she is no friend."

"She is the best friend any may have, Nortee."

"Mother, you saw her not. She insulted you and shamed me in the class to all there. Then her mind threw me across the room."

"You attacked her, Nortee."

"I will do so again when my mind recovers. She pretends to be a friend yet she is not the friend you believe."

"She insulted both at my request and defended herself with ease; and threw you across the room with equal ease."

Dragging her eyes away from Pose she looked at her mother in surprise, "You *asked* her to attack me?"

"I asked her to anger you, and she to defend herself."

Tears were forming in her eyes as she shook her head in disbelief, "You wanted her to attack me. Why, mother, why?"

"You have too much confidence, Nortee. You needed to be shown defeat, what someone may do when they are more powerful than their attacker, what may happen should you become over confident. Humility is part of being an enchantress, confidence, if misdirected, may kill you."

The tears dried slowly as her mother's words became clear, "You asked Pose to teach me a lesson?"

"I did."

"It was a hard lesson to bear."

"Only a hard lesson may sometimes teach what is needed."

"I have learned the lesson. Pose, I am sorry I did not see what you were trying to teach me."

"Had you seen I would not have taught."

"I am still your friend?"

"Now and always."

Pose eyed the students stood before the benches; "This morning each saw what happened, I will hear from you all in the order I have indicated."

With her eyes closed she sat on the chair and listened while each spoke of what had transpired between mentor and student. Placing her elbows on the desk and her head in her hands she shook it slowly.

"No, no, no. Does no one here understand? Ten students speak and I hear ten versions of facts plain for all to see by now."

Standing she walked around her now seated students, "With her mother's permission Nortee was part of my plan to test you; it seems all have failed." Once more she corrected the posture of the same student as she had done earlier in the morning before stopping at another, "You hair is much better, Aurorai Minlets, yet try it a little longer and let it fall around your cheeks, it will suit you all the more."

"Yes, Pose."

Reaching her desk she sat, her head still shaking, "There is far for you all to go. Nortee feigned anger to me for my insults, as she feigned the attack. Do any now see why?"

No one spoke.

"Oh, then best I explain it seems."

Her hand came down on the desk with force, snapping her student's wide-awake, her voice adding to the sharpness of the smack, "Anger! She feigned anger and pride! Both of which may get you killed. Nortee, explain to this sorrowful bunch of would be enchanters."

Taken a little aback she was momentarily lost for words, "Anger clouds the mind and as thoughts flee the mind becomes unfit fit to fight. You will lose reason and then your life."

Pose nodded, she had said enough and stopped her, "Exactly! Lose to anger and you will lose your life, the real the lesson of today. Caspo Kwil has a saying all here will do well to remember 'An angry enchantress is a dead enchantress'. Lessons for today are finished. You may go and think on what has been shown here, and think hard for it may save your life one day."

Standing they bowed to her before heading to the door.

"Stop! Nortee, approach me please."

As she stood before her Pose bowed low.

"Student, I apologise. You played your part well yet I used too much force on your mind and hurt you."

"No apologises are necessary."

With the class dismissed Nortee left with Aurorai, still a little shocked at the day's events.

"Nortee, why did you not speak to me of this lesson?"

"Aurorai, I could not. Life is for sharing yet not all is shared with us."

Pose offered a glass of wine of to Norty and sat beside her, "Nortee is powerful; you are a good mentor."

"Thank you."

"I like this place; I come here often to relax at night. Minlets serve the best white wine by far and they are used to me. Now I am mentor to Aurorai."

"She fast becomes friends to Nortee."

"I have watched these last weeks as they train, always together."

"I warned you of the mind of my daughter."

"I understood the warning yet not it's full meaning. I was expecting a simple thrust of her mind at me not the subtlety in which it was used, or the power she was able to apply. I am sorry I hurt her, please forgive me."

"There is no need to forgive. You used force to stop her and I would rather you hurt her than for overconfidence to kill her."

"Nevertheless you have my apologies. Is it your ways of teachings which made her mind so strong?"

"I believe it is to do with her hybrid self. Through the years I thought her powers would be weaker, to be split betwixt her two professions."

"It would seem to be a reasonable assumption."

"As I at first thought. Yet it seems she may use both enchantress and druid powers together and channel them as one."

"In what way?"

"I feel her mind is able to call on her enchantress and druid powers; one, therefore, adds to the other to make her attack more powerful."

"In her attack on me I thought to have caught a glimpse of a druid mind, I dismissed it as impossible; no druid could use their mind to attack."

"I agree yet I have also seen the druid mind within her."

"Never would I have thought a druid could attack in such a way."

"Yet it is not all of her ways. Animals trust druids and she is trusted by them also, her druid half has powers I have yet to see. I saw a bird come to her as a friend not charmed or forced but of its own will. Her enchantress mind saw its loneliness and she called it to her. It *responded* to her, never have I seen Finglas manage such a feat with a bird, only animals."

"It is as if she is the first of a new profession."

She took a sip of the wine, "One power within her complements the other; in essence she is able to use her powers together."

Lowering her voice she glanced towards the bar to ensure she would not be overheard, "I would speak of Aurorai, of her mind. I have taken to mentoring her; she is like all yet there is something.... I may think of no other word but strange, hidden within."

"In what way?"

"Her mind is the same as all who attend trainings, easy to see and study yet a part is closed to me."

"You wish me to see it also?"

"I would ask her to our study where we may enter her mind together and see what blocks us; to see if her mind is all it should be."

"You know what is there; you wish to be assured it is what you suspect."

"If it is such she will be different to all."

"Her life would change."

"Her mind is still frail, unused to the ways of the enchanter, she must be handled carefully."

"It is as you say. Her training must be changed or her mind will close the darkness and it will be lost to us."

"We must be careful, for her to know may change her."

"I have instructed the mentors nothing must be spoken to her of this."

"I saw this when I instructed her mind how to leave the body yet knew not what it was; my training taught me not what it was and I dismissed it thinking I would know later. She cannot be lost to us, Pose, she cannot."

Thoughts of Love

Kare E'Thelt shook his head; "Your control over casting is not how we are taught."
She could feel her cheeks redden a little with each compliment, whenever he could find an excuse to touch her. It was a habit she wished to encourage, "I cast in my own style and use less mana and, therefore, I fight longer than someone of a greater understanding than I."
"Your spells are more powerful than they should be; show me once again the style you use."
With a smile she watched as he did his best to mimic the ways she cast, but no spell resulted, "I will show you again. Relax; let me control your body. Cast again."
She helped him move his hands and arms but no spell resulted, "It seems only I may cast in this way. When my sisters try they also fail. I have wished to train another wizard to be sure; you are the first I have shown."
"You have trained none in your guild?"
"The gnomes are known for their ways and I will not be allowed to mentor for another two years."
"You may do so without the gnomes' knowledge."
"It is not our way, I have been forbidden to teach and it will be so."
"Your sisters and I are not gnomes, yet you would teach us your ways."
"I was forbidden to mentor gnomes."
"It seems you always get your wishes."
"The one I wish has yet to come my way."
"What is it you wait for?"
"Your love, Kare E'Thelt, your love."
"I have no wish for you to wait longer; I had thought not to be presumptuous."

Norty shook her as she lay on the bed, "Icee, you are lost in dreams."
"I know love, Norty. I thank the Gods they have sent him to me."
Once more her eyes closed; then sat bolt upright, "Sister!"
"Yes?"
"You travel the world and see much, I have a question."
"Ask."
"As a newborn you knew Finglas was for you."
"I knew from the moment of my birth when first he held me in his arms."
"And Malinna knew Flight was for her."
"The moment she saw him, yes, she knew."
"I knew Kare E'Thelt was for me the moment we met."
"What is your question?"
"Do all know when they meet they have found the one for them?"

"Only the elves are so blessed. Other races have a courtship period when each get to know the other to see if they are meant to be."

"It is a waste of time; their lives are short compared to ours so they should love sooner and not spend so much time in the learning."

"They are not gifted from the Gods as are we, their love is not instant. I cannot see an elf wishing to be with so many others in the vain hope of finding love."

Her eyes opened wide, "They go with others until love is found?"

"Sometimes with many I have heard."

"Unbelievable. I would go with none but my Kare."

"Many of them mate with each they go with in the search to find love."

"You tease."

"On my journey to the land of Messenger I was aboard a ship and the crew tried to capture me."

"I recall your tale."

"The imp spoke I would be sold into slavery, used as an object of desire and needs, and you know of which I speak."

Icee giggled, "I do, sister, yet you told the tale of the boat and its crew."

"Yet I missed part of the tale."

"No part of a tale should be missed as well you know; why did you do so?"

"With what he spoke I grew curious as to the habits of others. I enquired of them; it is how I know some have many lovers in their search."

"You tease, it cannot be so."

"There is more I found out."

"How may there be more?"

"I travel with mother to the cities of man when her duties call her. In those cities are females who sell their love to males for money. They do this and call it a profession."

"It cannot be so! How is this?"

"I know not. To love with another but my Finglas is revolting to me."

"I have my love yet we have not yet loved. I will wait not as you did for it to be. Should he not offer his love soon I will make the offer."

Her cheeks flushed once more, "I have a confession."

"It would seem to be a night for you to confess, sister."

"It was not Finglas who offered his love but I. No longer would I wait for his love after he gave me the ring. I gave my love to him, Icee."

"It was wrong for you yet you had your reasons. I will offer my love to Kare. If my sister may do so then so may I."

"No, it is not our way, you cannot do this."

"My sister waited for her love, it took its time to show. I will not wait as you did. I will love with him, whether or not he agrees."

"Icee, you must let it be natural."

"I have already spoken to him of my love."

"Before he spoke of it to you?"

"I would wait no longer."

"Yet you went against our ways, our Lore and tradition."

"Often have you spoken of changes coming to our lands; I also wish to change the ways, yet only for the better."

"Yet it seems unnatural to speak of love until the male does so first."

"I am elf and he dark elf, where is the natural part in all of this? Our love is strange yet meant to be. I will ensure it will be even stranger."

Watching her leave she remembered words spoken to her, 'you are correct, friend Kyna. Icee has fire within her; I pray he may be her match.'

To Train The Mind

Pose checked her students one last time, "You are ready to begin. Your partner is of many years experience so fear not. Try as you have been shown, enter the mind of the other gently, this is not a test of strength but of technique."

Her smile was designed to encourage Nortee as she sat nervously in front of her, "Begin. Enter my mind and see the thoughts there. I am not here to resist but to guide you."

The glance she cast did not go unnoticed.

"Aurorai has her own guide this day. Concentrate on what must be done."

Her mind traversed the small gap between them to seek the one in front of her. Then it was open before her, a mind so complex she was unsure of the direction to take. A single thought entered her, 'Look not for the way in, rather know the way.'

The voice in her head was unmistakably Pose, and she followed the thought back to its source. Never had she seen a mind so complex as the one she found open to her. All the years of training with her mother she had never been allowed to enter any persons mind, it had been made it a proviso of her training; 'You are never to enter, never to try to enter, any one's mind.' Her mother had so often instructed.

The rabbit had been a lesson to her; she had become lost in his simple mind but had learned her lesson well; as she followed Pose through her mind she marked the path she took. Making notes of fixed points in the mind and choosing to mark them as her favourite trees in the forest. Each tree in the woods of her home she knew well. Her father had taught her how to look at them, and she saw trees as individuals not as a whole. She knew each group of trees so well she could be taken blindfolded to any in the forest and would know instantly where she was. Her father had taught her the signs to look for; how they had sturdier girths when water was close to their roots. Thin when nourishment was lacking or had more branches when the forest floor needed shade for smaller plants to grow.

Now she marked the feelings in this new mind; pain was an obvious one. She saw it as the old oak atop the great waterfall of Sahera near her home, it had been struck by lightning a hundred years ago and it still seemed in pain to her. They were the same, the old oak looked as if it had suffered since its first shoot had seen the sun, and was how she saw the pain in the mind of mentor Pose. Slowly and carefully she marked her steps as she was beckoned deeper into the mind, each of the emotions were marked and numbered. Longing became the sapling near the glade where she trained, the one the sun never seemed to shine on, yet it longed to reach full height and bask in the sun. Happiness became a silver birch tree high on the hills of her home, for it seemed to shine the brightest in the forest.

Each and every feeling in this new mind was marked and numbered in meticulous order, and she was happy. Now she knew her way and had set the markers she could allow herself a little fun in her mentor's mind, to see if her mother's teachings were clearly set and understood.

It was as if Pose knew her thoughts and stopped her, instantly and without warning. Panic seized her for a moment before she calmed and thought it out; Pose was testing her, trying to see if she could find her way back. A task had been set to see if she was able to find the way out of her mind, or be trapped within its complexities. She would show her friend she would not be caught so easily, she had memorised the trees and the numbers, it would be no trouble to backtrack and leave the mind. She smiled inwardly; if Pose had thought to trick her she had a surprise for her.

Searching for the elm she found it almost immediately and headed for it, but something was wrong. She had marked the elm as happiness yet now it was hope; she wondered how it was possible. Looking around she saw the old oak tree and relief comforted her, the way out was there and she raced to it, but there was no exit, the oak was now happiness and she became confused. Mentally she sat down and calmed herself, Pose must have moved the markers, how and when she did not know, but move them she must have done.

'I have only to search for all my markers and one will be my way out.'

With all the markers she found a different emotion, each time she thought to have found a way out it was changed and frustration began to build in her, the old oak tree changed its number and emotion on three separate occasions, she was being thwarted at every turn, and it began to annoy her.

Then a new mind entered Pose and took control of her, leading the way with ease. Within moments she was out of the mind and relieved.

Bowing shakily she smiled to Caspo Kwil,, "Sir, thank you, I was lost."

"What was the point of the exercise, child?"

"To enter a mind and mark your path through it."

"As Pose had instructed; yet we are enchanters, in essence we are liars."

"I am no liar, sir."

"Has your mother not spoken of how she hates to lie?"

"Yes, on numerous occasions, sir. She has always hated to speak an untruth and sees no reason to lie, they only upset others."

"We enter another's mind to convince him or her we are not as we seem. We create illusions to fool others to believing we are different to what we appear. In all aspects we are liars."

"We are a profession reliant on deception, not lies."

"There is little difference."

"There is a world of difference, sir. I see what Pose did to me in her mind and it convinces me we are deceivers and not liars. She deceived me by changing the emotions of my markers; had she removed them altogether then it would have been a lie, she did not lie but caused deception."

"The very reason your mother hates to lie. There is enough deception in our profession."

Pose coughed, "If you would be so kind as to let me continue with the training. We have more than enough work to do and philosophising is not part of today's schedule."

"You are right, Pose, I will attend the others and ensure they are safe."

"You teach a good lesson, Pose. You changed my markers with stealth."

"You will never feel them move. You set the markers as something you know, something any would know and, with training, would be able to change. It is not the way to mark your passage."

"Yet I marked my way as mother instructed."

"I think not. She instructed you to mark your passage yet she would not have told you to do so with markers."

"Then how should it be done?"

"How do you memorise a passage in a book you would wish to read again?"

"By the number on the page."

"In the mind there are no numbers."

She thought a while, "I see. By taking note of what precedes and what follows the part I wish to read, so I can quickly get to the part I wish to read again."

"Enter my mind again but watch for lies."

She corrected herself, "No, watch for deceptions."

Happy to have her home she hugged her, "It is good you are back, if only during the festival."

"You attended training only at the month's end, mother. Why so?"

"Xandorian has been unwell. They are not the best of people when ill; their demand for attention is almost constant."

"Why was I not told of this?"

"Your studies are important and there was little need to worry. The gnomes are an inquisitive race and sometimes they fall to an illness due to this trait. I stayed a while to ensure he is well."

"He has odd ways yet I find I like them."

"He is one of the best mentors to the new classes I have seen. I watched as he trained them and told tales of his adventures."

"I am surprised you were permitted to watch."

"Icee holds sway over them or it would not be so. The students were enthralled with his tales, especially the first meeting of the Protectors."

"Each has spoken of how they met; the battle and the friendship which was to follow."

"Yet it was strange place for them to meet, Xandorian has no love for rocky land and normally does not travel such paths."

"The Gods decided where the battle was to be, so much is obvious. The goblins were far from home ground also."

"His love of travel led him to the spot they were to meet."

"How was it he came to travel such a path?"

"When he was younger he decided to travel once more after lessons which had bored him yet trod paths not normally used by gnomes, those covered with large rocks are not a favourite to them. In the late afternoon he witnessed a fight between rival bands of ogres and saw one run from the battle with a shield of great size. He followed him and watched as he threw the shield into a lake. It was almost dark and he decided to wait for the sun to rise to see if he could retrieve the shield. With the dawn he dived into the waters to search yet found nothing of the shield."

"I had not thought to ask as to why he was there, accepting the Gods placed him on the trail so they would meet."

"Xandorian is always one to be different and will travel where others do not. Eventually he gave up the search and decided to catch fish for his meal; you know well the ritual of their midday meal, it should be taken with friends yet he was far from home and had none with which to share. The thought upset him as he cooked the meal. Still he teases Keitun over the pot ruined in the fight."

"Never did he finish his meal. The goblins ensured it was not to be."

"A few years later he took your father and Keitun to where the meal should have been eaten. He had bought a new pot and insisted Keitun pay for it."

"Keitun has a mind to hold tightly to the money in his purse, never will he pay for a new one, and I believe he enjoys the teasing."

"His purse is free enough when ale is found, offering even Icee a drink."

"Why is it she has no love for drink?"

"She has none for any drink with alcohol. It dulls the senses and she must always be the one to have a clear head. Father was most upset when he discovered she had no taste for wine, only for her training. It was Icee who was the first of us to cast a spell."

"Ah, I remember what it is I wished to speak about. Why is it you attended training only for a while and I saw you not?"

"New ways are shown to us and are hard to master."

"Few are allowed in the classes and guards ensure no others come near, why so?"

"The ways are new and dangerous. Each is supervised by two others to ensure no harm befalls them."

"Rumours abound, it is unusual for doors to be locked, many are curious."

"Pose shows us ways different to what we know."

"She mentors also yet nothing has she spoken of new ways."

"Your understanding of the mind is only in its infancy, it will be many years before the ways are even mentioned to you. Learn well what she instructs, they will form the pillars on which new teaching are formed. "

"I would know of what you speak."

"Be silent on the subject, it is not yet.... He is hurt! I must go to him."

After four steps he sank to his knees, his left hand holding his right side to stem the blood oozing from the large gash. He could feel the strength ebbing from him; and with it his life. He had made it home; she would be near and feel his need for her and come to his aid. A strange feeling came over him and his mind closed to the world.

Slowly she came into view, worry easily visible on her face, as he tried to sit several hands held him steadfast to the bed.

"I seem to be home, and alive."

"You must remain still; Malinna still has much work to do with you."

His eyes flicked left to see Malinna casting another healing spell, before it finished blackness surrounded him as a spell from Icee ensured she could do her work.

Pain twisted his face as he opened his eyes once more; she was still at his side, her hand holding his, but less worry showing on her face.

"I will live it seems."

"Only until you are well, then I will take pleasure in killing you myself."

As he laughed the pain forced him to fight with all his might to stay conscious. He lost the fight.

"Worry not, sister, he is strong and will live."

"Thank you, sister. I am pleased this festival you return home. Too many you spend with the dwarves."

"They are almost to me as my own kind."

Once more he came around as Malinna finished her spell.

"Lay still and Malinna will have you well again."

He had learned, nodding he made no attempt to move, "I made it back. I knew I would, I have a lead on the ones who would kill Nortee; I found it this morning yet barely escaped."

"Quiet, lay still it will help Malinna."

"No! I had the one who would kill her, he escaped yet we can go and find him. Hurry, soon it will be too late."

"No rush, beloved, no rush. Lay still now."

"No rush? Our daughter is...."

His voice trailed off as, once more, a sleep spell from Icee claimed him.

As he woke she was with him, still smiling down and soothing him.

"We must go, I know where those are who would harm Nortee."

"Lay still and recover. Soon you may move."

He was getting annoyed, "We go before they leave. Come, hurry."

Sleep took him again, and she smiled at Icee.

Her voice called him from afar, quickly coming closer until he heard her distinctly.

"Time to wake; come to our world and open your eyes."

They flickered open and she was with him, but now seemed drained, all her liveliness gone, leaving her looking tired.

"We must go now."

"They departed one week ago."

"What?"

"You have been in our bed for one week. Your injuries were great; Malinna struggled to help you. Your body needs to rest, to recover."

He tried to sit up but the pain in his side made his eyes close.

"No, rest and recover."

"I had them trapped in the city, they came for me and we fought. I killed two of them before something came; I know not what it was, from the side and behind moving so fast. I knew I could not win the fight and had cast my Heart Stone spell to bring me home as it struck me."

"It was a grylok, its marks are there."

He shook his head, "No, they were hunted down and killed, all of them."

"It would seem not. I have soup for you, you need to eat and will do so."

"There is no time to eat, we must search."

Taking the bowl from Malinna she offered it to him, "Eat, do not force me to make you, husband."

He nodded; the look she gave him left no room for arguing.

He remembered waking several more times in the next few days, twice Nortee was with them insisting on her duty to look after her father, and he felt strange as she fed him the soup. This time his both were absent.

"Malinna, where is she?"

"We made her sleep, she fought the spells both Icee and I cast at her, as she succumbed she was cursing in high elf. Did you teach her such words?"

"She cursed? No, I did not teach her the words!"

"She cursed and Icee giggled."

"Never have I known her to use such words."

"Nortee stays with her; there will be trouble when she awakes."

"Then why make her sleep?"

"Eat the soup in front of you or I will call Nortee to feed you."

"I ask and expect an answer. Then I may eat."

"She has slept and eaten little while you lay here. We began to worry."

"She has not eaten? It is hard to believe."

"Shush, you may disturb her; she sleeps in the next room. Had we taken her elsewhere even Nortee would be hard pressed to calm her."

His laugh turned to a cough and before he could stop she was at his side.

"So my sisters would have me sleep while my husband lays ill in our bed?"

"We...."

A hand on her shoulder stopped her, "Enough, Icee, I jest." Bending she kissed him, "I am pleased to see back in our world, I admit for a time I worried."

"I ache as never before."

Sitting on the bed she glared at him, "And what thoughts ran through your head to have you attack, especially if a grylok were with them?"

Taken aback he almost spilled the soup, "I knew not it was there."

"You speak to Nortee sharply when she thinks not to use her druid ways, are you so different as not to deserve the same sharpness?"

"I was wrong, I know it. I was pleased to find the ones who would harm her, I stopped not to think."

Her arms enfolded him and held tight, thankful the Gods had spared him, "Haste kills, so many times have you spoken such to Nortee."

"We must search; they may have left clues to see."

"It is as it was with Old Jim's warehouse, nothing was found."

"You have not the druids' eyes, you may miss something."

"I could leave you not, Icee and Flight searched. I am proud of you, husband; this is your quest whilst away from us?"

"I do not explore, I hunt our daughter's would-be assassin. I will find him."

"Norty, please, I grow weary of this room."

"Our bedroom is now a place of weariness for you?"

The twinkle in her eyes had not gone unnoticed, "You twist my words as well you know. I grow weary of these walls, I yearn for open spaces."

"The answer is as it was yesterday; you may rise from where you lay when I feel you are well enough. The day has yet to arrive."

"I am well and need to move from here."

"Mother's duties call for her attention and I leave with her. This time Nortee will be allowed to travel with us, as was our promise to her. The minds of man are troubled once more yet if Malinna speaks well of you on my return I may let you rise, for a short time only. Watch him closely, sister, and heed not his words, he can be most persuasive."

"I will take care of him, sister. Be about your business and worry not."

The city seemed unusually active as she made her way to the centre and the silk shop. Elfin archers, dwarf warriors and high elf guards ran everywhere, heading the commands to assemble.

Entering the shop she touched the rolls of silk on the counter, feeling the quality and admiring the colours before picking out a green roll, "Mother wishes me to accompany her, Myra. This will make a suitable robe I feel."

"Well chosen, Norty."

"Such activity outside today; to what end?"

"A grylok is found and heads this way. But a few days' march it seems."

Dropping the roll back in its place she quickly left the shop, there was no need to ask why it was coming, or who its victim was to be.

Dressing slowly he turned to her, "I will not run; it will find me wherever I rest. I stand and fight with my people."

"It will seek you out from all others; ensure you are the first to die."

"Then let it come for me, I will fight and I will win."

"Bravado is not needed, husband. Now is the time to surround yourself with friends. You will need not to fight, but to tease."

"There is another way, mother. You know yet speak not of it."

She cast a glance at her daughter, one to stop her speaking.

"Mother, the Chosen Ones may fight and win as well you know. Help father and fewer lives will be lost."

Once more the look was cast her way.

"Many will lose their lives in this fight and you would not wish such. There are others now who would help, Flight and Sha'Dal, Kare E'Thelt and myself."

"No! You are not to be there."

"Mother your thoughts are muddled."

"I think with a clear mind."

"Fear for father and I cloud your thoughts."

"I cannot ask more of the protectors, it would be wrong for them to face such a being."

"The protectors fight with you as always. We have faced dangers before and this we face together. Nortee and Sha'Dal will remain here."

The top of the small hill looked out onto lush valleys on all sides, a few trees to the south blocked their view but it did not worry them, the grylok would come from the east if the reports were correct. They needed to see it coming; it was part of her plan. Although she hated the thought she held back some of the details from them. The plan in her head was not perfect, it was probable several of them would lose their lives; they were too few in number to ensure the fight would go their way against such a creature.

Sat in silence they watched and waited, lost in their own thoughts as to the battle and its outcome. They knew they were up against a creature whose very existence was to kill, placed on the world by the Gods for a purpose unbeknown to them. Yet none had thoughts of not entering the battle.

Xandorian glanced round at them, "All day we have waited and I worry over this battle, grylok's are the best of all fighters."

"We hope to not let it get close enough to fight."

Sharpening his axe a wide grin spread on his face, "I would fight it on my own. Axe against claw, knife against teeth."

"You are a good fighter, Keitun, but your time in this world would be measured in minutes."

"Then I go to the Gods as I would wish, in battle and not in bed."

Flight rose, "Someone comes from the south."

A figure emerged from the trees to wait there, as yet too far to see who it was. Others joined before moving in their direction.

"Warrior, paladin, wizard, enchantress and druids. Why are they here?"

All thoughts of formality were ignored as the newcomers stood in front of them. Embracing each in turn and talking excitedly.

Finally Icee stepped away, "You must forgive our poor manners my friends. I have introductions to make."

Her hand, palm upward, gestured towards the paladin, "I present to you Kyna, truest bow shot in all the lands of man, taught by mother."

Kyna bowed, "A pleasure to meet you all."

"How may I speak of Graforge? Warrior of the highest battle orders in the dwarfs' kingdom, self appointed protector of sister Malinna."

Stepping forward he took the forearm of Flight, "We meet again, elf."

Stepping back Flight rubbed his bruised arm and grinned back at him.

Icee shook her head at the dark elf stood before her, "When first we met this one I would have killed her for the words she spoke yet now it is so hard to believe. She is the truest friend any may have as this day proves. Welcome, Pose."

Stepping forward Kare nodded, "Pose, I have heard of you and the stories I see are true. It is strange to see one of us fight alongside of those they hate."

"I hate them not, and I see another of my people turn to their ways."

"To the ways of one of them."

Giggling she gestured, "This wizard quested for all our robes risking death, and worse, for the robe Norty wears. She saved our lives in the battle with the goblins and holds a place in all our hearts. Arabella, wizard of the sixtieth understanding."

Flight smiled, "Arabella, I have heard Malinna speak often of you."

"I am the same as all here. Except for the dark ones, I am not as they."

"He is not as he was, Arabella, he is mine and sees the light in his dark world. Pose you may remember, you met her after the battle of the goblins, when you worried as to her and Finglas."

"I thought I had seen her before. Friends of the Chosen Ones will be as friends to me, greetings, dark ones."

"I have heard of you, Arabella, from Icee and my own people."

"Your race speaks of me?"

"Some in reverence at your power and some in hatred for the many of my people you have killed."

"I have left a few dead, though not many. All died in their challenge to me, I never challenged but accept all issued."

"This is one who will never challenge. The saviour of my future wife is a friend to me."

"Your future wife! Permission to speak to father has not been given and I have not accepted. More; have no mind to."

"You have a mind to and so do I."

"Ha! I teach you new ways yet never have I mentioned wedlock. Think your place again."

"My place is at your side, accept what Lady Fate throws to us."

With head lowered Malinna bowed, "Mother, this fight is not for you, return to comfort Nortee and Sha'Dal if you would."

"Never have we fought alongside of you, daughter, we will not be dissuaded."

"Father, you will be needed to take care of them should the worse befall us."

"All will be needed in the fight, we stay."

Leaving them to their arguing he sat beside Norty, "Icee will wed; her voice is one of defiance while her posture is of love."

She nodded.

"I have seen the way he looks at her, the way I look at you."

She nodded.

He caught the mood she was in, "What children will they have?"

She nodded.

"They wish for ten children."

She nodded.

"I would have you consent here and now, love with me."

She nodded.

His hand moved to her face, slowly turning it to him, and saw tears flowing none stop down her face. Gently he wiped them away, "Why the tears?"

"Death stalks us. One will die; three should plans go wrong."

"Who is it to be?"

"Before the coming of others many could have died. Now it may be one of four, myself included. It depends on how the battle transpires. I fear the feelings my sisters will have for me when it happens."

"How did they know where to find us?"

"Nortee is our child in more ways than I would admit; she plans and thinks as do I. She has heard of the closeness of our friends many times, and has met each on many an occasion. She knows at the time of the festival where they will be and the great problems against the grylok."

"Yet she would not know the place you were to choose for the fight."

"It is obvious. We need to see where and when it comes, a place of open space to fight near to home, and for help when any are hurt."

"Many such places exist."

"She is still in my mind and knows our direction. Father would take her to our friends to ask for their help."

He was pleased with himself, the tears had dried and there was now a trace of a smile on her lips. He had deflected her troubled thoughts as she had done so often with him, but he had also been willing to let her deflect them.

Kare stood, "No battle plans have been mentioned and now it is too late. It comes."

They watched as it lumbered towards them in a slow but sure walk. They had seen the damage it could do with its claws, and those claws were almost eight inches long, with arms more powerful than any giant. The size of two large bears its looks was almost dragon-like, scales protecting its body as armour would protect a warrior. It looked dangerous, and was more dangerous than it looked.

Creatures of single purpose and mind when a victim had been selected they would hunt until they were dead, and none had been known to survive. A remorseless hunter they could track a victim wherever they hid in the lands. Once one had been seen heading for a village or town the cry would ring out. Every man in the town would ready for battle, every woman and child draw bow and arrow, yet few were ever killed.

The dwarves had fared better than most in their battles with them, but the cost in lives had been great. It was they who had first called on other races to help kill the creatures. There had never been a time when the terror of the grylok was unknown, yet they took few lives each year.

Then the killings changed; entire villages were wiped out, leaving their victims bodies ripped apart, lying where they had died. The senseless slaughter had united most of the races as the dwarves had asked, and they hunted down their common enemy, finally killing each and every one of the creatures, or so it was thought.

At her nod her sisters moved out, Icee right and Malinna left, their protectors moving with them, untold yet knowing their place, forming a horseshoe a hundred yards from the grylock. The others remaining on the top of the hill; as yet unsure of the part they had to play.
She turned to Pose, "Join Finglas with your pet."
"Join me, where do you expect me to be?"
"To the right, halfway between Icee and myself."
"I stay at your side."
"Do as I ask! If we are to survive I need not your arguments!"
As Pose cast her spell her fur ball appeared at her feet, the living glass shield wrapping around her, protecting its mistress.
"Arabella, keep it at bay with your spells let it not get close to Finglas. Mother, father, your cast your insect spells, they will annoy and confuse the beast. Kyna, use your bow. We wait for word from Icee; she will know when the time is right."

Icee watched as it walked towards the hill and saw it stop, it had found its intended victim and her battle cry echoed across the valley, "Trust to your instincts and look to your wards, and may the Gods welcome the losers."
Arabella cast, engulfing it in flame, but did not deflect its steady pace.
"Again, Arabella. Kyna stop it or Finglas dies, then we all die."
As she cast Kyna loosed her arrow and three other spells struck home; the wizards casting together, and it slowed down.
Kyna screamed as her arrow found to its target, "We will win."
Her arrow bounced harmlessly of its hide and she shot again, with the same result.
"Icee wishes you to concentrate your efforts, cast and shoot as one. She decides its eyes are the weakness. Kyna, aim for its eyes they are not protected."
Once more spells hit from all who could cast and the grylock stopped in its tracks, looking round as he decided who was the more dangerous to him.
Commanding her pet to attack and help the one Norty had ordered towards the enemy Pose knew they would do little harm to the beast; but would serve to muddle its thoughts.
"More." Cried Icee, "It falters, cast again."
This time Norty did not cast; her mind entered it, running amok within, calming his thoughts of it attacking Finglas, heightening those of sleep in its mind. Then left again almost immediately, wanting it to hate her, to come for her, to attack her, anything to take his mind off Finglas.

It turned towards her as she stood on the hill. Now, if all went according to plan, it would come for her and she did not care, as long as Finglas and Nortee were safe she did not mind. Yet there was never just one part to her plans, and she knew Icee would follow the second path carefully.

Now she had the most dangerous part to play, the part she hated so much, deliberately keeping it from her sisters. Entering his mind once more she stirred its thoughts before leaving, but still it headed for Icee. She could not let it happen, how could she let her face such a beast? Icee must be saved for Kare. She was not yet in wedlock, as yet unfulfilled, and Messenger had mentioned their unborn child.

She cast again, her most powerful spell, cursing the Gods withheld from the enchanters any spell powerful enough to cause real harm to such a powerful being. Yet in a way she was happy, Icee was far more able to deal with the creature than she was, than anyone except Arabella, and a slow smile started. It had forgotten about Finglas.

Pose called, "It knows its enemy and seeks to deal with Icee, defend her."

Swinging her staff round in a short arc Icee saw the shards of razor sharp ice strike the grylock. Blood flowed from several deep cuts, but still it advanced in its slow and steady way.

Norty lowed her staff, watching the jagged lightening strike the beast, yet still it moved towards her sister.

Now Pose entered its mind and found the turmoil left by Norty, and added to the confusion already there, wanting desperately to keep it from the elf she loved.

Arabella cast once more, her spell so powerful it stopped in its tracks, looking at her as if deciding which was the more powerful of the two. Its huge head turned towards Icee and resumed its pace towards her, but now less quickly.

Once more Norty entered his mind, this time to charm it, to make a pet of it and to leave immediately so its mind was free of her. He would hate her and concentrate all its attacks on her; she would be the one to die. She had not told Finglas who she thought would die in the battle.

Once more spells hit it and it and as it shrieked in pain, they sensed victory within their grasp. With more attacks timed to hit it at the same time they would win, or so they hoped.

Yet they were not the best killer without reason, it disappeared to appear only feet from Icee, its huge arm shooting forward at blinding speed.

Icee saw the claw swing up to her as her staff came down to block the attack, but somehow Xandorian was there in front of her, and its claws buried deep within his chest.

As more spells hit the creature it reeled and Xandorian dropped to the ground.

Icee lost all control, hatred flared up inside her, revenge shining bright in her eyes, "Curse you and curse the Gods!"

Her right arm shot upwards and left reached out, and all the mana she possessed surged from her in one pure blast of hatred, doubling it up as pain racked it from head to toe. It staggered, knees bending as other spells hit hard, forcing it down. Blows from the axes of Keitun and Graforge giving it little time to retaliate as it rolled over in its death throes, arms and legs twitching. A last movement of its arm caught Keitun and he screamed as a claw ripped open his right leg.

Calming thoughts from Norty and Pose slowed its mind as more spells hit before it lay still, finally its breathing stopped.

Before the swirling strands of mana had dissipated Malinna was at the side of Keitun, her spells healing his wounds. She had chosen to tend to Keitun first, knowing she could do nothing for Xandorian, yet she continued to heal her protector as tears began to mark her cheeks.

Bent over her protector, using her body to shield him from view, Icee did not want them to see his blood soaked robe. To the gnomes blood was sacred and she knew it, for others to see his life oozing from him was too much for her. It was now her turn to protect her protector. Her duty to him clear; she had to take him home for Final Rights.

As they approached she called to them, "No! Look not at him. Remember him as he was. He was *my* protector; he is mine to care for at this time. Finglas, take us to his resting place."

Her arms lifted him with care, but her voice was choked, "Cast your spell Finglas, hurry. Take us to Gronich. Hertish Munsil will recite the Rites Of Passage for him."

Once more her tears flowed freely as Hertish Munsil, his arms around her, tried to comfort her, yet knowing no words could do so.

Finally the tears stopped and she looked at him, "You are a kind, Hertish. I thank you for the reading of the Rites Of Passage, it will speed his journey to the Gods."

He motioned her to her feet. "Your sisters grieve also, take them home and light a beacon on the hill at midnight as you say your final farewell. Stay in prayer for him until the fire dies, then he will sit with the Gods."

Standing she bowed low to him, and with all the strength she could muster, slowly left the room.

To Help A Sister

For an hour he had tried but still she was oblivious to his words, not once offering to return to study, choosing to spend her time reading the scrolls and spell books used for those entering their first class. She was wasting her time and he knew it, pretending to be deep in study while she mourned the death of Xandorian, "Icee, I love you in a way far deeper than you know. It has been one month since Xandorian died and the time for mourning is past. I wish to join in wedlock with you and would do so now. Give permission to speak to your father, he knows of my feelings for you."

"I grant no such request!"

"Do you not understand? I am in love with you and wish you to be mine. True you mourn yet you must let him go, set him free to be with his God."

Her look was as cold as her name as she turned and walked quickly away.

The sound of her practicing her singing in the glade led him easily to the spot and he sat in front of her, waiting. For minutes he listened as each word sounded clear and sweet. He knew only an enchantress could sing in this way, even the bards could not match the beauty of their voices. When she stopped he was disappointed.

"You have taken your time in coming to see me, Kare."

"I wish to speak with regards to your sister, and I see why you sing of her."

"Your understanding of us grows. I know why you would speak with me and I will speak to her for you. Grief is still heavy in her heart; it is why I sing of her. You must wait; she is yours and will always be."

"My heart cries, it wants her as it has never wanted another."

"Your heart must wait for her grief to depart, it will be some time. The Oath of Protection bound her to Xandorian and he gave his life to save her. Death cannot break such a binding."

"Finglas has spoken to me of its meaning yet my heart is bound to hers as Xandorian was also bound. I must join your sister in wedlock, I must."

"Do not push her and she will come to you when she is ready, she will come and you will know."

"Have I not waited long enough?"

"Time is the healer, not Malinna or I; it will pass at its own pace."

"I feel I have waited too long, mayhap I should speak with Juin now."

With eyes still close she shook her head, "It would bring only an argument between you and at this time such words are not needed. Wait, time will play its part for you."

"You know love, as does Malinna?"

At last she opened her eyes, "We know love. Speak your mind."

"You would wish love to be withheld from you?"

"I know how it feels to have love withheld. I will do your bidding and speak with my sister."

"It is said the Chosen Ones read the others minds, they are as one."

"We know the others thoughts."

"You feel her love for me?"

"I do."

"Then her love is still there?"

"It is there yet hidden under grief."

"If love remains for me then I am happy, thank you."

"I will speak with her after meditation."

"I was soundless when I came yet you knew I was here, how so?"

"You were soundless, yet your mind screamed your thoughts."

"You saw my mind coming?"

"An enchantress sees the mind when she sees the person to whom it belongs."

"You could not see my mind, your eyes were closed."

"My mind is a gift from the Gods. Nortee and I may see a mind without seeing to whom it belongs first."

He stood to leave, "You call it a gift; I would call it a curse."

Sibling Rivalry

"Sister I would speak with you."

"Kare has spoken with you. I am in no mood to speak of him."

"He would join in wedlock with you, Xandorian would not have you this way, as well you know. Release him yet keep him in your heart."

"I will speak not of this or Xandorian. Leave!"

She had to push her sister; she saw the way her body reacted, Icee was getting angry, "You will speak, younger sister, and do so now!"

Icee slammed the book shut, "You will leave or face my wrath!"

Her plan was working. Icee was losing her temper, she had only to push a little harder; "I am the elder; you do as I demand!"

"Demand! Make none of me, *sister*."

"You will face me and speak of Xandorian or I will force you to do so."

"Force me? You are incapable of such!"

"It would be easy for me; you are but a mere wizard."

Her sister had pushed her past her limits by insulting her profession and would stand it no longer. Spinning round on the stool she faced her tormentor, "Beware! If you were not my sister you would be already dead!"

"Dead? A wizard knows little the ways an enchantress may use to best them, or the courage needed to face us."

"You would dare to speak I have not the courage to face my sister, a lowly enchantress?"

"Hear yourself; a wizard believes she may best an enchantress. Many of your kind have I faced, none have fared well against me. You are as children facing the mighty!"

"For such words I would be within my rights to offer the challenge."

"Then I consider myself challenged. You will meet me in the arena within the hour. Be there, *wizard*, or all will know you have not the courage to face me."

She hissed the words, "Make your peace with the Gods; soon you are to meet them!"

Finglas was shocked, "You cannot fight Icee. I forbid it."

"I must be in the arena; she grieves and must be released from her feelings. This is the only way I may help her."

"You cannot beat her in a fight. She would kill you with ease."

"She is my sister and will harm me not. She has anger in her and I have the power to release it."

"You have seen her fight, all her mana will be loosed at you in one spell. You could not survive."

"She will not harm me this I promise, the challenge has been accepted. We fight within the hour."

Her pet spell cast long before Icee walked into the arena she turned to face her, "I stand ready for the challenge."

"I must harm you if you stay, leave."

"I stand ready for the challenge."

"Once more I ask you to leave."

"I stand ready for the challenge."

"So be it. Prepare to die!"

"Attack, my pet."

Her fur ball surged forward from behind Icee interrupting the spell she was casting; she had little time to complete her task. She had to enter her sister's mind while her fur ball annoyed Icee. Quickly her mind sped to her sister and, as she entered, pain coursed through her and she sank to her knees, to be in her sisters mind was almost as much pain as she could bear.

In the balcony above them Finglas caught Malinna as she slumped forwards holding her head. As he watched he saw Icee and Norty, hands holding their heads, the sisters were in agony, and his thoughts were for his wife. The Oath of Protection surged up inside of him and he moved towards her.

"No, Finglas, no."

The memory of swearing to his wife he would do her sister's bidding, even if she was in dire trouble, flooded back to him; and found no comfort in the thought as he stayed with Malinna.

Desperately Norty searched for what she knew to be there, she could not spend too long in her sister's mind, it was too painful; she was almost on the point of collapse. Throughout the years her enchantress mind had often wondered how the link with her sisters worked, and now she knew. A part of her own mind was in her sister; she could see her own thoughts and it caused pain; the nearer she got to those thoughts the greater the pain became. Her hidden thoughts should never be seen, and she knew it. Yet she would not listen as they screamed at her to get out of her sister's mind, screamed she should not be here, and the thoughts were right, it was no place for her to be. She had to continue the search, no matter what her mind told her or how much it hurt. She had a duty to her sister she would perform and nothing would stop her search, nothing, even her own mind. Then she found it, the single thought troubling Icee, the one cause of the pain in her sister's heart. The reason all her thoughts were troubled, and why she could not give up her protector. Gently she touched the thought, highlighting it before leaving her sister's mind and, as she did so, the pain eased and was gone.

She found herself lying on the ground and raised her head to find her sister on hands and knees; the pain had been in her also. Breathing deep she looked towards her husband and Malinna, and saw the worry in them slowly fade. Now it was up to Icee to play her part.

In her mind Icee saw Xandorian once more, whole and alive, calling to her, almost pleading with her to come to him, and with great happiness she headed the plea, hugging her protector as the tears started over again.

'Xandorian you are with me once more, where you should always be. I have missed you so much.'

'Icee, I ask you to let me go.'

'No! Never!'

'Let me rest with the Gods.'

'You are my protector, my friend. I need you with me.'

'No, Icee, say your goodbyes to me, let me join my ancestors.'

'I do not want you to go.'

'We knew this day would come, Icee, for me it is here.'

'Stay with me a while longer.'

'I cannot stay, you must let me go.'

'I love you.'

'I love you and will miss you, yet we will be together one day.'

She held him tighter, 'Please do not go; you are my protector, my friend.'

'No, Icee, another is now your protector. He loves you and your love must belong to him. Say goodbye to me and hello to him.'

He was right, and deep down she knew it, 'Yet I will miss you, Xandorian.'

'I will always be here to talk to. I live in your heart and your mind; never will I be far from you.'

She nodded, her tears slowly drying, 'Goodbye, Xandorian. You have been good to me. I will always remember you.'

'It is all I ask. Think of me on the anniversary of my death, think and light the fire. Goodbye, Icee.'

'Goodbye, Xandorian.'

In her mind she watched him walk away and tears fell once more, and were reflected down her cheeks as she knelt in the arena.

Shaking her head she looked at the fur ball still attacking her, the robe she wore ripped to shreds; deep cuts covered her body, "Be gone!"

Her spell turned it to dust as she looked at her sister still on the ground in the arena, then slowly walked towards her, arms coming down as she did so, encircled her, helping her to her feet.

"Thank you, sister. You make my life worth the living again. You have won and I have offended you."

Kneeing before her sister, Icee let her forehead touch the earth in elfin shame; "Forgive your foolish sister, if it is within your heart."

"You cause no ill feelings in me, sister, rise."

"Mine is the best of sisters."

"Malinna is here to heal you. I apologise for the harm my pet caused you."

"Had he not done so I may have harmed or killed you."

"You would not have done so; my sister would never do such."

Finglas hugged her, "I should trust you more, yet when I saw you in pain..."

"I knew not how much pain there can be. I entered her mind and saw my own; we should not see our own mind."

He held her tight; it had hurt him to see her in such pain.

"And I am proud once more of you. You stayed your ground and remembered your promise to me."

"Malinna reminded me, yet it is the hardest of tasks for me to do."

"I felt your feelings."

"Enough of this, explain how Icee is herself once more."

"Icee grieved for she had never spoken to him of the day he would die, never spoken her farewells. He was more than her protector; she had a love for him to match any and needed to say those words. I entered her mind to have him appear to her so she may speak them. Still she misses him so much yet now the words are spoken she is herself once more."

"Will she not hate you as other do when you leave their heads?"

"I had not tried to charm her and she had more hatred of herself for not saying goodbye than she would for me. She is Icee, sister and wizard; she could no more hate me than I could hate you. And a poor sister I would be if I could help her not."

"You gave her back her protector so her goodbyes may be said."

"The mind is powerful. I had only to place the thought of him in hers."

"And if your plan had failed and she had attacked with full force?"

"She could not; there is something stronger than grief."

"What is stronger?"

"Love is stronger."

"I have a mind to love with you."

"It would seem you must wait. Caspo Kwil arrives and in a hurry I have never seen before."

"What is it to cause such haste in him?"

Opening the door she bid him enter, "Soon we shall see."

The Attack

The attack on the little band as they journeyed between high elf and wood elves city had taken them completely by surprise, none had escaped. As leader Nortee blamed herself, cursing under her breath it had happened today of all days. She had been given the greatest of honours, to be placed in charge of young elves, barely out of their fourth year, and instructed to show them the sights before returning in four days.

The honour granted had sent her a sleepless night as she planned the sights she would show them. The great waterfall of Sahera and the beautiful colours the rainbow greeted each sunrise with. Hondyns cave, glowing with so many colours, forever changing as you walked its length. The view from Saseens Point, so beautiful you could watch from sunrise to sunset in one day and never tire of the view. Yet most of all she would see her mother and father and let them know the honour bestowed on her.

The pride flowing through her had disappeared with the attack; she was their captive, caught within the boundaries of the elfin realm, where safety should have been guaranteed.

She hardly felt the whip as it came down on her but she screamed, not in pain but as her mother had instructed long ago, and was thankful for all the lessons she had thought valueless at the time, yet heeded her teaching well. She knew they dealt in pain and any not wise enough to show pain suffered yet more. As she feigned a slip from the whip she began to wonder how her mother seemed to know so much of life, how she was always right, always had the right advice and somehow, it seemed to her, even managed to prepare her for this encounter. Her mind turned to think of Messenger, had he also known of this encounter and made her robe like armour in readiness?

She did not know the answers, and it seemed as if she never would, but she would not let her thoughts turn to despair, her parents had taught her better, there was always a way out of any problem.

The scream of pain from one of her wards being whipped was almost as much as she could bear, and wished she could take the pain for them, they received the whip for no reason she could see. She longed for her mother to be linked with her so she could get help, but the possibility of the link connecting once more seemed slim, they were headed slightly away from wood elf city, more to the west than she would have liked, it would be too much to ask for them to venture close to home. Too much and too foolish, her mother and father had sent word they were to travel to the land of the gnomes, too far to be linked, and would return the next morning.

As they travelled she noted the direction they took, the position of the sun and of strange shaped trees or rocks as her father had taught her for when she journeyed in unknown lands. She marked them in her mind and in the correct order, not realising why she was doing it, she knew her lands, every inch, but somehow the druid training took hold, it was becoming automatic. Each detail was held fast in her mind, each turn in the path and rise and fall of the land. Yet she never marked the noises of the forest, least of all the screech of a hawk as it flew overhead several time during the day.

Her mother had taught her most of the languages known to her; she had disliked several of them finding most boring, the orcs had such a language and she had hated to learn it. It was not the sweet whispering tones of the elves or the fairies. It was of throaty grunts and snorts, more like the snarls of a mad dog. Yet she had studied hard and accepted it as part of her duty to her mother.

Now, in one way, she wished she had not learned this particular language, she heard how they spoke of her, and what would happen to her before they reached they reached home. She had listened to their grunts and noted the looks they gave her, and it filled her with a dread she had never known. But what was to happen to the little band filled her with hatred enough to make her blood boil. She knew what to expect, enslavement and pain in the mines for a short time until they were killed. They never let a captive live long; when a prisoner received the gift of mana death would be their reward, and they were the lucky ones.

Her life was to be so different, she would be allowed to live well past two hundred and suffer pain every day. The others were of various professions, she alone was an enchantress. Of the whole group only she could enter a mind to make them to work harder for their captors. But she would not do it; she would refuse and deny them her prowess, refuse and die for it. Better a short life than years of pain and being used by any passing male with thoughts of lust.

As she watched their progress she had, at first, thought the way they changed direction was to confuse pursuers. Now she thought different. It was as if they knew the paths taken by the patrols and changed direction purposely. She could not rely on a passing patrol to find and help them, she was in charge and it was for her to find a way out of the mess. Once they entered the land of the desert people escape was less likely and, once in the land of the orc, almost impossible.

Now, after a full day of running through the forest, this change of direction surprised her, they were headed more south towards dense forest. Why they would head into an area dangerous to them eluded her?

As they ran she studied them, the leader obvious and always in the lead, once in a while stopping to let them pass, and whip his men. Then the elves would be whipped in retaliation, and her hatred for him grew stronger by the hour, it was because of him her group were treated so harshly. Gritting her teeth as the whip came down on her once more she vowed he would die if she could make it happen, and with as much pain as she could inflict. He was the one using the whip on his own men, revelling in the pain he gave, and he had thoughts on her.

The grain of an idea came to her at the next food stop. Given only meagre scraps of bread and a little water she has secretly passed them to those in her charge. Her body did not need as much food as the young elves required to grow strong and true. She could be without for another day before the running began to take its toll. As she tried to think the plan though she cursed the hawk as it screeched overhead distracting her, denying her the concentration she needed, there would be no second chance.

Only when she realised the whip was once more on her back did she open her eyes, and wonder how many times had she been struck. If it had been a few times and had shown no pain they would investigate, and find the secret of her robe. Crying aloud she rolled onto her back as if in protection. The whip was raised to strike, but the leader caught his arm, growling a threat to him as his lips pulled back in a snarl. She was not only worried for her charges but for herself now, the leader had plans for her as night fell and did not want to see whip marks on her chest. She shuddered at the thought of what she knew he was going to do with her. Their ways with prisoners was well known; often the female did not live through the ordeal.

They were nothing like the elves, in either looks or ways, yet most races believed they were related, becoming more and more grotesque as they neared the evil to which they seemed born. None of the races were friendly to them, even the trolls and ogres, yet a few tolerated them, allowing them into their city for provisions. They were large and stocky with powerful legs and arms, their fingernails an inch long. It was easy to see how they could do such incredible damage to an enemy even when disarmed.

Before she was five years old her mother first instructed her on the other races dwelling in the lands, and had her own thoughts on the orcs as she saw them in study books, and in the book to which her grandmother so often scribed. Though her mother's illusions she had studied the image of them and her mind was set, to her it seemed unmistakeable; they were not related to the elves, but to the wolves.

Yellow eyes with a mouth and nose joining to form a short muzzle they looked the same as wolves. Long canines protruding past the lips give them an even more wolf like appearance, but their hair finally convinced her of their origins. It was long and grey, how much more werewolf-like could they be? Yet these creatures ran on hind legs and had the intelligence and mannerisms of man, she could almost see some the traits and physical characteristics in them. Her eyes cast a glance towards the heavens as she thought, 'With these beings you made an error.'

Her plan was poor and left many gaps she had no time to think about and, for a moment, a feeling of shame passed over her. Her parents had taught her to think much more clearly, and she felt a slight feeling of inadequacy. In any battle her mother had always a plan and countless parts to the plan to cover every eventuality. Never had she known her mother's plans to contain errors, while hers was riddled with holes and doubts.

Resolution hit her, when she got back, *if* she got back, she would ask her mother to explain once again the ways she planned, how she saw the numerous ways of telling how a plan would play out, and maybe, with a lot of practice and help, she too would become a good planner. Hers were poor and she realised it, but it would have to suffice, she would play it as it occurred but her mother had warned her so many times about fighting in such a way. As she rose to her feet she breathed a sigh of relief, the whip had struck her just the once.

The opportunity to mend a few the holes in her plans had come quicker than she could have hoped; when a pack member gave her an unmistakeable look, he too would have her after the leader had finished, and now smaller pieces of the plan slipped into place. The next time they stopped she would be ready; she planned with care, and more than a little excitement.

Always out in front when they travelled she half believed she would be able to see help coming and warn those behind her in time to save a few. If the orcs thought they were in danger they would kill prisoners before fighting to the death, it was their way, their only way. If she could warn them in time one or two might manage to escape, and she would die a little more contented.

'Messenger, why do you not come as promised? I have called to you so many times this day and your promise was to come in my time of need.'

It was useless to call to him again, yet she had to try once more. His promise to her had been broken, yet he was not elfin kind, not bound by a promise, as were the eves.

Letting the others catch up slowly she whispered to Lethin, hands tied behind his back, a rope securing his neck to the elf behind him in the typical orc way of travelling, "When next we stop we escape then or never."

Several hours later they stopped again, but they were only short giving little time in which to act. Carefully she let her mind slip past those in her charge and enter the mind of the orc who had given her the look earlier. The thought was still there, foremost in his mind.

Pose had taught her the first steps in the secret of increasing the power of a thought; it had taken her a long time of pleading, begging and cajoling until she had succumbed. Her mother would not have been pleased if she knew how she had pushed Pose into showing her how it was done. She had been promised the dark elves, or Pose, would train her in the ways of thought manipulation after she had passed her fifteenth year, she had been unwilling to wait. Now she was thankful she knew a little of the secret, hopefully it would save all their lives. Her training had been brief, thrice in the early evenings for a few hours only. She knew she needed to practice the technique for years, but her life seemed it might be short.

The thought was still in his mind, but her powers were too low to capture it. Time and time again she tried until, in desperation, her mind grabbed at it once more as it flew fleetingly past her.

The lust in him for the elf suddenly took control, the food halfway to his mouth all but forgotten as he rose. He wanted her now, not after the pack leader had finished, she would be his while he was away.

He pulled her from her sitting position with such force her mind almost lost its contact. But she could take no chances, it had to be now or they would be too far from home and any reasonable chance of a rescue. The mountains were clearly visible on the horizon now; to the left of them was the orc's domain. She had to continue to push the thought even harder as he tried to rip the robe from her body

Fear caused through her; the leader had to be here soon, he was vital to her plan. If he stayed away this orc would have her here and now, the lust was too prominent in his thoughts. A form of relief flooded through her as the leader grabbed him, growling a threat to him to keep him in line it had the opposite effect. His hand went for the short sword at his side to give battle; and she would be the winner's prize.

It was time to seek another guard and push the same thought into him, if she could. He would come for her and the leader would have two to deal with and, she hoped, cause a fight within the group. The plan had worked so far, as she turned she saw there was no need, a revolt had started.

For moments she watched as it transpired, they were more like a pack than she at first thought; once a fight started all fought, like the wolves. It was a point to remember should she ever have need for them to fight them at a later date in her life. Nodding to the others they slipped away without a sound, running northeast, yet not directly towards wood elf city.

Within moments she was far ahead of them, stopping constantly for them to catch up. 'So slow, why do they run so slow, surely they know we will be run to ground at this pace?'

"You have run but one day, surely you are not weary?"

Her eyes turned to the heavens once more, 'Messenger, why is it you lie to me? I have wronged you not; I did all I was asked at your anvil yet still you answer not my call. Is it mother was wrong to trust you as I am also?"

She had hoped for five minutes while the fight raged, they had been running for three before the howling of pursuit reached her ears. Once more she cursed; with their great running ability they would catch them. In her planning she tried to think of a way out for the band but always they led to one conclusion, she would have to sacrifice herself to let them escape.

'Damn it! Why does the hawk scream so incessantly?'

"Run, do not stop and never look back. Keep the sun to your left shoulder for two hours and then place it at your backs. May the Gods bless you."

Her mind was made up, she would not die submissively but fight to the death, never would she let herself be captured again, never subjected to the thoughts they had for her. She had found the spot where she would fight and die, they would escape if she could keep the orcs busy long enough. The trees were plentiful here and would protect, they were her friends; she would use them as a wood elf should, as Keitun had taken such pains to instruct. She could not let her body be found with a wound in her back as if she were running from an enemy.

She would die yet make her parents proud; her death would be one of an elf. Reaching the old tree she began to climb, as she had never done before, giving thanks she was at home in them as on the ground. The girth of the trunk would shield her from their eyes; it would be all she needed. Moments later they raced past, they had not seen her. She hated to use their language but it was the quickest ways to gain their attention. With all the hatred she could place into their tongue she slipped round the other side of the tree and called to them.

"Warriors? Ha! More like pigs for the slaughter. I kill pigs such as you."

They stopped, looking around as to where her voice had come from, they wanted this elf and they would have her, she had called them pigs!

It was imperative she gave her wards all the extra minutes she could, each moment she could delay them gave a better chance of escape; if she could keep them here for ten minutes they might reach safety.

"Can pigs not take a lone elf, or has fear of me grabbed your feeble hearts?" Glancing round the tree she saw their faces, her teaching were right, they hated to be called pigs, it showed in their faces and snarls.

Reaching up to grab the branch above she swung easily up, and they raced towards her, somehow she was finding the thought of battle thrilling. Three began the climb, and she had to admit they were fast, their long arms helping them, but trees were her home, they were no match for her while she was in them. She noted the leader motion the others to stay on the ground, probably hoping to catch her should she fall, but she was happy to let them stay there. The fewer in the trees to chase her would mean it would take so much longer; her wards would get further away. Her hopes were dashed as he called to those still on the ground.

"Kill them all, we take her back alone."

Panic seized her, this was not part of her plan; she had not set aside any part for this, she would have to stop them from chasing them down.

A song sprang from her lips "Pigs love the mud, pigs love the mud. Pigs cannot fight; pigs cannot fight. Leave others to climb, leave others to climb." The effect was too much, grabbing the tree two more started upwards.

Reaching the top branch she grinned at them; she must keep their thoughts on her, just a few minutes longer, "Pigs good to roast, pigs good to roast."

Howls rent the air as they reached for her and she knew the threats they called were to be carried out, yet she was pleased, her wards were getting further away with each moment. They were a few feet below when she leapt backwards to the next tree, "Pigs in trees, so funny to see."

She had given her wards more than the ten minutes needed if they were to reach safety. They had suffered so much under the orcs, if she could hurt them before her death she would have repaid just a little of her debt to them. Quickly her mind reached out for the leader, she could not hope to keep out of their reach forever; she must have help.

He felt her enter his mind and fought back, howling in delight, "Elf not good enough to make others work hard. We have fun with you, enjoy you, all enjoy you."

"Never! Pigs cannot enjoy anything but the mud. You are all pigs."

Dropping to the next branch she taunted them on the way down before leaping to the forest floor, into the arms of one still waiting below.

His arms gripped tight across her chest as he started to squeeze, "Elf not so good, your kind easy to fool."

For a moment fear took control of her but she fought it down, she had been trained so much better than this and she knew it. Fear would only lead to a slow death at their hands, after they had carried out their threats. Searching for his mind she found it, and it was not as strong as the leader, she entered it with ease and he released her. Pleased with herself she stepped forward and the leader was suddenly standing there, his arm reaching to grab her throat.

Ducking and moving sideways she evaded his grasp easily, enjoying the fight somehow.

They were attacking his mistress, and he was wild with rage. With sword drawn he lunged forward, any who would dare attack her must die.

Under attack from a new direction the leader swung his sword round, to remove the head from the body of his onetime subordinate, disinterested he had killed one of the pack.

The severed head rolling around on the ground almost made her sick, the only fights she had been in were when she was protected by her parents or in practice with the staff. Caspo Kwil carefully controlled all the fights between the other enchanters; they were but training sessions for life. Fighting down the feeling she looked round and moved to place her back to the tree as her father had taught her, she reached the old tree easily.

Then he stood in front of her once more, and still it seemed he moved so slowly. She had been instructed they were fast and very agile; his lack of speed and agility puzzled her. Once more, as his hand reached out, she ducked, kicking her leg out and back, taking pleasure as she caught him between the legs. Now was the time to fight, it could be put off no longer, grabbing the branch above her she kicked out once more as she swung easily upwards. The orc with thoughts on her found her foot in his face, and it gave her a strange feeling of satisfaction as she heard flesh squash into bone.

The others were encircling and she knew she could not fight five of them for much longer. She would die here, but her wards should escape, if only they would learn to run. Dropping from the branch and rolling over she kicked out once more at the one nearest to her, and he went down, encouraging her as, for a brief moment, hope sprang up inside of her. If they were this easy to harm she might just stand a chance, mayhap to live. A leap took her to the branch of the tree and she grabbed it, swinging round and letting go of the branch her slight weight forced another to the ground, her foot stamped hard on his neck, and grimaced at the sound of the snap.

Now she needed the trees again, to be in them and the comfort they offered. In her haste to reach the trees once more she had not seen the arrow enter the orc's chest just before she had dropped on him, as she did she see the arm as it encircled her, pulling her into the trees; and she screamed.

The leader stood once more, vengeance on his mind; the elf would die in great pain, his fingernails would rip her slowly to shreds, inch by inch. His snarl was cut short as an arrow to found his throat.

She barely had time to see the rest of them fall as arrows from unseen archers found their marks.

The Reckoning

With hands on knees she sat patiently, but nervously, as her mother and father read the scroll she given them from Caspo Kwil, he had been adamant about the speed in which it was to be delivered.

Rolling up the scroll he placed it on the table, "Are you aware of the contents, Nortee?"

"No, father, I was instructed to deliver it with all haste. I believe it contains the details the poor stewardship of those in my charge."

"It contains the account, yes."

Her head hung, eyes refusing to meet theirs, "I am to be chastised and accept any punishment you deem fit. Am I to be dismissed from the enchanters' guild?"

His hand hit the table sharply, "You are elfin! Look to those who would speak with you."

Her head rose, "I apologise, father."

Shaking her head she let her voice become firm, "Is it my teachings have fallen on infertile ground?"

The words stung her, "Mother I have listened to all your teachings, I try *so* hard to please you, *so* hard to please father."

"You have missed several points to this, Nortee. Had you thought you would never have been caught; not have started out on your journey."

"I missed nothing, mother."

Standing she moved behind her daughter, hands resting gently on her shoulders, "Words to hide the truth. Let us begin part way through this affair. How was it you were so easily captured?"

"We.... I was not ready for an encounter. The fault is mine alone."

"Why was your mind not searching for danger as I instruct so often?"

"I thought no danger to be present so near to home."

"An excuse not a reason. Eight wards were in your charge, you should always expect danger no matter how safe the situation appears to be."

"Yes, mother."

"You failed to see their tracks, why so?"

"I was not looking for dangers, father, as I should have been."

"Not looking the same as being ignorant of dangers, Nortee."

Her eyes flicked down then back up again as she corrected herself, "It is as you say, father."

"When you were captured you did nothing to stop the whipping of your wards?"

"I did not, mother, I might have been killed and be unable to help them."

Behind her daughter's back she smiled, "Ah, a thought runs true."

Inwardly she signed; she had done something right at last.

He caught her smugness, "Yet you ignored several signs of help."

"There was none, father. None knew of our departure save Caspo Kwil."

"This does not strike you as strange? Which profession have you chosen?"

"I am an enchantress, mother, as well you know."

"And it is all you are, daughter?"

"I am druid also, though it is my second calling."

"An enchantress must be capable of thought; it would seem you have not done so."

Finglas shook his head slowly, "I had thought you trained in the ways of the druids much more than you are. You failed to see signs left for you."

They had their say, it was time to stop being defensive, "I think clearly, mother, as I have been taught; no signs were left father."

"Only druids and rangers may move through the woods and leave no sign of their passing. Several were left for you yet you chose to see them not."

She had been too confident in her reply and knew it, once more she let her head drop again, "I did not, father."

His hand slapped the table again, "Head up, child! Remember your heritage. You did not see three rangers and a druid hidden in the trees?"

"I did not, father."

"They were there and you saw them not? A poor druid you will make."

Giving him a short nod Norty let go of her daughter's shoulders and sat again, the smile she had fought hard to control had passed, "As you chose to ignore the hawk calling to you all the day?"

"I heard the hawk; it annoyed me in my planning."

"The hawk you befriended is now an annoyance?"

"I knew not it to be the same hawk."

"Your mind should have told you, should have reached out and listened."

"I was not to know, mother."

"You were in charge of them. It is your duty to know."

"I am sorry, father."

"Sorry does not return the dead, daughter."

"None have died as I have been told. Please tell me none died."

"None have died."

Her breath came out in a sigh of relief.

She glanced towards her husband, "It is time for an explanation."

He nodded his agreement.

Reaching over the table she touched her daughter's hand, "Think this through from the time you were asked to undertake this task. Think of why you were chosen."

This time when her head lowered it was in thought, "There was no reason to choose me above others; I saw only the honour bestowed on me."

"To take your mind off the reason you were asked. Why would Caspo Kwil ask you walk there?"

"I was told they were to see the land, yet it seems strange to me now, they would know the way to our city."

"Now she begins to think, it is a pity it is so late."

"In her defence she did use her mind to turn them against each other."

"You know of this, mother?"

"The druid and rangers watched."

"Yet they did not help us! Why so?"

"You started to think, continue please."

"We were followed, it is obvious. A test; but to test whom?"

For several minutes she was totally silent, "They wished to test me. Do they think I am not good enough to be an enchantress?"

"Dismiss the thought. What plan was in your mind when you escaped?"

"To run for help, the shortest direction most likely where help would be found. Study maps show the common paths taken by those patrolling our lands."

"You used druid ways at least, you knew the direction and which way was best."

A small smile crossed her lips, "I remember your training, father."

"I have not yet taught you to fight in trees, or how to kick an enemy."

"You know of the fight?"

"In detail."

"I fought as an enchantress yet it was hard to control their minds; therefore I fought as a druid."

"Your father has been known to fight in trees, and once I believe he did kick an ogre in his most sensitive spot."

"I thought to fight with my back to a tree, also as you taught me."

"Yet still you saw no help to hand, daughter, I feel your training needs to be refreshed."

"Yes, father. Yet I feel now our talk is about to finish. I believe I have been rejected as an enchantress and will now train only as a druid."

"Why do you think such?"

"You spoke of my need to train. After the way I handled my stewardship why else would you say such?"

Norty rose to walk slowly round the room, "Caspo Kwil directs the ways in which watch is kept on our borders and, therefore, he was the first to know of their incursion into our lands. He asked they were not to be killed but to be watched so you could be tested. Only once in a while does an opportunity present itself for any to be tested to the limits. You were sent purposefully to them knowing you would be captured; it was desired."

She stopped behind her once more, "When first they crossed our borders he approached us and asked permission. Did it not seem evident to you we were away when no plans had been made for such travel?"

"Now it is obvious, mother. You were to be away so I could not link with you. It would spoil his plans for I would rely on your rescue of me."

"You were captured, but it was not the test Caspo Kwil had in mind for you. You passed his test, passed it with ease."

"I failed in all respects! I failed to get my wards to their destination, failed to get them to safety, failed to stop them from being whipped and failed to ensure their safe return to high elf city for the rangers escorted us there. In what way did I pass the test?"

"You did not run and save yourself; you were prepared to sacrifice yourself in order to save your wards. No greater courage could have been shown."

"Yet the poor children, they took the beatings so I may be tested?"

"They were told of your prowess, each was willing to go each a volunteer."

"My training as an enchantress is to continue?"

"Yes, daughter, it is to continue. This day you make us both so proud."

Eating while she talked over the scroll with them twice she explained to her father the ways she used the trees in the fight. As she talked her mind was on other things, not only was she to continue her training as an enchantress it seemed the high elves held her in esteem. She realised the young elves may have been hurt badly before the rangers could intervene and made a promise to herself. She would seek out each and every one of them in her charge and thank them in a way she knew they would wish. For one whole day she would treat them to the sights they had missed and at the end of the day she would take them to a little shop she knew and they would have the pick of anything their hearts desired. The shop called Minlets, where sweet offering from distant lands adorned the counter, but for her it was to be the sweet white wine Pose had introduced her to. She would speak with her dear friend Aurorai Minlets and this time she would have an adventure to speak of, her very first.

The feel of her father's hand squeezing hers brought her back to reality.

For over an hour they talked of her training, but each time it returned to the same subject of her prowess in the trees. How she had learned to swing on a branch and where to kick to make it effective.

"I have not yet taught these to you, daughter, and none in guild would do so for another year."

Finally she could keep the secret no longer and leaned forward to him as if someone might overhear, "Keitun asked I speak not of this to you. He taught me the ways in the trees, saying if a wood elf cannot use the trees to fight then why be a wood elf. I think he will not mind if I tell you now. He knows a lot of how to fight and says at times it does not matter how good you are but how dirty you fight."

He roared with laughter, "Keitun! I should have realised. You were spending so much time with him but looked so innocent whenever I called to see you."

"The linking made it easy for me to know when you were near, as it did with mother."

"He is a great fighter. Once an ogre called him...."

A look from his wife stopped him, "Ack, I cannot remember now, it was a nasty insult to a dwarf"

She giggled, "I must ask Malinna what it may have been."

Her father's eyes flicked sideways, she understood immediately, "Mother?"

"Yes?"

"You are quiet and have been for so long, of what are you thinking?"

"There is an explanation missing, I would know of it."

"There is nothing else, mother. This is my first tale and have spoken of it at length, you know all there is to know."

"Not all do I know, outside if you will."

They followed her as she pointed to the boulder five hundred paces away, "Race to the boulder and back, all speed now."

"Nortee tires and would sleep."

"All speed now."

Raising an eyebrow to his daughter they began the race at full speed.

As she watched the race her eyes turned towards the heavens, "Thank you, Messenger."

"You are back before your father; do you think is the way it should be?"

"Father is a much better and should easily beat me."

"Why is it you may beat your father?"

"I should not be able to, I do not know."

"Remove the amulet please; give it to your father."

She did as instructed, still puzzled.

"Race again. Fast as possible."

Once more they ran for the boulder, neck and neck for the first ten yards, he beat his daughter back with ease.

"The report says you stopped several times to wait as your wards caught up, indeed it says the ranger's struggled keep up with you."

"The amulet! Messenger gave magic to it, the gift of speed!"

"Yet the gift is for you only. Your father may not use its powers. You spoke of hearing the wolf as Messenger forged it for you."

"I will thank Messenger when next I see him, it is a wonderful gift."

The Gift

The glade was full of sweet fragrances and warmth as she hugged him tight, kissing him gently, "No, your city."
The kiss was returned, "I will hear no arguments."
"We are not yet in wedlock so you may not say what is to be. Always the female decides on the place of union, and such it will be for us."
Kare shook his head, "It is too dangerous to join in wedlock there. Many would see you dead, my own family included."
She giggled, "They will come to love me, as do you."
"They are against the union of our people. I will be disbarred from them the moment they know of my love for you."
"You give up so much for me. Why?"
"You have need to ask when you feel as I do?"
"Then be with me, it is my wish."
"It will be as you say; I have a love for you as no other."
Her robe slipped off her shoulders as she thought of it, "It is time for us, love with me."

Finglas paced the floor, "I am unsure of this. If they wed in his city trouble would ensue, there is no doubt."
"It is her wish and she must join with him as she feels best, it is the way females of all races would have it."
"I was happy we joined at the druid stones, yet I would have joined wedlock wherever you wished."
"I knew of your wish to join at the stones. Icee wishes it to be in dark elf city yet would be just as happy in our glade."
"Then why not join in wedlock there?"
"She wishes it to be in his city as a sign to all, unity is possible."
Her smile grew wider and excitement entered her voice, "Nortee comes as promised, in time to celebrate the tenth year of her birth. She has been away but a week and I have missed her. I must return more often to the guild, I have ignored my training and mentor duties too often."

The meal was taken slowly, all the family attending to celebrate; much to her surprise there were gnome sweet meats.
Finglas offered the plate around, "Arkie insisted we have them."
"A favourite of Xandorian and himself."
Glancing at each as they sat at the table, her family to the right and friends to the left, Aurorai immediately her left, she was pleased, every one of whom she cared for was present.

Sipping the wine she gave a silent toast, 'to friends no longer able to return the toast. Xandorian, may you rest well with the Gods. To my grandparents parents, wherever they lay in rest let it be in peace.'

She smiled to herself, the time was right and she had waited all evening for this moment. She had noticed the way her mother watched her, knowing she wished to say something but never dreaming of spoiling the occasion by asking. Lifting the glass to her lips once more she finished the remains before snapping the stem and tapping the two pieces together.

Instantly there was quiet as they looked expectantly at her.

Standing she bowed to those assembled around the table, "My family and friends. Tomorrow I become of age and my parents duty to me is fulfilled."

Her hand rose to stop arguments, "I know of what you would speak yet I will continue. Pose has been far more to me in my studies than any have asked. And my special thanks to Caspo Kwil, without whose permission I would not have been accepted and trained for some years."

He rose slowly, age showing in his body, to return the bow.

"Tomorrow I celebrate my tenth year and may take my place at the enchanters' guild. This time it will be official."

Pausing she looked at their nodding heads, noting her mother's face remained impassive. She knew she suspected something but was unsure if she really knew what she was about to say. Now she would change the nodding, and mayhap even surprise her mother, "Yet it would seem they must wait. I follow father to the guild of druids."

The effect was exactly as she expected, her father looked stunned yet her mother's face still retained her impassive look. She had hoped to change it and could not understand how she had failed to do so.

Her gaze turned to Icee and Malinna; their mouths wide open, while her grandparents looked at each other in shock. With more than a little satisfaction she noted Aurorai was, for the first time since she had known her, at a loss for words. Waiting until she judged they had recovered and might speak she continued, "I am accepted in the enchanters guild and may return at anytime to continue my training. I have the permission of Caspo Kwil to return whenever I wish. I need not enter dark elf city to train there, Pose is willing to undertake my initial training upon my fifteenth year. I am also druid born, yet have not yet trained in those ways. This I will correct and, the Gods willing, take both understandings in my stride. Father, as I am to enter your guild I believe you should speak first."

He drew a long slow breath, "I am stunned. I had wished you to enter my guild yet had thought it not possible. You know not how pleased I am."

"I know how pleased you are, father, and it is possible, as you will see. Mother, all this day your face remains the same, I had thought to change it with my words."

"I have thought your change late in the coming; however, it was expected."

"You knew I would heed the call of the druids first?"

"I had surmised as much."

"How so?"

"I have watched as you concentrated more on your path of an enchantress than your druid ways. After your adventure with the orcs I knew the change would come."

Three chairs were sent hurtling backwards as the sisters were suddenly at her side, holding her moments before glowing blue-green bands of shimmering mana descended on her. They had sensed the slight change in her body, the way it alters just before the mana descends.

Her face filled with pleasure as she bathed in the glow, each band seemed to fill yet pass through her. As each strand ran through her body she felt as if she wanted to hold it, to keep it close, to always have it with her. The thrill was almost a living thing as she wished it would never stop, her body tingling as each thread slowly drifted from her head to her feet. Untold joy entered her heart; the Gods had finally given her their blessing.

She had wanted the mana to be in her as it had been in her aunts long before their coming of age. Each day as she awoke she had prayed to the Gods to let it be the day, yet each day brought only disappointment. Each evening she returned to her room to sleep and offer another prayer for tomorrow to be the day. She wished, above all else, to walk to her parents with the mana in her, tall and proud.

Then the ribbons began to fade, to take an age before they finally stopped and she saw her mother checking her over, a worried look on her face.

"No pain, mother, only pleasure. Cease your worries, it creases your face."

Malinna shook her head, "The mana took time to end, far longer than is normal."

"It fills me, my very being tingles with the power within me. I feel I could do anything."

She glanced at each in the room, deciding whom she should choose to test her. Malinna was a cleric, her spells healing based; she dismissed the idea. Icee was a wizard, renowned for her skills and power, yet her spells were the longest of any class to cast, she realised she could think of several ways to reply before any spell came her way, Icee was also dismissed. Aurorai was a friend and a fellow enchantress with whom she had trained many times, she knew each move she was likely to make, and how to deal with it. Another enchantress would not be the challenge she desired. Her mother and Pose would not attack her, they were strict in the ways they instructed and would never attack for fun. They were dismissed also. Her grandparents would never attack her; they loved her too much. It left only one who she could turn, one who would be pleased to test her.

"Test me, father, test me now!"

He moved fast, his fist glowing green as the spell started, growing brighter until it hurled towards her at frightening speed.

Her left arm rose quickly from her waist to her head as she uttered a spell and a wall of force appeared before her, deflecting the spell with ease, "Slow, father you are too slow. Try to stop this!"

As her spell ball sped towards him another deflected its path

"Desist! Desist I say! Enough! Magic is not for play. Desist, and do so now."

Her voice brought Nortee to her side, "I have the need to be tested, mother. Father tried to grant my wish, scold him not."

She spun round to face her daughter, "Magic is not for play, how many times do you need to be so told? Many are harmed in such foolery when the mana enters them, you will not succumb to such behaviour! Hear me, child?"

She realised how upset her mother was, she was only called a child on rare occasions when she acted as such, "You are correct, mother. Accept my apologises."

"Mine also."

Calming herself she smiled at them both. She had watched what had happened and was happy; her daughter had reacted with thought and not instinct, it pleased her. Now she had to control the exhilaration and channel it the right way, "Soon you enter your guild with mana already in you, and few do so. You have a duty to show you are worthy of the mana and of the guild. I expect high things for I am proud of you. Let me continue to be so."

"I promise you will be proud of me."

She hugged her daughter, as never before, "There is an end to it."

"Nortee."

The voice brought her out of her thoughts as she gazed from the treetop home of her grandparents, "Yes, Aurorai?"

"Your mother wishes you only to think before you act."

Her arm went over her shoulder, "This I understand."

"You were sad when your mother spoke sharply to you. It is understandable yet I would have a smile back on the face of my friend."

"I am no longer sad. I think of my path and of the new one I will soon tread. Aurorai, a fear starts within me and grows."

"Never have you been afraid, I do not believe you to be so now."

"It is in me, Aurorai, a fear I may let father or mother down."

"Place the fear to one side, yet if you have the need I am here to listen."

Taking her by the arm she led her out of earshot of her family, "I have dwelt little on my druid ways, Aurorai, now they now cause me to worry. "

"Yet you spoke of entering the guild to all at the table."

"I must enter the guild, to prove I am also as my father."

"You have little to prove and your father would not wish you to do so."

"I have much to prove and the fear grows ever stronger in me. I am proud of my parents for both have been gifted above the ways of others. Father knows so much above his station whilst mother has a mind unlike any before her. You see yourself the esteem in which she is held, the way all ask to train with her."

"She mentors others before she should be allowed. Many come to her to ask if she would help their children, never have I known her to refuse and all those she helps speak highly of her skills. It is she who also taught my mind to leave the body."

"I knew not of this."

"She speaks not of those she trains yet has ways above others."

"How may I compare to them, be as them?"

"You need only be yourself."

"If I were to let them down what would they think of me, what would they say to me?"

"They would say they love you as they do now, as they will always do. All know you are also gifted, except yourself it would seem."

She laughed, "I bless the day you helped me choose at your mother's counter. Your words are wise yet do not remove my fears."

"As I saw you there I knew you would be a friend. You have far to travel yet fear may oft bar your way. I offer to share those fears with you."

"Not here, mother will feel them in me. When I return will you listen and speak not of them to her?"

"I make no such promise. If I were asked I would speak of them to her. She has taken the role of mentor to me, how could I withhold from a mentor words which may help a friend?"

Her arm pulled her tight, "Had I a sister I would wish for you to be her."

"Then the fears depart?"

"They do not, yet they are eased, I have a friend to whom I may turn."

Druid Ways

One week later, on the new moon, she stood at the entrance to the guildhall as she waited her turn, second in line to be called before the elder. The elf standing beside her was ready to take on the duties of the druids. As his name was called he smiled to encourage her before turning to take the short walk down the aisle. He was familiar to her and she knew he must be a little older to be called first, as was his right. Yet his smile had helped her in a way in which it had not been offered. Though the elves knew her most were a little uncomfortable in her presence. This druid was not nervous of her as they stood there, but of the ceremony itself. Whispering words of encouragement to him she watched as he walked to the elder's rostrum; he did not know she had already taken a walk such as this before, when she had joined the enchanters.

As he walked the aisle she glanced to her family sat on the front bench. By Lore only her father and grandparents should be in the hall, they alone were druids. Yet her mother and aunts were there, as was Pose and Kare, she was pleased beyond belief. Never before had dark elves attended an elfin ceremony, except the wedlock of her parents, Pose had attended also.

As she heard her name being called her shoulders went back and with head high she walked the short way to the rostrum, her hooded cloak of druid colours rustling softly as she moved. In moments she stood before the elder as so many had done before her. With a bow she waited for his words.

"Nortee; you are of age and come before this assembly to join the druids. Are you ready to accept your calling?"

The reply she knew by heart, her father had spent over an hour instructing her on conduct and etiquette, she knew every move to make and just when to make it, "Elder, I am of age and I come before you as I was called to do so. I accept my calling with pride."

"Nortee, daughter of Finglas and Norty, you know not the happiness within me as I reject your application."

She was unable to comprehend what was happening; she was being rejected but knew not why.

He saw she was flustered and it pleased him, after all these years he was in the right position to take revenge, "You are as your mother before you, an abomination with no right to life and none to be here. Leave in shame, this guild has no use for the likes of you."

She was at her daughter's side, as her mother had been at hers when she had rejected the druid ways, but Finglas was already there, speaking to the elder with an a calmness she found hard to understand. The elder was rejecting their daughter yet he smiled at him as if he understood the reasons, and accepted them.

"Elder, you lead our guild and have the right to make this decision."

His glance moved to those not of the druids and distain showed in his face, "I have the right; druids only should be welcome in this guild hall."

"My daughter is druid born and has the right to enter this guild. I invoke the Test of Trial."

His head shook slowly, "Test denied. Leave now for what you bring forth before this guild."

"Elder, the test may not be denied. I invoke the Test of Trial!"

He almost screamed his reply, "Test denied. Leave!"

"Lore says the test may not be denied. As all who stand in the guildhall are my witnesses, I invoke the Test of Trial."

Back in their home she could contain herself no longer, "What is the Test of Trial, father?"

"A series of tests to show you have druid ways."

Norty stopped her pacing of the room, "How is it you know of this test?"

"I have heard of it before, it is a story told from time to time to the fledglings of the guild. Yet I thought it never to be used."

"I have heard no such talk."

"You are no druid so would not know, as you know not the elder."

"He was not the elder when I rejected the druid ways."

"Think on the other elder, the one you fought and killed."

Old feelings returned; he had been her first kill, "I know him not."

"If the guild leader dies his son has the right to stand in his place for he follows his father. He is the son of the elder you killed and, therefore, has the right to replace him as leader. He has reasons to reject Nortee."

"It is wrong to make the child suffer for the actions of the parents."

"He follows not only his footsteps but also his ways."

"For his rejection I have the right to duel him."

"To challenge him would only widen further the split between guilds. There are other ways. Tomorrow my plans begin to see the light."

"You scheme, Finglas."

"From her birth I have thought of this and knew she may be rejected and laid my plans. I have ensured she knows all needed to take the test, and to pass it. This is not the end of my planning but the beginning. Tomorrow Nortee becomes a druid."

Waking her daughter early she gave her the clothes folded over her arm, "You should not be asked to undertake druid tests while dressed as an enchantress. These are more fitting for the occasion."

Trying them on she found them a near perfect fit, "I had thought not to change to druid clothes. You made them for me?"

"They are your grandmothers; she was your size in her younger days. She kept them for me and is happy they will be worn once more."

"Thank you; I will do my best for you today."

Checking the fit of the clothes she smoothed them, "Do your best yet do so for yourself. This day is yours and you should think only of yourself."

With the city far below them in the distance the elder called a halt, "Saseens Point, here we find I am right, she has no right to our guild. Should she fail I demand she be banished as an Undesirable Elf."

The group of judges stood ready and nodded, Finglas relaxed and happy, Nortee ill at ease, and it showed.

"They will ask nothing you have not done on many occasions."

"In front of them I wish not to let you down."

"Banish those fears and be as you would with me, all will be well."

A sneer entered his voice, "The test of hiding is first. Hide if you can."

Moving to a tree her arms spread along a branch as she concentrated on becoming one with it, and slowly it became almost impossible to distinguish her from the tree.

"Test failed! She cannot hide with yellow hair, any would see her."

Finglas let his feelings for the elder enter his voice, "She passes the test; her body is hidden. Nowhere does it mention the hair of the one under test. Only the body is to be hidden."

As the druid peers consulted the old scrolls their heads nodded in agreement. She had passed the first test.

As his daughter stood once more beside him he placed his arm around her, "First test passed with ease. The Mother of All guides you."

The anger in his face was plain as he insisted on continuing the tests, "Find the nearest creature to you; say what and where it is."

This test pleased her, one she could pass as both druid and enchantress. Her mind could see so many others around her, the druid side of her could sense them as her father did, "My friend the hawk on the first branch."

"You fail! A hawk is not an animal! Entry to the guild denied."

"You asked for the nearest creature, elder, and not the nearest animal. Find the nearest animal for them, daughter."

Her eyes closed as she saw the creatures in her mind so many she became confused, the more she tried to find the nearest to her the more they seemed to move. Panic entered her at the thought of letting her father down, she tried harder before remembering his teachings and paused to compose herself, and found the animal with ease, "The squirrel is nearest, on the branch to our left."

"No! She cheats on the test. No druid is she but an abomination; never must she enter our guild. She must die!"

Dafon Artith shook his head; "It is plain leadership weighs heavily on your shoulders for you reject one with druid ways. You will return the gems of leadership you wear, another will be chosen in your place. Nortee, you pass the tests set forth in the scribing of our Lore and we see no need to continue with them. Welcome Nortee, daughter of Finglas and Norty. Welcome to the druids' guild."

Hugging his wife he was happy, pride flowed through him, "She found the tests easy and passed both. They decided to accept her to the guild before the testing was over. I am so proud of her. She begins her training on the morrow, yet unlike the enchanters she will not start until after breakfast."
"To try to study in both guilds will be a strain on her."

Holding out her left arm the hawk flew to her, drawing it to her chest she stroked him, "Hello again, my friend. There are happy thoughts in your head now, a new mate you have found and she has young ones."
He screeched in reply and she smiled back at him, "Come see my mother and father before you fly back to them."
Watching as he flew over the trees she waved to him, "Mother, it is time for me to prepare with father for tomorrow. I feel our time is the glade will be forfeit this night."
"For many nights I fear. You must speak and sort things together."
"Soon our training will resume again in the glade and in guild. I do not reject the enchantress ways."

With her head high she entered the guild hall side by side with her father, slightly nervous but eager as she bowed before the instructor, "Sir, I am here to take my position with the guild."
His bow was stiff but his sharp eyes checked her over, "Welcome, Nortee. Take your place with the others in the first class of druids. We begin with plants and roots; each has its own ways."
Turning she walked to them as they sat on small benches as her father left.
Handing each student six roots he gave each a firm look, "Now, who is to describe them to me?"
Walking along the row of seated students he watched them carefully, it was their first day and he wanted the lesson to inspire them, not demoralize them. He needed to find the one who he was sure could answer his questions, "We start with, hmm, young Nortee. Speak of the roots."
"Not all are all edible; this one would make any sleepy. The sap from this is poison except the wild cattle of the scrublands. "
"Verith, explain the roots Nortee as not yet mentioned. Once I am sure the roots will be forever in your minds we turn to leaves, those your parents were bid not to speak of until you enter the guild."
"Why were they forbidden?"

He let his voice take an air of mystery, "Leaves are more to us than you will know; one is a friend to all druids and one a friend who would protect us, to help us in our ways of healing. Learn well the roots and I will teach of leaves."

Finglas greeted her on her return, "All was well, daughter?"
"He is sweet, father. I like him and he ensures the teachings remain in the head by the questions he asks. I found it odd he spoke of roots when all knew from childhood of them."
"There is method in his ways. Do you remember all I taught of roots?"
"His ways refreshed your teachings. Why is it the teaching of leaves are withheld from us?"
"More than leaves are withheld from the young ones as you will see. Training is not over for this day; your mother waits in the glade."
"A bite to eat first, father?"
"Your mother's daughter you are, she also likes her food."
"Mother are you ill? You saw me not as I entered the glade."
"My mind was far away."
"Never are you unaware others are near, so often you scold me if I see not a mind as it approaches. What is the cause of this?"
"My dream bothers me. The land I see is strange and the people stranger. Fear and loneliness confuses the one who once lay on the bed as others chase her. She will be caught; this I know. "
"I would have Malinna ensure you are well. Come we speak with her."
"She is with the dwarves and needs to see me not."
"The day Malinna refuses to speak with her sister will never come. Father will take us there this instant."
"There is little need to trouble him."
"If father heard you speak such he would be most displeased with you. We journey there and Malinna will see you. There is an end to it."

Sitting next to her he relaxed in the chair, "You look happy."

"Nortee trains in your guild and now returns to mine. No mother could wish for more."

"Even now I miss her."

"She has been gone but one day."

"Her time here was only one month, I miss watching her as she trained, and the hawk was always nearby. The others speak of the way none may take him from her."

"She spoke of the tree craft and the ways to drop from branch to branch, it causes me to worry. She is not a full druid as are you."

"She is born for the trees, as are your sisters, as are you."

"I move freely in the trees yet I am not as agile as the druids, even the rangers cannot match you in them."

"As we cannot match them on the ground."

"I hear as she speaks to you of your younger days."

"She asks how I was raised and trained."

"Often has she asked, I wonder why she does so once more?"

"Her training makes her think as to how I was trained with no parents to guide me. I spoke of all who took to my training, of those I call friend for their actions. Elesee once trained those in their first class as she did to me also. I came to admire her and the way she taught. After six months I asked she give me more instruction after the others had left, she refused."

"I would not have thought her to do so."

"I asked when her ambassador duties called, unaware of her role to man. I believed she wished not to train me for I knew too little of the ways of druids and must learn more in classes. It is the reason I left the guild early to travel; I wished to prove to her my worth."

Frowning she saw the mind of Pose as she ran towards their home, "Strange, Pose comes, and she is troubled."

Pose rushed to her, her face reflecting her thoughts, "Her mind has been entered and closed to all. She sits and does not move. Come."

Kneeling at the head of the bed she examined her daughter, resisting the urge to fold her arms around her, to take her in them and beg her to return to her. It was useless to try and she knew it, yet the mother in her wanted to hold her daughter. Thoughts of her husband entered her head, he should not see what was needed to be done, or the strain it would place on her, "Leave, Finglas, this is not for you to see."

"I stay."

"Let me do as I must with no distractions!"

With her arm in his Pose guided him out of the room, "Do as she asks, it is best she is with others who may be of help in her task. Caspo Kwil asks you stay with him."

With Finglas in the study of Caspo Kwil she made her way back, worry constantly playing on her mind, not only for Nortee but also for Norty. The task ahead was dangerous, for both of them.

She spun round as Pose entered the room, "Her mind has been entered and locked from the world. Who did this?"

"None know. She came to Caspo Kwil to speak of returning for training. When she failed to keep the appointment he came in search of her and this is how she was found. He bid I bring you here with all haste."

"I am sworn to find the one who attacks her, Pose, when I do he will beg me for his death and, and I will ignore his pleadings. By the Gods he will suffer as none before him as ever done."

"My promise will be to grant him his request with all my pleasure."

"You understand what must be done, the part I may call on you to play?"

"Caspo Kwil spoke you would know her mind and its ways above all others so the task would be easier for you."

"I cannot count the times our minds have met, yet there is risk for you, she may see you as a foe and defend herself."

"I will take any risk, do as you must."

The entrance to her daughter's mind had been cleverly hidden, but the thought also comforted her a little, there could not be many enchanters capable of such a feat. She would speak to each of them until she found the one she was looking for. It was one of her kind; it would make the search so much easier. For almost two hours she struggled to find the path into her daughter's mind, and noted the way in which it had been hidden. It narrowed down the number of enchanters capable of such a feat to the dark elves. Under the illusion of an elf they could easily fool the guards and gain entry to the city. But she began to wonder why the enchanters' patrolling with them, for just such occasions, had not seen through their illusion. The thought was pushed to the back of her mind; she would ponder the reasons later, at the moment she had a more important task.

The path was narrow and difficult to tread, to each side traps lay in wait, cleverly hidden but traps just the same. Whoever had closed her mind in this way, was very skilful in their profession, she had never seen it done but had heard in training of the possibilities, and of the ways it could be done. Yet in each case the perpetrator had to leave a way out of the mind for them to escape, in so doing a way back into the mind of the victim was left.

The path was thin to tread, and was getting narrower, as if she were treading a narrow ledge high on a mountain, one false step would mean starting over again. Each footstep had to be carefully planned, and precious time was being wasted. Then the way started to become a little easier and hope began to show in her face. The sudden appearance of the wall across the path she trod changed her feelings.

The style was easily recognisable; her daughter had placed the wall in her way. She knew someone was trying to enter her mind, and had moved to stop them; while she could still react there was a chance she was not too far gone to get her back. Instantly she began to sooth her mind with calming thoughts but the wall did not crumble, it grew higher and wider the harder she tried. Her soothing stopped immediately; realising her daughter was fighting her but did not understand why. She was here to help and she should realise it, not fight her.

She rethought her approach; her daughter knew someone was in her mind even though it was locked from the world. All minds were capable of stopping an enchanter if they knew they were there, or if they thought the encroaching mind meant them harm. It seemed her daughter thought of her as harming her and it not only worried her, it saddened her.

It was going to be hard to battle through to her but she was her daughter; nothing was going to stop her from getting her back. Nothing! It would be easy to smash the wall down, her mind was so much stronger then her daughters, but she did not know what harm it may cause to her. Another way lay open and she would prefer the gentle approach.

"Pose, speak with Nortee. Send your soothing from the path I have marked yet be careful, danger lies close to the beginning."

She felt the anxiousness in Pose but noted she did as she was asked without question, and instantly. She watched as she saw the mind of Pose enter her daughters, begin the process of carefully following the marked path until she had passed the traps. Then heard her thoughts as Pose called to the mind of Nortee.

Instantly Pose saw a wall appear before her, blocking her way forward while from the side's vines sprang to grasp her. Nortee was using her druid self to attack, the vines were proof. As they lashed at her she fought back, her mind fighting the visions Nortee had planted in her thoughts.

The plan was simple; to convince her daughter she had withdrawn further out from her mind. She could not understand how she had fooled her daughter but Pose would keep her occupied while she proceeded, 'Pose, keep fighting; do not stop. While she fights my task will be all he easier.'

'The vines cause little strain yet the noises I hear noises beyond the wall worries me, as if someone were in torment. Bring her back, my friend, before she is lost to us.'

She trod the path more carefully now, watching for any signs of her passage being blocked, but careful to keep her thoughts calm and to herself, she knew she would not fool her daughter so easily a second time.

For the rest of the afternoon she moved carefully in her daughter's mind aware Pose and herself were rapidly tiring of keeping the link with Nortee, Never had they been in the mind of any other for so long. Yet she could not hurry, any false step and she would have to start over again. She could not lose the time; the longer she remained locked away the less chance she would have of recovering completely. Then she saw the cause of the closing of her daughters mind, and anger brewed within her, anger so terrible she began to shake. Her resolve to find the one who did this heightened.

To close a mind to the world an enchanter must use the subject's own fears, to lock it away within the boundary of those fears, for it to surround them and leave no way out, and this enchanter had used the same technique. She could see her fears laid out before her daughter, encircling, tormenting her.

This enchanter had entered her daughter's mind, defiling it, using her own fears to cause her pain in a way she had never thought possible. As she began to move forward she heard her scream, and it sent ripples of sadness through her, and tears began to fall down her cheeks.

In horror she watched her mother approach, screaming as she did; he nearer she came the more she screamed but could not back away, her tormentors were all around, everywhere. She wanted to run but it was no use, images of her mother were all around and there was no escape. Her arms stretched out in front of her, palms facing her mother in elfin denial, it was too much for her; falling to the floor her body shook uncontrollably.

At her daughter's posture she almost stopped, forcing herself onwards through the elfin denial, she was going to reach her daughter and nothing was going to stop her. Finally she understood her deepest fears, there, all around her daughter, the forms of Finglas and herself taunted her for imagined failings to them in their guilds. Heartache crushed her as she thought of the fears within her daughter; fears she never knew were there, fears with no reason to exist. Nortee was living a constant nightmare; there was little wonder the path back could not be found.

Then she was at her side as Nortee collapsed in a heap, head twisted away, hands still held forth in denial, the sobbing changing to a flood of uncontrollable tears.

'Why will you and father not forgive me? I work so hard to please yet all I do is never good enough for either.'

Kneeling beside her she took her hands in hers, her fingers entwining with her daughters, 'You work hard, we are pleased with you.'

'You laugh and scorn. I wish only to please, only to please!''

Gripping her tighter she placed all the love she could in her words, 'Untrue, Nortee. You are our pride and we love you. Never have you done anything to displease us; never will we be displeased with you.'

'You mock me as does father. Go! Leave me alone!'

'Look to me, Nortee; see what I am, not what you believe me to be.'

'I will look not at your laughing face. Go, leave me alone!'

Love would not bring her daughter back; firmness entered her voice; 'I did not bring you up in this way, Nortee. Face your mother as you have always faced me, with the pride your heritage demands of you. With pride, Nortee, with pride!'

Still she would not look at the one she thought hated her, could not face her.

'Look to me, look and see what you are to me. Look to me, Nortee.'

Her head slowly turned to see her mother smiling down at her.

'I love you, Nortee, never have I been displeased with you, never have you displeased me, never will you displease me. I am proud of you, so proud.'

Her head shook violently, 'You laugh at me, you think me wrong to be of both professions.'

'I have never been more proud of any. Stand; be at my side as you were meant to be. Stand and see my feelings for you.'

Slowly, with her mother's help, she stood and faced her, and the ghosts and fears in her faulted, turned to mist and were gone.

Her eyes flicked open to see her mother knelt in front of her and drew back a moment, the thoughts and fears still in her memory.

"You may be confused for a while, little one, you faced your fears for a long time; they will take a while to settle."

"I wish not to let you or father down."

"I knew not such thoughts were in you."

"I try hard not to do so, mother, I try so hard."

"Cease your trying, be one with yourself, it is all to those who love you."

Her arms flew around her mother's neck, squeezing her tight, "I wish only for you to be proud of me."

"I am proud, Nortee. I am *so* proud. I must sleep, I tire as never before."

Finglas leaned towards Pose as he slipped the silken sheet over her, "This must have been so hard for both; Norty slipped into sleep before I could speak

She could only remember him leaving her room as he laid her on the bed, and cursed herself for her tiredness, and missing such an opportunity.

The Beginning

Gently she shook her, "Mother, awaken. You sleep too long."
Her eyes opened and she smiled up at her, "You are well?"
"Yes, mother. Father prevented my sleep saying I should train yet I knew his thoughts."
"He does as he must for your good; he loves you as do I."
"Those fears are no longer within me."
"Pose, I wish to thank you, I am forever in your debt."
"There is no debt."
"Do you know the one who locked your mind?"
"No, mother, I have never seen the high elf before."
"High elf? Surely not, this is the work of a dark elf."
"Illusions fool me not, I know him to be high elf."
"Have any others trained with the dark elves but I?"
"Vague rumours spread of one who strays there."
"If he be high elf Caspo Kwil will know of him."

Scribing the names he handed the list to her, "There are a few able to do this to a mind; none have been back in over a year."
Finglas was getting annoyed; once more his daughter had been attacked, this time they had been subtle, "We see all until we find the one we want."
"He is right, Caspo Kwil, we wish this enchanter and I would speak with him. He will know the one who hired him to harm Nortee. Two of these I know and have trained with. We start with those; may the Gods help the one who did this to her."
With the names in her hand she could feel the hunt was coming to a close, and it encouraged her. She wanted the enchanter who had done this to her daughter, "Vento Greth used to train the young ones in the guild when first they joined. He was part of my training and has lived in the land of the gnomes for almost two years. We start with him. Best you accompany us, Nortee, you will put the one ill at ease and it will show in him."

Vento Greth looked up from his sitting position on the grass as he saw them. His attention always with the gnomes he had befriended; yet it pleased him when others visited, "'Tis a while since I had elfin visitors. You are all most welcome."
Refusing to bow was hard for her, but she would not do so to any who held intentions of harm towards her daughter, "Is it customary for a high elf to remain seated when visitors call?"
"Is it customary for a wood elf not to bow when she addresses someone?"
"I came not to bandy words but to see if you recognise my daughter."

"I do not, yet I remember you and our training. They were fun and useful for both. You are well?"

"You speak with truth."

"I know her not yet have heard of her, her likeness is of you."

"I am sorry to have disturbed you."

Half turning she stopped and bowed to him, "I ask you forgive my poor manners."

"You are forgiven, yet my manners are not so poor."

"You do not rise in greeting nor do you bow, what am I to think?"

Opening his robe he gestured, "My legs were shattered in battle. Now I live here with the gnomes, I may look at them face to face."

"And you have a guard it would seem."

"Still your mind sees others without the need to see them first. A gift I would have gladly given my legs to receive."

"Your words were always kind."

"It is safe to come out. Norty knew you were there long before now."

From the tall grass he appeared, dressed in light blue and scarcely able to control the thoughts darting across his face.

"Had you tried to harm my friend I would kill all of you."

Nortee bowed before kneeling in front of him, "No intention of harm was intended to one who caused no harm, Arkie."

"Plain it is now, Nortee. Yet to see the way you approached there was anger within you all."

"You know us to be friends yet still you would protect him?"

"His legs are as they are when he came to my aid. In the battle he was crippled and no longer able to walk."

"You protect him when your life may also be taken?"

"I follow Xandorian in his ways, as he protected Icee I protect Vento Greth."

"Xandorian spoke often of you, yet sometimes with worry."

"Why so?"

"He would speak of your youth to Icee. I believe he would have you be more careful before you act."

"I saw you as you came, I would not see a friend harmed."

"I thank you for the sweet meats for my coming of age."

"Xandorian spoke often of your love for them."

"Thank you once more, Arkie. Be safe."

Crossing another name from the list she sighed, "We have seen four in as many days. I grow weary."

"I agree, yet I wish to find him, and find him I will."

"I understand your desires yet do not bear the same wish, our last meeting did not go well for me."

"You tried to resist his mind?"

"I had not the opportunity, he was there and then my fears overtook me."

"I know not they existed within your mind, you hid them well."

"I should have spoken of them to you."

"Speak of them now."

"Father should be with us. When he arrives home we will speak of them."

Finglas wrapped his arms around his daughter, "Such thoughts should not be in your head."

Returning the hug she pulled away, "Father, we have not trained in almost two weeks, the guild will be ashamed of me."

"We are not as strict as the enchanters. Druids have a wander lust in their soul, many stay away for months with no training."

"The druid is within me. I long to see our world and all within it."

"Then you shall, daughter. We visit soon, after you spend a few days in the guild, and this time you shall choose where to go."

"An easy answer, I shall first see the trolls."

"They hate the elves. I am sorry, we cannot go there."

"Correct, father, *we* cannot go yet Malinna and Flight see them often. I ask if I may go with them. I more than ask, I plead with you."

To Beat A Troll

Flight grinned as his teleport spell took them close to the trolls, this time two others were with them, and he liked the thought. The more he could get to mix amongst the trolls better it would be, for both the trolls and elves, "We walk from here but you must look relaxed, Nortee, they sense when someone is tense and like it not."

"I have listened to all you have spoken to me, Flight. I will be as I should."

"Be yourself, they do not like it when deceived."

With the way still a little to the northeast she had time to ask more questions and study the answers. Although deep in discussion as to how she should behave towards the trolls she was aware of a little feeling within her, a feeling of excitement. The booming voice caught her unawares, bringing back her mother's words to always be on guard, her mind searching and, momentarily, she felt shame.

"Elves invade! To arms!"

Racing forward Malinna grabbed him by the belt, clinging on as if she could hold his great bulk, "I have this one. Quick, get one each...."

Slowly he lifted her, "Malinna back. Grugt happy."

Laughing aloud she clung to his neck, "It is good to see you again, Grugt. I have not seen you for ages."

"Malinna come more. Grugt miss Malinna."

"I miss you too, Grugt. Now I bring my child and the child of my sister."

"Grugt see. Many elves. Invasion."

Letting go of his neck she slipped to the floor and grabbed his hand, "Show me to the town square and the trader's shops. We have much to speak of."

It had long been her dream to see the troll's village. Each time Malinna and Flight returned she had questioned them constantly, wanting to know each and every detail of the village and the trolls, their ways and habits, the food and drink. From two years of age she had been asking they take her to see them yet each time she received the same answer, 'you are not old enough yet, Nortee. Maybe when you come of age we will speak of this.'

Finally she had pushed enough and was of age, and the answer was different, "Enough, Nortee. Ask your father, if he says you may join us then you may do so."

Following Malinna and Grugt her eyes missed nothing, she wanted to see it all and she was determined to. The houses were little more than mud huts or branches with hides wrapped around them, placed where the owners decided. It was confusing to thread their way through them and remember the directions. The village did not have the openness or the formality of her home as it nestled at the foot of the great Waterfall of Sahera.

Elfin homes were of wood, each home separate yet still part of the rest. The shops were to the north of the town and on the ground, convenient for both elf and traveller alike. Elves had easy access to them while travellers walked hundreds of feet below the living area nestling high in the eighty-foot girth of the trees, elves still preferring to keep their private lives separate. Wood elf city had grown this way over the last few centuries as more and more they allowed strangers into their town.

Here were shops of all types, but placed where the owners thought to get customers to which to sell wares. The smells of the blacksmith shop in the centre of the village caused her to shake her head in dismay, it would never have been allowed at home, and she wondered how anyone could eat food with such a mixture of smells in the air.

One thought crept constantly into her mind and she turned to Flight, her voice low, "They do not look to us. I had thought they would stare as we passed."

"They are used to seeing elves in their village; Malinna and I are here often. Do not whisper, elfish is understood not by them but is a form of insult, a minor one yet an insult."

"Their minds are strange and hard to see clearly."

"They are slow to think but their bodies are strong. Have you noticed the way they speak?"

"Mother taught me troll when I was three, I thought she exaggerated the speech to make the learning easier, it seems she did not."

"Their minds cannot think in long sentences, if you use them they either become bored or attack, thinking you mock them."

Grugt called back to them, "Echo, we here. Gryt move. Last place bad he say."

Nodding he pulled back the bearskin acting as a door to the shop before grabbing the trolls forearm, "Friend, it is good to see you again."

"Echo brings more?"

"Yes, more for you to sell."

Nortee was amused, "Echo? You have a story of which to speak I believe."

"One day I will explain it all to you."

Slowly he emptied first his backpack and then those the others had with them on the trip, "All I have, friend. Many things to sell."

"Echo good. Me am rich. Lot to sell now."

"What do you like the next time we come, herbs or scrolls?"

"All Echo carry. Many come. All want elf stuff."

"Next time I will bring more elves to help and you will be very rich."

As Gryt grabbed him and squeezed he felt the pain as he was hugged too tight, but he still laughed.

With the evening Nortee finally settled back to take in all the day had shown to her, but one thing still puzzled her, "Flight, how is it the trader is your friend and you trade only with him?"

Rearranging the bearskin bed he made it more comfortable, "He was the first troll I saw. My mind was made up to be friends with him and I followed him everywhere he hunted."

"You have told me the story, yet in parts only. The name you were called, I have heard it before as Malinna spoke it to you; I was younger and did not understand the meaning."

"Always it seemed you had to run off and do something when I began my tale. This has taken the longest of all my stories."

"None may want me now, continue your story please."

Placing his hands behind his head he lay down on the bed, "I made so many mistakes as I tried to become friends with him. Ran when I should have held my ground; hid when I should be seen. So many mistakes."

"I would hear of them all. It is also your name I wish to hear of."

"In time, it is part of a long story."

"I have the time to listen it would seem."

Malinna pushed aside the hide forming the door, "Another time, Nortee, I would have your help please. A young troll has a tooth ache."

"Coming, Malinna."

As they left he called after her, "Even here I may not finish this tale."

Sliding through the water with ease there was hardly a ripple showing behind her, but try as hard as she could she was unable to gain on him as he swam ahead of her. In his wake the water swirled and boiled, but he was beating her, and this was not the first time he had done so. He was on the grass bank and laughing with a low roar as she stepped out of the water.

"You good, fast. Hard to beat."

"You are good, Trag, you were taught well."

"Father teaches. Malinna save me when young. Me like her. Like you."

"Thank you, Trag, I like you also."

"Now fight. You good like Malinna?"

"No, I am poor with the staff yet I train hard."

"Me help train Nortee. Me good. Malinna teach. And father. He only one beat her. All fight Malinna. None beat."

Smiling back at him she remembered Malinna telling her they always challenged her. Grugt had told them of her prowess with the staff and how she had beaten him when his son lay dying from the bloater fish bite. Now she had beaten just about all the guards, but she had let Grugt beat her after a heavy fight. She had explained the captain of the guards should beat her, to save face to the others.

They faced each other and his club swung round at her, fast; stepping back the club missed her by an inch. It was too close, she was not quite ready and it had taken her by surprise. Ducking as the club swung back from its peak to her right her staff came up hitting him in the stomach.

"Nortee not tickle me."

"I wish not to hurt you, Trag."

Grabbing the end of her staff he rammed it into his chest, "See, not hurt. You hit Trag."

After twenty minutes of fighting he had not managed to hit her; he was big and powerful yet, just as with the orcs, he seemed to be slow; as if telling her the next way he was going to attack.

"Stop, Trag. We rest a minute."

"No rest, me not tired. Fight more."

"Let me rest and think."

"Elves weak. No make fighters."

"And trolls are strong and make good fighters. I need to think, Trag, give me a minute."

"Wish Trag think good."

Waiting while she sat with her eyes closed he mimicked her, closing his as he tried to think.

"We can fight again now, I realised something and need to try it."

"Trag ready."

His club swung upwards from the ground but she was already out of its reach.

"Slow, Trag, too slow."

Grunting he swung at her once more and the club went over her head as she ducked. Letting his club carry on its momentum he spun on his heels, expecting his speed to catch her by surprise. He was facing where she should be but she was nowhere to be seen.

"Behind you, Trag."

Lowering his club he turned, "How Nortee gets there?"

"My secret. Want to race to the tree and climb?"

She had confirming what she had first thought when she fought the orcs, yet at the time had dismissed it as just the excitement of the battle. Now she knew different, but she had to take his mind of the fight, for now.

"Me good tree climber. Best troll climber ever."

She set off running to the tree, beginning the climb before he was half way to it. Her mind caught the danger as they came down the hill behind her and she stopped, calling to him with all her might, "Run! Do not look back, Trag. Run for your life!"

He did as she instructed as he heard the hooves behind him, knowing exactly what was running him down he would never make the tree.

Three colts had split from the herd as they moved east along the top of the ridge; his only companion was an elf so he would be an easy kill and a way to win favour with the leader. The half horse half man centaurs hated the trolls, there had been more wars fought between them than any other of the races. From their first meeting of troll and centaur it had happened, hatred for each other for no other reason than hate itself. They would take any opportunity to rid themselves of another enemy.

Her mind reached out to the furthest of them and entered his, to charm him, offering a prayer to the Gods she could do it. Cursing she tried again, it seemed the Gods had not headed her prayer. On the sixth attempt she finally managed to charm him, but she had been lucky, and knew it.

The centaur knew his brothers would kill the troll, but did not care what happened to him. Then they would then turn their attention to his mistress, and he could not allow her to be harmed. She must be protected. Drawing back his bow he fired at the centaur in front of him, his aim pleasing him as the arrow pierced his left shoulder.

Screaming in pain as the arrow struck he turned to look where the attacker might be hidden. They had only seen the troll and the elf, there must be others around and set a trap for them. His eyes searched the tall grass and then the tress, no sign of an enemy. Looking towards his brother for help he saw him drawing back to shoot again. Rage filled him as he reached for his sword, he would pay for his treacherous attack.

As the centaur reached for his sword her bolt of fire burned the soft flesh of his arm. It was her first cast in anger but her aim was not true, she had cast at his body, the largest target. She found little comfort in the pain she had caused but it was enough to make him rejoin the rest of the herd, now almost out of sight as they dropped down the lea of the hill.

Twisting round on the branch she prepared to cast once more, just as the arrow found its mark. Pain shot through her shoulder as if it were on fire, causing her to fall fifteen feet to the ground below; her ankle twisting as she landed. She had been inattentive to the battle and knew it, dwelling too long on her feelings for an enemy. She saw the centaur grin with satisfaction, vengeance was on his mind, and with her arm disabled she was unable to cast, helpless as she lay there.

With a cry of delight as yet another troll fell to her staff, tripped as he lunged at her, Malinna brought it down to his throat to pin him gently beneath it, "You are good, my friend, yet your balance is lacking."

To be beaten by Malinna had become a badge of honour to them, a form of pride to have fought her, "Me try hard. Watch Malinna when she fights. Think me beat her. Find weakness."

"You had me worried for a moment, friend, you are good."

"Beat Malinna one day. Then good as Grugt."

Her hand snatched at her left shoulder as she felt the pain in her niece, "They attack Nortee and Trag by the river, too many for them to fight."

Instantly she was running, guided by the link with her niece, running faster then she had done before, Flight, Sha'Dal, Grugt and a few troll guards close on her heels. She knew Nortee was not far away, but she also knew she could not reach her in time. Three centaurs were easily more than they could handle and desperation flooded through her at the thought of what may happen to her niece and how she could ever face her sister again. A faint hope stirred in her heart; there was still a link with Nortee, she must still be alive.

Suddenly they were ahead of them, Trag leading a centaur at a run, Nortee riding on his back, her hand pressed to her chest, an arrow protruding from it. Four more centaurs were rapidly bearing down on them.

"Faster, Trag they gain on us."

Turning back she saw three spells cast from their rescuers smash into the centaurs, two stumbled, the others turning to run back to the herd.

As Trag reached out to help her off the centaur she smiled at them, "Thank you for the rescue, we could not have fought off four more."

Malinna was unsure of her emotions, anger and relief fighting to be the first to show in her, "Nortee, how could you? You know of your mother's thoughts on this."

Through the dizziness rapidly overtaking her she turned to her mount, "Return to your herd, I thank you for your help."

It was all she could remember as darkness closed about her and the pain in her shoulder ceased.

The flash of pain in her shoulder brought consciousness back, and it was not the way she had wished to be wakened. As she tried to move several hands held her firmly down.

"Lay still, Nortee. I am sorry for the pain yet I must remove the arrow."

"Remove it, Malinna I will take the pain."

"It is barbed, the pain will be great."

"I have felt pain, Malinna. Remove the arrow please."

"Your robe saved you; if not for its powers the arrow would have smashed the bones beyond my abilities to mend them."

She passed out as Malinna pulled at the arrow.

"How did you manage to fight three and win? It is hard to beat one, ask Icee, she has fought them."

"I have spoken to Icee of her fights with them. Trag and I fought together. I charmed one to help us; the Gods must have smiled, it was an all but impossible task for me. I had him attack the other while Trag fought the third one. It kicked him hard and he was stunned for a moment. Then an arrow hit me and I fell from the tree."

"Him shoots Nortee. Makes Trag mad. Me hit him good. He kicks me so me kicks him. We wrestle and me break his neck. Him not good fighter like Trag."

Nortee squeezed his arm, "He is stronger then he looks."

"Me put her on centaur, she no walk and arrow in her. More come so we run."

"Malinna, Trag can run so fast, I was amazed."

"Nortee good now? How chest?"

"The wound is almost gone thanks to Malinna; I have but a limp now."

"Nortee! You wish trouble for me with your mother, how may I take you back with a limp? Let me heal you."

Checking her leg she cast her spell, the fine blue mana from her fingers healing her niece, "She will be angry with me even now and I have little wish to face her wrath."

"Mother will not be angry with you, Malinna, but with me. This I know."

Trag looked puzzled, "Why mad with Nortee?"

"I have helped in the taking a life, Trag, she will not be best pleased."

Up before the sun had risen she shook him, "Trag, get up you lazy troll."

His eyes blinked open, "Nortee crazy. Is early. Go sleep."

"Get up Trag, get up. We never raced to the top of the tree. You won the swimming and I wish to win the climbing. Get up now."

Standing he rubbed his eyes, "Mad. Nortee mad."

"No, not mad. I want to beat you just once. I can beat you at tree climbing. I know I can. Come."

Pointing to the tree they had intended to climb she nudged him, "I will not race until you are half way there. Go."

"Unfair to Nortee. We go together."

"I run as swift as the wolf. Go."

With amusement she watched the lolloping gait they used, and had to admit it was a very fast way for them to run, using their great weight to help them run rather than have it as a hindrance. She had to wait until he reached the halfway mark, it was her promise to herself, and she set off as fast as she could, passing him well before he was at the tree.

"Come on, you are too slow."

"Nortee fast. See if Nortee climb good."

Setting off up the tree at first his height advantage showed, but soon she was along side of him, by the time she stood on the upper branches he was less than a third of the way up the tree.

"How Nortee so good? How you climb fast?"

Hooking a leg over a branch she let go with her hand, swinging upside down with her face in front of his, "I am a *wood elf*, trees are home to us. Father has taught me to climb since I was six weeks of age; there is no tree I cannot climb, even the skater tree."

"Skater tree?"

"A tree covered in a slippery sap, home to the few creatures who climb it. Predators are unable to chase them up the tree. None may climb the tree but a wood elf."

"Where tree? I climb easy. Like trees. See everything from trees."

"The trees are many miles from here, maybe Flight will take us one day and we can see if you can climb it."

Straightening her leg she let herself fall to catch a branch and swing round to face him, "I have just thought."

"What think?"

"I am druid as well as an enchantress so I should be able to teleport us there soon. I will work hard and we will travel there and see if you are as good as you say."

"Me good. Me best troll tree climber ever. Learn. Take there. Learn soon."

"Race you down?"

"Go."

Leaning backwards she checked the height to the ground below, a good forty feet, she had never fallen so far, even in training. Once she had managed thirty feet but even so it had been a risk. As she climbed she had noted the braches and their positions, her father had instilled it into her each and every time she climbed, to take notice of not only the tree she was in, but of those around her.

'There may be times it is advisable to change trees.' He had told her.

She knew each tree around the one she was in, and exactly where they were, how many could be reached easily and those at a distance she might manage if she needed to try and make the leap. Each branch below was firmly implanted in her memory and decided she could manage the distance in two drops. Letting go of the branch she fell the twenty feet to another and caught it with ease, slowing her fall, as she swung round to land feet first on the one below. Knowing the drop was now easy she jumped clear of the rest of the branches, rolling over and standing up as if she had just dropped a few feet.

"Come on Trag, you are too slow."

"Nortee good. Teach Trag?"

"I cannot teach you, my friend, you need the agility you do not have. You are better than me at and wrestling and fighting."

"Nortee right. Me good. You good. Best way."

"You are wise, Trag. Come, time to go home."

"Nortee right. Trag hungry."

For the next week they remained in the land of the trolls, but with all the items brought by them now sold, and the trolls eager for still more, they decided it was time to return home.

"My sister will wish to continue the hunt the attacker of Nortee, Grugt."

"Hunt attacker. Kill. No mercy."

"It draws time for Icee to wed in dark elf city."

"Icee good if Malinna sister. Trolls see wedding. Be happy for Icee."

"Are you welcome in the city?"

"Not happy with troll. Not turn troll away. Trolls see Icee. See wedding."

Waving goodbye her feelings were running high, the trolls would attend an elfish wedding in a city a wood elf would only see as a prisoner. Norty had spoken the ways of the elves were to change; now it was so obvious, "Take us home, husband, though I have now to face my sister's wrath and I look forward not to it."

Hushing Nortee, Malinna bowed low, whoever told tell the tale of how Nortee was wounded would find the sharp end of her mother's tongue. To her it was her own fault; she had been hurt while under her protection, failing in her promise to look after her niece.

As her story finished she readied herself for any punishment her sister deemed fit.

Closing her daughter's robe carefully over the small scar she turned to Malinna, "Sister, I thank you for her safe return and the healing, I am grateful. If you have a wish you have but to ask of me."

"I have no wish you may fulfil, sister."

"Should one present itself ask of me, it shall be yours."

Turning back to her daughter she smiled, "It would seem you learn well, I am proud of you."

"I have helped in the taking of a life and you are proud of me?"

"Why should I not be proud? Your mind was looking for danger when engaged in fun. You remembered well your training and sought to protect the one you were with. Had you not helped Trag would have lost his life, and you may also have died. Yes, I am proud of you."

"I had thought when you heard I had taken a life you would be angry."

"There are times when the taking of a life is unavoidable, this was one such time. They attacked you; you did not attack them, they were ready to risk their lives. You did well and I am happy you return to us."

"Your mother is right; any who attack must be prepared to pay the price."

"It was not a nice experience, father."

Taking the wine offered she looked at her inquisitively.

"You like the wine do you not?"

"I love Minlets white wine, yet I have tasted others."

"Xandorian always did spoil you."

"Mother?"

"You stayed with Xandorian for a few days while your father and I had matters needing attention. You were young, still not a year in age, and talked him into tasting his wine, yet he let you drink too much. Through the linking I could feel the wine in your head."

"I remember my head the next day. I did not know you knew of it."

"The link was strong even then."

"If Xandorian had a fault it was his generosity. I miss him, mother."

"We all do."

"Now, what did you do while I was away?"

"We spoke with two more from the list."

"Without me?"

"You believe we should wait for your return?"

"I had hoped I would be here when next you looked for my attacker."

"Only a few remain, as the list shortens your mother's anger grows beyond bounds."

"Anger clouds the mind and Caspo Kwil warns of anger when he sees it."

"An anger I feel she needs."

"Yet still an anger."

"Anger I have in me and it will remain until the one who would harm you is in my power."

"It may cloud your thoughts, mother."

"The anger guides my movements, my thoughts."

"You offer meat?"

"Arkie was most adamant as to your tastes in meat. He came to see us yesterday to thank you for your words. It would seem he has heeded them and Hertish Munsil has offered to him a new position within the class."

"Which position has he obtained?"

"He would speak not of it, asking I say to you he is no longer a tender to the waters of ice. I know not his meaning."

"Then Hertish Munsil is most pleased with him."

"In which way?"

"You must speak to Icee of the first spell she was instructed to cast by Hertish Munsil, and of the events afterwards."

"I believe his visit was to bring the meats as a thank you."

"It is their way of saying much without the need for words. The gnomes have a way with their cooking of the meats to make them special. With fish they season them the moment they are caught. May I offer a suggestion?"

"Of course."

"Most meats are the better served warm, this is one such meat."

"It seems I have much to learn. I will warm it for you."

"It is fine as it is thank you."

Taking a bite her eyes closed as she savoured it, before turning to her father, "It takes so long to track them; ten days to find two?"

"They travel far and wide leaving one place with no word of where they go next. Yet there are places they like to visit and return often to them."

"It is how you traced them, father?"

"Once a pattern becomes obvious it is easy to see where to wait for them."

"Where do we look next, and for whom?"

"It seems Veldeth oft visits the city of the cat people, Melthest. He should return within two days if friends may be believed."

"Never have I seen the cat people. I hunger not, may we go now?"

"You eat, Nortee. Tomorrow we go."

"Father...."

The city was nothing as she had imagined, the buildings spaced apart yet often three stories high. The inhabitants as tall as her and walking on two legs yet took little notice of them as they journeyed through the city. She compared their movements with those of the elves; they were more graceful and far superior in their ability to jump; watching one leap ten feet to a balcony before climbing, there were no apparent footholds.

"They are born warriors, Nortee, natural agility make then so. Should they choose to attack any would have a fight on their hands."

"As it would seem, father, I would like not to fight one."

Opening the door to an inn he motioned them forward, "We need a room for the night, and their beds may surprise you."

"In what way, father?"

Placing an elfin gem on the counter he took the wooden peg offered, "How may there be a surprise if I tell you? Their ways differ much to others, even to the locking of a door."

"Still I find it strange others have need to lock a door."

Closing the door he swung the large latch round and over, to let it drop in the metal cup fastened to the frame, before pushing it forwards into the wall itself. Finally he dropped the peg in to the metal cup where the latch rested, "A lock almost impossible to pick. The latch may not be moved with the peg in place, and the peg may not be moved from the outside. Simple and almost perfect."

"It would seem you know well their ways, husband."

"I like this city and have been here often."

"I feel there is more to your love for this city."

He sighed, his wife thought she knew him only too well; "I admit their drinks are pleasing to the palette."

"I know you have a fondness for milk, father."

"It is not for milk he comes, daughter, but for drinks made with alcohol."

"I have oft brought Icee here, she loves the drinks also."

"Icee drinks here? I find this hard to believe."

"How is it you manage to speak with them, father? I find their language hard to understand."

"The language is not so hard once you realise how simple it is, it is their gestures which are complex."

"It would seem you might have to take the role of tutor for this language."

"Not so much a spoken language as one of gestures."

"I have seen their minds as we moved in the city, mother, they are strange. So unlike any I have seen before."

"They love to tease their victims, toying with them beyond belief before killing them. Yet their minds are easy to control."

"You have done so?"

"Once one was injured and sought help in wood elf city. I was called to control him while he was treated, infected wounds send them wild."

A soft scraping at the door ceased the conversation, "Ah, the drinks I ordered. You have never tasted the like before."

Returning with a tray he offered them the drinks, "Your mother knows I like a drink or two yet I come here with Icee for these, they contain no alcohol."

He watched as they exchanged looks, their eyes wide open after tasting the drinks. He knew he would surprise them, as he was when Keitun first introduced him to them. He had been persuaded to come here after Keitun had spent many hours talking to him about the drinks served. His first tastes were a disappointment; the range of alcohol was poor. 'The cats hate it' he remembered Keitun saying, 'but they love milk. Try one of these.'

He loved them from the first sip; made from milk and a brown bean he had seen growing nowhere else except just outside the city. No matter how hard he tried he could never understand what it was called, or how they used it to produce the drink.

"They also make it in a brown bar for eating when they travel, yet I have not tasted it in such a form. I see the drink is to your liking."

"It is wonderful, father. I would like to return and try more."

"There is little need. I ordered a few bottles for the morrow."

"Where do we sleep?"

He pointed to a small building, "The house we asked for is to the right. Be prepared and let us be about our business."

The door opening puzzled him; the cats of the city knocked. Only an elf would enter unannounced yet there had been no visitors since he decided to settle here. Turning round he let surprise show on his face.

"It would seem you remember me."

"I know not how you escaped the locking of your mind, and to be honest I care not."

"I suggest you make it your duty to care."

"Payment was accepted to kill you and I was left to my own ends as to the way to do so. I will correct my mistake."

As his arms moved a spell from the still open door knocked him backwards into the room. His eyes flicked to the caster he realised her mother and father were standing close by. Unsure of whether to be angry and kill them instantly or to let them think themselves safe before he killed them it took a few extra moments before he realised why they might have come for him.

"So, they send you to return me to the city?"

Quivering with pleasure at the thought of what she would like to do to him a sneer entered her voice, "We come not to take you back yet you may wish it preferable we do."

"I broke no law for which you are capable of extracting revenge."

"You broke the law of parentage! Now the price you pay."

"You are but wood elf, powerless against me."

"I am capable, as you will discover."

Too long the patient father he decided it would be his turn, "Who hired you to attack her?"

"I do not say, *druid*."

Pushing him forcibly into a chair he was happy to be hurting him, if only a little, he knew his wife would ensure he hurt a lot more, "Speak!"

"I choose not to speak."

Leaning close to him her voice became little more than a whisper, "Not to say is a choice you have not, *swik*."

His face reddened in anger as she used their word for the lowest of all enchanters, a word for a traitor to the guild; used for any who would turn on their own kind, "I will deal with the child and the druid. Then take great pleasure in showing you the true ways of the enchanter; the ways all will be taught when I lead the guild. All should tremble in fear when they face us!"

"The wrong path you would show us. Few friends will we find if all fear us. None will come to our aid in times of need!"

"Words of the weak! You are unworthy of our profession."

His mind leapt to Nortee, to charm her into attacking her mother whilst he dealt with the father; he knew exactly how to play this fight. He had fought and won where there were more than three to contend with, usually by devious means. But this fight was to be different, never had he had a child attack her mother and the thought brought forth a feeling of pleasure. Later, after he had dealt with these, he would look for others, mother and daughter or father and son, and have them fight the other. Then he would kill the victor, or lock their minds from the world by letting them see their own deeds.

Suddenly a high elf guard was attacking from behind and for a moment lost concentration. Then the attacker was gone and he realised the truth, she had placed the thought in his mind to place him off guard.

'Once before you have attacked my daughter. Never again!'

As their minds clashed he felt his being forced back, she was gaining ground as their wills fought for supremacy. He had believed his mind to be like a fortress, impregnable. Now his defences were crumbling under her assault. His mind struggled for words, it was going to be a hard fight, 'Your mind is strong for a wood elf, yet mine is better. Desist now and I will kill you all painlessly.'

'I came not to die but to show you how a mind could be ripped apart, how a single thought may be taken, plucked at will. I would know who hired you and then I leave you as you left my daughter.'

'Brave words, yet all three cannot beat me. I am, and will always be, superior to any wood elf!'

'This fight is for me alone, and long have I looked forward to it."

From the first moment their minds met she knew she could beat him, his mind was strong but hers was the stronger, and deep down she knew the love for her daughter gave her the power needed, but let him push her mind back just a little. In doing so she would give him a feeling of hope, a feeling she would take and crush, and the pleasures she would feel would be all the greater. His mind was strong, there was no doubt, but she had trained with Caspo Kwil, and his mind was easily the strongest of all the enchanters she had met, even this one.

Desperation took hold, he did not want to die but it seemed as if he had misjudged her prowess. When he was hired to kill a wood elf he had thought it not to be a problem. When he had heard of her wishes to be an enchantresses he became angry and had taken only half the money offered. He wanted to show this upstart the profession belonged to the high elves.

Then he found her mother in his mind and he could do nothing to stop her as she searched his thoughts. He had not known a mind as powerful as it ripped thoughts from him, discarding his memories like unwanted articles. Her mind was full of desire to find its needs and he began to wonder how it was possible to see individual thoughts, how anyone could examine them and throw away those not needed. Regret for not returning to his dark elf friend for so long entered him, it seemed new methods had been found and this female had been trained in them. Advances such as these could help him in his battles; make them worth the fight once more. He had not enjoyed a fight for so long, most of his opponents were of a far less professional level than he, it was hard to find any good enough these days to even warrant the effort.

Finally the thought she searched for surfaced and she grabbed it, examined it, and her voice echoed around in his head, 'I have what I need, Veldeth, and you will see the way a mind should be locked from the world. Your attack on my daughter has earned you my wrath. Many have suffered under you; no more shall you attack another. This is my one, my only, promise to you.'

His mind saw his victims, all those he had fought and killed in the past, or whose minds he had trapped within their bodies. They came for him, each taking a piece of his mind before reaching for more. He could feel himself losing it to them, and began to scream, to call to them for his mind to be returned. Yet the more he pleaded the more they took, his greatest fear was being realised; he was slowly losing his mind. He had to run from them, but there was nowhere to go, only his mind's darkness all around, and so many people grabbing at him. His arms covered his head in protection but still they took his mind. His scream turned to sobbing.

Leaving his mind she looked down at him, "No more will he be feared. Never again will he attack another."

Nortee glanced at the crumpled figure on the floor, arms covering his head as he sobbed uncontrollably, "I watched as you did this to him, mother, I have been there and feel sorry for him."

"A natural feeling. Did you count the minds he locked from the world?"

"I saw many images of people."

"Four hundred and six minds he locked away, and then those he has killed for pleasure. He makes me ashamed of our profession."

Wanting to leave she turned to her husband, "Beloved, what is it?"

Quickly she moved to him, "His mind may have caught our fight, Nortee."

"Enter it, mother, show him the way back to us."

Quickly she entered his mind and it enfolded her, caressed her, filled her with love, "Rogue, you scared me!"

"It is not just an enchantress who may fool others. You know who paid him to attack Nortee?"

"I know she paid for his services in elfin jewels as I know my mother was mentioned with hatred. Now we find her, and she will lead us to the one responsible."

"Druids spend so long away from the guild. Adventure is deep in their soul; it may be months before she returns."

"She will never return. She has forsaken the guild for a pursuit of revenge against me. Attacking Nortee is her way."

"If a druid attacks then the fight is mine."

"To trap her," Began Nortee, "you must first know where to look."

Hunted

Glancing at the trees around her Nortee knew she was at least three days from home, even with the speed of the amulet to help her, and her pursuers were near. Yet she had a friend, and with his help she may evade them. Raising her arm the hawk flew to her instantly to settle there, screeching frantically as she stroked his chest with her forefinger.

"I know, little friend. They come for me and I see no way to evade them. Mother spoke such a day may happen and to plan what I was to do, yet she did not say in what way I should be prepared. It is unlike her not to say what to do, she is always there and her advice is sound."

Once more his screech seemed as if he were begging her.

"Shush, little friend, you will alert them as to where we are. A distraction is needed if I am to escape. Are you willing?"

In answer he flew above the trees to circle slowly.

"Let them see you, they know of you and will follow where you lead. Do not get too far ahead of them or they may give up and return. Thank you, little friend."

High above them he knew he had been seen and he turned towards the sun, now half way down to the horizon, the opposite direction she had taken. He knew they must soon catch her and it would be over. He wanted to give her the time she needed and flew ahead of them; always letting them keep him in sight, never getting too far ahead, every moment he could give to her would mean a better chance of escape.

They followed him for an hour before turning and heading back, taking no notice as he dived close in his efforts to have them follow him once more, he had fooled them once and would listen to him no more. Kneeling to examine her tracks where they had first seen the hawk they had to admit she had covered them well, but a few broken strands of grass was all they needed. They were on her again and this time she would not get away, they had a score to settle with her, she had evaded them for too long.

She was cunning; her tracks disappeared on more than one occasion, once it had taken almost three minutes of searching before they saw the slight mark on the branch of a tree she had climbed, before swinging to several more and dropping to the ground again. They wanted her and they would catch her, it was just a matter of time.

Moving carefully backwards for two minutes she decided she had set enough of a false trail. They would pick up her tracks and follow them in the wrong direction; she would leave none in the next part of her plan.

Moving quickly to the rocks on her right she set of running along them, even without using the speed the amulet gave her she was atop the rocky cliff within minutes and looking down the ravine at the water far below.

The rocks along the top edge seemed barely able to cling on the sides of the ravine, as if they were about to fall into the river below as it quickly flowed on its everlasting journey. Her options were few; she could run the gauntlet and hope they would not see her, but she dismissed the thought almost as quickly as it entered her head. They would see her; there was no doubt, even wearing her druid trousers and top, which would allow her to hide more easily. For once she smiled at the thought of how her hair would stand out so well from the trees if she tried such a trick.

The thought of her clothes made her admit how comfortable they were, although not like the comfort her robe afforded, but she was happy to be wearing them; they hid her well and were much better for running in the forest than her robe. If she could find a way to join the robes of an enchantress to the trousers and tunic of a druid she knew she would have the best of both her professions. Although she had not had the mana in her for long she could feel it slowly seeping in to her trousers and tunic, they were becoming part of her, and the same was happening to her robe.

With a quick shake of the head she turned her attention back to the task in hand; escape. She could try and backtrack down the rocks but would almost certainly run into them. She dismissed the thought. The second choice was the only real option, the river far below, and the thought of what she had to do made her swallow.

'Eighty feet; mayhap eighty-five, never have I managed such distance, yet there is a first time to try.'

Her eyes closed for a moment of prayer before she slipped off the edge, twisting on the way down to catch the roots of a tree to halt her fall. As she caught them a sharp pain in her right side caused her to grunt, her ribs had struck the rocks buried under the thin layer of soil, bruising and knocking the breath out of her. For a few moments she screwed up her face until the sharpness of the pain subsided, 'and now a broken rib, you must be more careful, Nortee. There is time so do not hurry.'

With her breathing easing she checked the drop below her, 'Seventy feet, still too far for safe fall. You must go lower, Nortee.'

Kicking her legs forwards and back she began to swing in mid air, building up the rhythm until she judged she had enough momentum and let go of the roots, to once more begin her decent to the trees below.

Snatching at a branch she winced once more, her shoulder had been dislocated and her hand had caught a sharp knot, gouging a line in her palm, 'You must train more, father would not be pleased the way you miss such an easy drop, thirty feet and you injure yourself, ack.'

Steadying herself she checked the drop below, dismayed there was still too far for safe fall, 'Still forty five feet, too much for one drop yet I run out of options, and branches.'

Her head lifted to the heavens to utter a small prayer before letting go of the branch to fall to the ground below, rolling over twice she entered the river without a break in movement. There was no splash or noise, but with her left arm hanging almost useless at her side she dived deep to let the river refresh her as it gently took her to the surface. Gulping a lung full of air she let the water close above her head once more as she began to swim to the waterfall she had seen from the top of the trees some while ago. Swimming was not as easy for her now with her arm hanging in the cooling waters, and her ribs had taken more injury with the drop, but she pushed herself all the harder. She must reach safety, and the waterfall was her best, her only, hope of evading capture.

Kneeling beside the tracks they found at the foot of the rocks they saw the false trail, she had made a big mistake. Walking backwards was one of the oldest and easiest tricks to spot. She had taken to the rocks, an obvious move, and it was going to be hard to follow her over them, but she would leave telltale marks no matter how careful she was.

They always left a clue of their passing; she would be no exception. Five minutes later they saw the pebble she had disturbed, the sun had not shone on this side of it for a long time. They were on her scent once more and grinned at each other, she was not far now, and soon they would have her.

Reaching the peak they looked down at the water below, shaking their heads; surely she would not try to evade them by such a dangerous route. There must be another way and they began the search once more, before finding the fresh soil moved from around the roots just below the peak, displaced as they moved in the earth, and a rock open to the sun, its surface still damp from recent exposure. She had gone down to the river below and they agreed her courage was high, if misplaced. But they also knew the chase was almost at its end, she was theirs now. The direction she had taken was now obvious, and they saw the next clue after as short search, blood on the branch of the tree below, as they looked to the river for a spot she might hide and saw the waterfall, now they had her.

As they reached the top of the ravine she saw them and instinctively pushed herself closer to the rocks behind the waterfall. With luck they would leave and she could hide there for another few hours before slipping away. The call of the hawk caught her attention and she smiled through the pain of her shoulder and ribs, he had led them away from her and given her the time she needed.

Finglas thanked Malinna as her spell eased the pain in his daughter's ribs, "I am thankful you are here, Malinna."

"Verin and Rinini bound her ribs well yet there is work to be done with the healing and the cut to her hand. Then I feel you and my sister have many questions to ask."

As her spell finished Nortee felt the pain in her ribs cease, another spell and the deep cut all but vanished leaving the outline of a scar in the palm of her hand.

"Thank you, Malinna, the ribs and shoulder were a great pain, the cut was nothing but uncomfortable. I have thanked them for their binding yet at the cost of a forfeit."

"Of what do you speak, and why have they claimed such?"

"It was given to Verin in confidence, I may speak no more."

"I cannot heal the wound completely. I should be able, I am at a loss."

"Worry not, sister, thank you for all you have done."

"I worry, it is but a cut and I know I can heal it. I will speak with Grud Hearthstone on this matter. I will ask Flight to take us on the morrow if such is your wish."

Now, as they sat around the table once more she knew the questions would start, but this time she had thought long and hard about what had happened and was ready for anything they might ask. Her father's first words caught her by surprise.

"Never have I been more proud of you. You learn well the druid ways."

"I had thought I was poor in hiding my tracks, father, they found me."

"They are druids and rangers, trained to track .You were told before the test they are the best in the guilds, the elite amongst all the trackers. With them was a new one to the trackers, Rinini, there to learn the art to its full."

"It took all you have shown and the help of the hawk to avoid them, yes they are good."

"So you know why it is I am proud. You used your training and your wits to avoid them. I have questions."

"Ask."

He smiled; she sounded so like her mother when she used the word, "Why did you not use the amulet? Its speed would have made it easier for you to outrun them."

"Speed was not the test today, they were to track me and I was to use my training to avoid capture. It was a test of my skills, a test I failed."

"You did not fail, daughter."

"Yet found me, father. I have failed."

"Do you know how long it takes them to track another to earth, whether they be druid or ranger?"

"None would speak to me of this and I asked so many. I was to evade them for as long as possible is all any would say to me."

"In these tests they give their quarry two hours start; normally they catch them within four hours. How long was it before they found you?"

"A little over six hours, father."

"Longer than is normal."

"You have taken the test?"

"All take the test; they found me after six hours also. This is but the first of the tests all must face, four others await you as your skills grow."

"During our return I spoke with Rinini, it was her first hunt, elected by the members it seems."

"The members of each party decide whom they would have with them. To be on the hunts is the greatest of all honours."

For an hour she remained quiet as he questioned their daughter, the ways of druids strange to her, but knew they would find her moments after they had found her tracks, she could do nothing to prevent it. True she was an elf and could easily evade most creatures, given a forest in which to use her elfin ways. She was no druid yet he had explained so many of their ways. Now warm feelings in her heart grew for them both, pride foremost in those feeling. She listened with interest as they discussed the ways in which her daughter had avoided them, the tricks her husband had taught her, many of them he had learned on his own expeditions. Her thoughts turned once more to why he was so much better than any druid of his training.

He had been born fifteen years before her and the Gods had prepared him even then for the quest, and for her. They had given him abilities no druid had before him, but as with all gifts from the Gods, it had come at a price.

To him it had been a terrible price; they had ensured his parents were killed by giants on a quest to find him the amulet he wore around his neck. It had pushed him away from his guild, and away from her in the beginning, in his relentless search for it. This was part of the ways the Gods had prepared him; no other had left the guild so early in life and survived. To her it was all so plain; he had been prepared before she was born for the quest, before she was thought of by her parents, then so newly in wedlock. In her mind she gave thanks to the Gods; thanks he had been gifted and she was his wife, thanks their daughter was here to be taught.

Taking a glass of wine from the table her fingers gave a light squeeze to the stem, it was time to enter the conversation; "I have a question."

"Ask."

"When you injured your ribs and shoulder what were your thoughts?"

"Mother?"

"I am no druid yet it seems to me the drop to the ground from the rocks was dangerous, even for one trained how to fall."

"It was, mother."

"I am pleased you understand. Why did you risk yourself in such a way?"

"It was the only way open to me, a ranger cannot track a quarry in the water, and I was asked to make their tracking of me difficult. I have a question for you. In my short life you have guided me, trained me to think, to be who I am."

"Ask your question."

"You spoke to me the day after I entered the druid guild, one day I may find myself out alone somewhere and being pursued, yet offered no advice and it is so unlike you."

"What advice do you believe I should have offered?"

"I know not, it is why I ask."

Offering her husband a glass of wine he smiled, it seemed he knew of her plan.

"None for me, mother?"

"Minlets white wine, your favourite."

As she took the glass the stem fell to the floor and shattered, "I am sorry, mother, I have broken it."

"You did not. I snapped the stem whilst your attention was with your father and his questions. I keep the stem in my hand to make it seem as if it were whole."

She looked at her mother, puzzled.

"Stand the glass up please."

Sinking back into his chair Finglas smiled. He had heard the stem snap and knew his daughter had not. She would show Nortee the way but knew she would not be direct in her answer.

"I cannot, there is no way it may stand."

"So it will fall, as would you if you were you the glass?"

"Yes."

"Yet here you are to tell of your adventure. So, if the glass were you would it not stand now?"

"No, mother, there is no way the glass would stand."

"It will stand, Nortee."

Taking the glass from her daughter she raised it to her lips, slowly draining the contents, "Now will it stand?"

"Father has spoken often of your riddles. No, still it will not stand."

With the glass lightly in her hand she held it above the table for long seconds, but did not move.

"I wait, mother."

"Then wait no longer."

Turning the glass over she placed it by its rim on the table, "Now it stands."

"I think I see. If there seems no way out of a situation you must look at the problem from another angle."

"I cannot be with you every step in this life, it is yours and you must guide yourself. No advice is as good as teaching someone to think."

"Grud Hearthstone, you remember my niece Nortee."

"Yes, yes, so many times you call yet never do we have the time to speak. I have been anxious for this day to arrive."

Placing the quill back in the receptacle he turned round in the chair and looked up as she stood in front of him, "You are dressed as a druid yet you are firstly an enchantress, how so? Oh, welcome to my study."

"Sir, thank you for the warm welcome. Yet why would you wish to speak to me, and on what subject?"

"Your hybrid ways intrigue me, I would talk of them."

"It would be a pleasure, sir."

"Is now good for you?"

"It is, sir."

"My name is Grud Hearthstone, not sir."

"As is your wish."

"You have...."

Malinna coughed, "We come with reason, mayhap the discussions may continue at a later time?"

"Yes, yes, of course, I forget myself. Show me the hand, child."

Offering her hand she watched as he examined the scar, turning her hand over, feeling every part of it.

"There is nothing unusual here. Malinna, feel the scar, you feel the pain?"

"I do not, and have tried thrice."

"Then let there be a fourth time never give up after only three attempts."

As she examined the scar once more a young dwarf rushed into the room.

"Grud Hearthstone, Volk Stonebroom is in the halls demanding you see him this instant."

"I have wanted to see the idiot for years. I'll be back, Malinna."

"Do not look so concerned, Nortee, they are friends yet call the other names. The story goes back to their childhood and is very funny."

"You feel no pain in the scar, Malinna?"

"None, yet when I feel the pain I may heal."

"Thrice you have examined it and still he asks you to look at it yet again."

"Had I examined it a hundred times he would ask I make the examination for the hundred and first time. He ensures I miss nothing."

"He is so like mother, she would have me try several times to ensure I know them well."

Lost in thought she hardly heard her niece as she once more turned her hand over, her voice soft and low, "So if there is no pain I cannot heal, and if there is nothing to heal I may not remove the scar. Yet why a scar when none should be there. Why do I feel no pain, why?"

Her eyes closed in concentration, opening them as a gleam started to show in her face, "Oh Malinna you are foolish in the extreme. You see not what the Gods place so obviously before you."

"Malinna?"

"The feathers! It is as the feathers."

She let her lack of understanding show.

"It is so plain. There is no pain and therefore I cannot take the scar away."

"I fail to see where you lead me, Malinna."

"Our feathers may not be touched."

"This I know."

"It is our symbol."

"Also known by many now."

"Think, Nortee, when you dropped to the trees could you hold on with but one hand?"

"I had a task to accomplish."

"Think of what happened."

"I was injured through my own folly; I looked not where I was to grip as I dropped, nothing more."

"No, Nortee. Were you just injured I would be able to help and to heal the wound. It is a symbol for you, as are the feathers for the Chosen Ones. Your symbol also cannot be taken away; it is yours alone. See the scar and its pattern; is it not like a feather? Your mother will be well pleased."

"May I ask something of you, and please speak not of it to mother?"

"Ask and I will see."

"Mother knows an enchantress must be beautiful, if you tell her the scar is to remain she will be upset. Please, remind her not of this."

Throwing her arms around her she hugged her tightly, "She will care not of the scar, you are her daughter and to her you will always be beautiful. Worry not over it, beauty is which the eyes behold."

The door being thrown almost off its hinges made them look round. An old dwarf with a beard showing white with age seemed to be totally ignorant they were in the room.

"Malinna, you remember Volk Stonebroom?"

"Indeed, greetings to you."

"And this is her niece, Volk Stonebroom, her name is Nortee."

Looking her over he shook his head, "You ask I believe such rumours?"

His voice was high pitched in excitement, "Neither would you believe in the Chosen Ones."

"Different, different as well you know. Their powers are still singular."

"Yet each became something not of their birth. Born to change their profession and each is the best."

"Never has any been born with the magic of two guilds. The Gods decree what is to be and never have they gifted any with the powers of more than one profession. I have seen the wedlock of cleric to hunter and never has the offspring been give the powers of both guilds. I believe you not!"

"You will owe me yet another apology, Stonebroom, and yet another cask of your special ale."

"It is six to five and I will prove you wrong again. Sit, elf. We have much to discuss."

Almost in a daze with his rough ways and speech she sat and glanced to Malinna, smiling as she saw her mouthing, "Time to even the score."

To Kill A Friend

The journey to dark elf city had been without incident. Camped for the day in an outcrop of rock within sight of the city they had discussed their plans. Yet Icee was impatient; she needed to see the leader of the wizard guild; the only one who could grant her wish.

"I had thought younger sister to have more patience."

Turning she cast a glance to Norty, "I ache inside. I must see him and he is so close."

Kare pulled her back behind the rock, "Should we move before nightfall my people would be the last you see. Our eyes are poor with the setting of the sun, it is then we move."

"If he grants not my wish...."

Once more he pulled her back down, "It is his decision, and his alone."

"Over one hundred guards I count, how may we pass them?"

Pose held her down as she moved to look over the rocks once again, "Come the night many will leave; the gates are not the only way into the city. Trust to Kare and I, soon you will see the one you must speak with."

Reluctantly she lay back against the rock, "Many times have I waited in my life. I have waited for Finglas to show his love for sister; waited whilst enemies have passed me by in their search for me; waited for my love to come to me. Now I must wait for the one I must speak to. So often are things beyond my control yet it seems it will forever be my fate."

Norty nodded, "First you see the one you need; then we see Mel D'elith."

Slipping to the walls of the city had been easy; the guards so few in number. Now, as Pose moved the stone to open a secret passage into the town Icee realised her sister's tale of the city, it was full of such hidden passages, "If an enemy were to know of these, Pose."

"Should invaders be seen then every guild will send forth their best to the passageways to guard them. Come; with those I know and those known to Kare our task will be all the easier."

Befla J'Orrow sat and listened as Icee explained why the wedlock should be in dark elf city. As she finished he unfolded his arms to spread them across the marble table, "I sympathise with your feeling but it is impossible, your wedlock cannot take place here. I am sorry."

"You know why I feel as I do, the wedlock must be here."

"I will not risk open war and this is what your wedlock will bring! There would be bloodshed on the streets, and would not stop until many of my people are dead."

"Yet if no war were to come what would be your answer?"

"Even the Chosen Ones cannot give such a guarantee."

"If I give those guarantees?"

"It is not possible; prove your words and I will preside at the wedlock myself."

Excitement grew within her, "Then you are for the re-union?"

"I am not. Your wedlock I object to in principle, yet I also know love."

She looked inquisitively at him.

"You think it is because I am against the re-union I refuse your wedlock? No, you are wrong. I know love and all should know of it. I refuse the wedlock for fear you or he may be harmed. I wish not for your wedlock to start with the death of one of you."

"We will be safe."

He turned to Kare, "Your parents approve of the wedlock?"

"They do not. Mother refuses to attend or even to mention her name."

"There are those who could hold back the war, guarantee it would not start on the day of their joining."

Glancing up at the others standing behind her, all white elves except for Pose, he shook his head, "The Chosen Ones hold no such a power!"

"I speak of those who hold power far greater than ours. If their guarantee meets with your approval may we be joined?"

"Who is it who could give such a guarantee?"

"Pose, we must keep to the shadows, any knowing we are here would send our quarry scuttling and we would lose them."

"This I know, Finglas, trust to me. Follow and all will be well."

Leading him along narrow dark passages to a small building she opened the door without hesitation, embracing the figure standing alone in the dark.

As they stepped forward he nodded, "We meet once more."

"Come; I know where the one you seek is staying. He does little to cover his tracks."

Quickly she pulled a cover from the old wooden floor and opened a trapdoor, "In here, it leads close to the river and his home."

"Long have I waited for this day to arrive."

"As have I, there are old scores to settle and this night they begin."

As Finglas descended the steps he felt a mind enter his with force, sending him tumbling into the darkness and, as his head struck the floor, vaguely felt someone fall on top of him.

Her eyes widened in disbelief, "Father is unconscious."

"We were prepared; still it troubles me."

"You knew this would happen yet still they go ahead of us?"

"Think on what has happened."

"I know not where to start."

Icee prompted her, "When it was known the wife of the elder we killed had thought herself disgraced where would she go?"

"To where none would search it would seem, dark elf city. Yet how could she gain entry and not be killed once seen?"

"Through lies and deceptions. Giving promises of how to defeat other elfin races would ensure her safety."

"It would take many a year."

"She has time, Nortee. Our suspicions are all but confirmed. Two enemies we seek this day."

"So you wake at last, Finglas."

"I have an ache in my head as when I first tasted ale."

Feeling around in the darkness her hands found him and she let her fingers run through his hair, "A lump on your head yet the pain will go."

"I will be well when we find the one we seek."

Her voice became silky, "So, what to do 'til help arrives?"

"The answer is obvious; to find a way out of the trap set for us."

'Alone for once and he wishes to escape, damn him.'

"Sister, the darkest part of the night arrives."

All their plans had been thought through. With Icee watching the battle's flow and Malinna to guide them through the fight she knew they would win. They had not sat in thought and planned since the quest ended and it gave her a feeling of satisfaction once more. She had been born to plan, to think each part of every action through to its inevitable outcome, and once more she was planning, "Thank you, Malinna; time to find my Finglas and our quarry."

"He is well?"

"A headache; he will live another day."

"You feel him so well?"

"I believe it to get the better the more our minds join."

Icee was up and impatient, "Come, I hunger for a fight. They would wage war and stop my wedlock to the one I would have as mine."

Kare took her hand, "Not so long ago this day seemed so far away."

"The day is still far away, should things not happen as planned."

"They will go as planned, sister."

"Icee, in the dark we are almost blind, lead where I instructed."

Giggling Icee cast her spell, "A simple lock, hardly worthy of being called such.

They emerged, Malinna running her fingers to find the lump, I will remove the headache."

"If you would, it dulls the thoughts."

Icee turned to Pose, "You are well?"

"I have no lump yet my pride hurts, I am shamed for my guild."
"Then this day we will banish the shame."

Reaching the anteroom to the great hall Norty motioned them to stop, "Kare only for now. Others must believe Pose and Finglas dealt with. Remain here until I call."
The door was locked and at her urgent knocking was slowly opened, "Norty, what is you which brings you here?"
"I would speak with you Mel D'elith."
"The time is inconvenient. Visitors I wait for."
"Yet you ensure the door is locked? I must enter and speak with you and your visitors."
"No! You must leave before they arrive, speak with me on the morrow."
Kare pushed the door open. "Norty wishes entry, and this shall she have."
Back-stepping through the door she tried to close it as he pushed his way past her into the shadows of the great hall.
Lit by several torches casting shadows along the length of the hall the alcoves were darker patches in the gloom. It had been used for all the important ceremonies in the lives of the dark elves, throughout its long history it had been the place where discussions were held, plans were laid and fights were settled. Now it was just a part of ancient history, almost forgotten, disused by most, yet it suited the purpose of some of them.

Her mind reached out to him to push him back, "Bah, a wizard believes he may best me, mentor to all enchanters?"
Then her mind was blocked from entering his as if some, almost, unseen force barred its way. It began to force her mind back, and with it her body.
In her life she had never felt such power, never believed she could be toyed with as she could a student of the first classes. A voice entered her mind to call to her loud and clear; unmistakably the voice belonged to Norty, 'Think not to attack one who wishes only the truth. I had thought you a friend yet you show your true self, a betrayer of your friends, a *swik*.'
'The Gods betray us when they gave to the elves the quest; to us it should have gone. You are elf yet not dark; I correct the mistake the Gods make.'
With all her might her mind fought back but she was powerless against the attack. In their training together she had not realised the might her student possessed, now it was shown to her and worry began to find its way into her thoughts.
'I have suspected you may harbour ill thoughts towards me, Mel D'elith, yet I believed you incapable of such deeds as to attack a child! What may cause this, what has twisted such a fine mind?'
Then she was in her mind, but it was not the mind she has seen so often in training. It was no longer the Mel D'elith she had known, it had been corrupted. Desperately she searched for its source, and found it; a death had turned her this way; hatred only a lost love may bring.

A pang of sorrow momentarily swept over her but she dismissed it; it was beyond her power to correct what had happened, even if she had been willing. She would end the threats to kill her daughter, once and forever. She needed the weakness found in her instructors mind, and, ignoring all the attempts to thwart her moved towards the thought she knew would defeat her one time friend.

Desperately she tried to stop her reaching the thoughts she had suppressed for so long, the thought she knew would be used against her, 'You left and my Lyris was killed the next day, you had a hand in this, I know it.'
'The quest was upon us, I had to go; this I explained to you. I had nothing to do with his death. I grieved for you as well you know.'
'Lies all lies! I swore an oath I would have my revenge; I waited until the time was right. When you bore a child I saw my revenge would be sweet, willingly I joined the ones who hate you.'
A slight feeling of pity found its way to her heart but she could not be weak in front of the one who would harm Nortee. She would remind her of the elf she loved; he would be the one to tell her.

In her mind Lyris returned to her, standing proud before her, yet a bitter look on his face.
'You betrayed me! Long did I fight for reunion with you at my side.'
'They killed you. She and the re-unionists; I hate them for what they did to you, for what they did to me. They took you away, never to be mine, never to be in wedlock, to remain alone and childless.'
'The anti-unionists killed me and now you fight for the ones who caused my death. How can we be in wedlock when you succor to the ones who killed me?'
'They did not kill you; she and the re-unionists killed you!'
'I did for the cause what was in my heart, the cause you now abandon, the cause we swore to uphold.'
'How was I to uphold a cause which took you from me?'
'It was your duty to my memory, as well you know. All of our teachings demand it of you, our Lore and our times together demand it.'
Tears rolled down her face to reflect the ones in her mind, 'I could not; I missed you so.'
'You are elfin kind! Where is your pride, your heritage? You choose not an easy way for peace of mind. Were we wed I would have it undone!'
'No, you could not do such.'
'The choice I would make with pride!'
Her head shook in desperation, 'No wedlock has ever been put aside, ever.'
'Then ours would be the first. I wish not to be with one who would betray me so easily.
'It would bring shame to me, shame my family, shame to our guild.'
'I bring none. You bring this on yourself!'

Falling to her knees her forehead touched the ground in elfin shame, 'Forgive me, I had no desire to act against your will.'

'Forgiveness you will not receive, your shame should know no bounds.'

'Forgive me, I beseech you; for our love.'

'I cannot forgive your deeds.'

Drawing her stiletto from its sheath her head did not leave the floor, 'There is nothing left for me. I ask you see the love I bear for you, a love so strong it will not let me bring more shame to you.'

Placing the stiletto under her body she sank down on it, making no sound as it pierced her heart.

Shaking her head she looked away from the body, "All may join me."

With his wife in obvious distress he held her.

"A friend I had thought her."

"You saw not the betrayal in her body?"

"When Jol E'ath was killed she cried my arms. I felt the sadness of her loss yet no compassion was in her."

"You knew all then?"

"When we went to see her I spoke I came 'to find the one who hired a wood elf druid to harm my little one.' She asked if I knew *his* name. I said naught about the one I sought being male. Jol E'ath hired the druid yet he was her instrument. When we came she knew I would discover the truth and she would be shown to be the one who arranged the meeting. To remain hidden she must kill him; it was the only way. There was only sadness in her heart for what she had done, no remorse. This I felt in her as I held her, the reason I held her."

"Enchanters come, mother, ten I count."

"Everyone to the shadows. Kare, greet them they must see one of their own here."

Entering at his bidding they saw Mel D'elith on the floor, blood showing as a dark stain on her robe. One of the enchanters bent to examine the body, "She is still warm. You killed her!"

"I did not. The one you seek is here."

"Show me!"

Stepping from the shadows she gave a sharp nod, "I was the cause of her death."

"A white elf, I should have known. None of ours would harm her. Die!"

"I wish no harm to any. She died through her betrayal not mine. Think! Why are you watched so closely?"

"Those for re-union seek a weakness in us to exploit."

"They worry for the cause and would have you join them."

"It is impossible to believe you. You have trained here, how may you betray us?"

"You are Byntha, student in the class I saw on my visit here. I remember the look on your face when you sat, too low to offer the challenge."

"No longer too low. I will kill you; a friend to us you are not."

"I am still your friend and I come now to help your guild. Why is it you believed Mel D'elith?"

"She was our leader in all."

"Yet it was she who killed Jol E'ath."

"Another lie! Why should we believe one with murder on her mind?"

At her beckoning Pose stepped forward, "Then believe one of your own."

The words she had once spoken to Pose had come to pass; she was revered as the first dark elf to be trained by high elves. A place in history was assured for her; other could only follow where Pose led. Pose would lead them away from the poisoning of their minds, and into a new time for all.

Pose gave a sharp nod in greeting, "Mel D'elith betrayed her guild for her own ends. We are the true friends to the guild."

Exchanging glanced they began to kneel in front of Pose, accepting her words and offering allegiance. They had accepted her as leader; to show them the way.

Feelings she had never known threatened to overwhelm her as she held her place steadfast at their head as the last one to kneel sank to the floor. She had to be strong; they needed leadership and had accepted her as the one chosen to do so.

Norty smiled as she thought how far Pose had come from the day she had first met her, first tempted her in to journeying to high elf city and to train. The leadership in her she had seen then, although Pose would never have admitted it. Her dream was to roam the world in search of adventure, or so she may have thought. The Gods had decreed a different path for Pose to tread on, and had gifted her also. New ideas of where the elves destiny may lay began to filter through her mind to merge with plans already laid. Her mind went back to their first meeting, when Pose had challenged her to a duel over Finglas. Even then she had seen her potential; the ease in which people would listen to her, do anything for her. She was an enchantress and most people could not help but listen, to do as she asked. Pose had an extra something which made all she spoke to believe in her, to want to be a part of whatever she was.

As Pose gestured they rose, unsure of the actions they should take, "It is not wise you leave at this time. Others will know things are amiss and return to their guilds. For now you will remain here with us. Nothing is to happen to you. Later we repair the damage to our guild and reputations. You will be held in esteem should we have our way this day; and have our way we will."

Showing the enchanters where to stand and the actions they must take Pose returned to Norty, "It is as if I watched another do and say all."

"It was you, Pose. They know your name and reputation. They are yours to command."

"I have no wish to command them; or to lead the guild."

"You think the Gods seek not to help your people? You were chosen by them to take your place at the head of the guild. Only you may bring the enchanters back from the brink of the abyss on which they stand."

"I will speak to them, nervousness is still deep within."

Watching Pose speaking with the enchanters her mind began to drift. It took several moments before she realised she was being spoke to.

"Come back to us, sister."

"I am sorry, Icee, I am full of pride for Pose. When first we met I knew she was special yet not why until now. The Gods bless her also."

"Sister, I yearn for wedlock. After the battle is won I would speak with you. I ask for something I have no right to ask, even as a sister. You may refuse if such is your wish for I ask you to face your greatest fear."

"Ask of me now."

"We concentrate on the battle to come first. Nortee must be safe in our world, it is the reason all are here."

"You intrigue me as to the question, ask it of ne now."

"First a battle we must win; then I will ask, I will beg if you ask of me and if such will bring me my desires."

"I must know now, ask of me."

Turning she walked quickly away to speak with Kare, leaving Norty shaking her head and her voice trailing behind her, "Icee...."

Battle plans had been discussed for ten minutes before Norty sensed them as they came along the corridor. All her will was used to prevent her from running and attacking them, to kill as many as she could before she fell in battle. When she had entered her daughters mind she had seen the thought kept hidden from her. With each stranger she saw one thought ran through her daughter's mind, 'is this the one who will take my life?'

Enemy Mine

Kare opened the door, counting forty as they filed passed, dark elves all. Mostly knights with a few wizards in attendance, he despised each and every wizard as they passed, knowing they were blind to the ways of the elves. As blind as he was before he knew Icee. They were part of the plan to cause civil war and he hated them, only some wizards wanted the war he realized, but even so it would reflect badly on his guild.

Nodding to them as they passed he gestured to the seats provided around the oblong table in the center of the hall, "Take a seat all, others wait 'til you are seated."

Few words accompanied the scraping of the seats on the stone floor. Each knew civil war was at hand, and relished it. They would rule the dark elves first; whichever side won the battle. They had worked hard under the leadership of the druid who so long ago had talked them into listening to his plans of making civil war possible and, by dividing, rule the dark elves. They would then turn their attention to each of the races in turn, and each would bow to their rule. They and they alone would rule the known lands, and do so by sword and magic. But first they needed the enchanters' power to help them; they and the necromancers were held in both fear and awe for what they could do to both friend and enemy. The necromancers would follow them if they won the first battle, but they needed the enchanters to ensure they did win.

Her voice penetrated the torch lit hall, strong and no fear within it, "It is good to see so many enemies in one room."

Some looked up while others spun in their chairs to see who the voice belonged, the general noise adding to confusion she had started. Stepping from behind a torch a small smile played on her lips, "Good evening to all, though I fear for many it will be your last in this world."

The words the Chosen One made her smile all the brighter.

"Sit! Do so now!"

Kare watched those seated at the table carefully. The wizards he knew would watch the knights and their reactions to the situation and not start a fight, and had voiced his thoughts. His attention turned to the knights; they were always ready to kill, never needing an excuse or reason. They would be the ones to start the fight, if there was to be one, and he trusted Norty enough to believe her when she had told him there would be, and who would start it.

He had studied the sisters as he stayed with them, and he liked what he saw. Never once had he seen them make a move for selfish reasons. Never do anything for their own gain. He loved the way they were, and he loved Icee. Yet it was Malinna who had shown him new ways of looking at life, and of the races within their lands. In her he had seen compassion for every race, watched as she treated all with equal respect and care, her healing skills given to any needing her.

His eyes settled once more on their leader, a knight he knew only by reputation. He fought for the love of the kill, and they had been many. It was he who had started the way the knights marked their kills, by adding a small metal ring to the broad belt around their waist. It had become a symbol of their power which made him feel sick as, involuntarily, he looked down to the belt of the knight sat beside him. The three rows of rings continued past the middle of his back, he could see no further.

Now, as the confrontation seemed to be reaching breaking point, he glanced at the others around him. His training had taught him how to look into the eyes of any he confronted, to see what was in them. If there was fear he had been taught how to handle the situation, to play it to his own advantage. But if he saw none in their eyes he had been taught how to back away, to keep both his life and respect. Now he saw what was in the eyes of most of the knights around the table, and he knew they would sit and hope the others would resolve the situation. There was no fear of fighting, but fighting the Chosen One was different, they knew the Gods protected her, and it was this he saw reflected in their eyes.

The wizards were a different; they would sit and watch the proceedings, to join in at the first opportunity. Yet he watched Kerist, the Knights' leader, the closest.

"So the Chosen One comes to die. Not the first in our war and not the last." Kerist moved forward, stopping as Icee and Malinna entered the torch light to stand side by side with their sister.

He felt himself getting nervous, "So, they all come to die."

Icee shook her head, "It is not us Death will visit this day."

"Kill the Chosen Ones and many will bow before us without a fight. There are only three, an easy kill!"

At the slight movement from her hand Finglas stepped from the other end of the room and Pose moved from the shadows to stand right of them.

Juin called as he and Elesee stood at his side, "I now count seven."

Kare pushed his chair back to stand with Pose, "Eight."

Pose was pleased, the plan was going as Norty had foretold, entering this way from different directions and increasing numbers served to unnerve and confuse them. If they had all appeared at once the battle may have started instantly, and been very bloody.

Nortee and Sha'Dal stepped forward, "Ten!"

Flight cried from the right, "I am the eleventh."

Kerist was desperate to show leadership to those under him who were looking decidedly nervous, if they would not fight now, if he could not rally them to his side, the battle was as good as lost, "We have them four to one, an easy kill!"

Some moved to draw swords but the enchanters appearing changed their minds; most sat down.

Icee giggled, "The odds are now two to one. Think again."

Swords were sheathed once more; a fight with druids and a few others they saw as no real challenge, but against twelve enchanters the odds were changed. Knowing the force against them the intelligent chose not to fight.

Norty was annoyed with herself; she had seen their minds approaching down the hall and had not checked if druids were amongst them. She had made an error and realized it might cost dearly. It was obvious Death stalked them and several would die; most of them the enchanters, they were not high enough in understanding or fighting skills; they would be the easier targets for those seated before her. These men would take advantage of the fact; their kind had always done, and would always do so.

Try as she might she could see no reason why Mel D'elith had invited only enchanters of a surprisingly low understanding, except Byntha, to attend.

Slowly her hands gestured to the two vacant seats, "Sit and be comfortable while we will wait until all are taken."

They did as instructed, watching as the others slowly drifted back into the shadows, the enchanters remaining behind the tall backed seats of the knights, their hands resting on the tops of the chairs.

For five minutes they sat as the tension mounted, none daring to be the first to move or speak, knowing it might well be the last thing they did. The creaking of the old oak door opening heightened the strain. As all eyes turned towards the door as Velsin and Bindra entered.

Seeing knights and wizards at the table and the enchanters behind the seats they nodded, the assembly was strong and none would be able to stand in their way.

Taking his seat he gestured, "Worries I see on your faces, it is without cause; calm your fears tonight we plan the future of the lands, of *our* lands."

Her voice came soft in his ear, "Those lands you will never know, *druid.*"

"So the disgraced being comes to die!"

Bindra was not waiting for her to harm her son; now it was obvious why the look of fear was on the faces of those around the table, she was here to take her son's life. As her hands moved to cast a spell a hand caught her arm.

Nortee glared at her, "Father would speak to you, have you the time."

Turning she screamed at Finglas, "Think of the disgrace you bring when you bring forth such an abomination!"

"She is no disgrace as you will see. *Midwife Bindra.*"

Velsin recovered, his spell blackening the wall behind where she stood.

"You think me careless when you attack? Your family has twice cast on me. Never will they do so again."

Once more a spell hurled at her but it was far off its mark, "Your chances to kill me desert you. "

Norty let her mind reach out to find his, and it was filled with fear; everywhere on his body his mind saw insects crawling and biting at him.

He had hated insects all his life; to him they were an indescribable horror haunting him. They had bit him since childhood and always seemed to choose him to attack; he knew not why. As his hands brushed them away he stamped on those falling to the floor as more took their place, surging upward towards his neck, biting and chewing as they went, covering his face and hair. There was no place the crawling and slithering creatures did not reach. As he cried out for help they crawled in his mouth, he spat them out looking for help from his mother.

She was standing next to him, pointing and laughing as she urged them to bite him. His eyes widened in disbelief as he fell to the floor in pain from the bites. He could not shout for help or even dare to scream, the insects wanted him to open his mouth; he knew it.

Finglas saw how fast his daughter had moved to stop the spell Bindra was casting. He was pleased, with the amulet she moved at a speed unthought-of until now. His turn had come and his spell struck Bindra in the chest to send her sprawling across the table, a second spell hitting her legs, crippling her as the bones snapped under the force.

Elesee cast on Bindra, her spell gouging flesh from bone, "You deserted me in my time of need and brought shame on yourself. Others were made of caring ways and stayed with me."

"You are no elf! You are an affront to us all."

"Finglas would have your life and there is little mercy within him."

As she lay across the table Kerist seized his opportunity. Standing with sword drawn he bought it across the chest of the enchanter to his right. Years of training had taught him how to inflict pain enough to stop a foe and give the opportunity for a second attack; without a pause in movement his sword sliced open her throat.

As she fell to the floor the remaining enchanters erupted in fury, joining the battle with spells and mind control. Yet it was as how Norty had predicted; they were far too weak to control the knights, their attempt to even the odds brought the other knights into the battle.

Icee was livid at the scene; four enchanters were dead before she had cast a single spell to help, but would change it now. Her spell scythed through a wizard, mortally wounding the knight behind him. From the corner of her eyes she saw Kare cast, and a wizard double up in pain. She was proud of him; he was fighting on their side and against members of his own guild. He was fighting against some she knew must be his friends, she could ask nothing more of him. As she turned back to cast again she saw the spell hit him and he writhed in pain, yet he was still trying to cast to help the enchanters.

Screaming at the caster she turned on him, her spell punching a hole through his chest. Then her thoughts were for her elf, looking back she saw Malinna crouched over him, her light blue spell healing his wounds. Malinna had not entered the fight; Norty had ensured she would stay in the darker lit section of the hall to heal the wounded in relative safety. With a nod from her sister Icee knew he would live but the anger in her needed to be sated. They had hurt him and she would make them pay, heavily.

Sha'Dal and Nortee joined as a single force, hurling spells at the same target, and each time they went down, dead or with serious wounds. It sickened Sha'Dal, he was like his mother, born to heal; he hated to kill yet knew for each life taken this day mayhap a thousand might be saved later.

Watching the mind of the elder as he fought the fear in him Norty was not going to be robbed of the chance to inflict pain for all he had done to her daughter. Realising another had entered his mind to place the thoughts within him she looked round for who it could be.

Her first thought was of Pose and cast a glance her way to find she had charmed a wizard and had no problems instructing him to fight on her side. She could not be the one who held his mind. Of the dark enchanters only Byntha had reached a proficiency were she could enter his mind in such a way, yet immediately she ruled her out, she was casting a spell, it could not possibly be her. As she saw her daughter she was helping those in need; she could not possibly be the one in his mind. No others were near of sufficient training; there was only one conclusion she could make. An unseen friend was close at hand.

Quickly he mind scanned the room and ignored all within, they were too busy in their own tasks. As her mind scanned outside the room she found no one close and settled on the only option open to her, and looked towards her daughter to find her mind more active then she had ever known.

Icee saw the danger her sister was obviously unaware of and for a moment wondered why. Her spell severed the knight's arm as he held his sword ready to strike, "Sister should look to her own defence as well as to those of others."

As her spell took the life of the knight she turned to Icee, "Thank you, sister, much is on my mind. I will be attentive."

Moments later Nortee was at her side her eyes ensuring her mother had not been hurt, "My revenge is sated; he is your do with as you wish."

As suddenly as they had appeared the insects vanished, as did the stings and bite marks they had inflicted on him. Hate flooded through him as thoughts of revenge crashed into his mind. Turning to look for the one who had caused the feeling in him his eyes caught those of her mother.

"Now my turn comes to show you the ways of the enchanter. The most painful ways I can devise is my promise to you."

Somehow he was out of the battle and in a small pasture shaded by trees; breathing deep he sat to lean on a tree. Somewhere a battle raged but could not remember where or why it had started. He would sit and rest, it had been so long since he had, and think of the battle later. Enjoying the warmth of the day his eyes slowly opened to see his hated enemy stood over him. Instantly anger cursed through his very being but as he tried to rise something stopped him, the branch of the tree was wrapping around his leg, slowly creeping up and preventing him from moving.

In disbelief he watched a branch arc down to grab his wrist and move up his arm; smiling at the sight as the branch seemed almost alive the way it wound up his arm and felt the gentle pressure as it pulled at him. The feeling of pain came a moment later, turning to agony as the branch pulled with such a force he thought his arm would be ripped from his body.

Grabbing the branch with his free hand he pulled hard, the pain was getting too intense and feelings of giddiness were overcoming him. Through his blurred vision he saw another branch wrapping round his free hand and drag it back, to grip ever tighter and pull all the harder. Then the branches stopped their relentless pulling and, as his vision began to clear, saw an old grey wolf sat in front of him. Relief took hold of him, a friend at last, "Rip the branches away my friend; help me."

"Why should I help you? You ignore the trees and animals you once cared for. You are no longer worthy to be a druid; the time for you has passed. "

"I am a druid, elder of the guild, you must help me."

"Leadership was taken for your wrong deeds. You are brought here to die before your schemes may harm the forest. You bring only death to the land and animals you once cared for."

"I care for the lands, the rivers and the trees. I am your friend, help me."

The branches began their pulling once more and the pain returned.

"You are no longer one with the rivers, no longer one with the trees or the lands. You bring this upon yourself, never has a druid betrayed the ways as you have done."

Raising his head he let forth a howl into the evening air, a dozen wolves entered the clearing where the elder was held captive.

"The betrayer is before you, brothers, do with him as is your will."

He screamed at the wolf, "I have no plans to harm the forest or the river, only to bring together the races of the lands in harmony and peace."

The wolf looked at him, his head shaking as if he could hear the lies in his voice, "You lie. I see it in your eyes. There is no love in your heart as there is none in mine for you."

Turning he trotted slowly away, never once looking back.

He tried to scream for him to return, to gnaw at the roots and free him, but he could not, a branch wound its way around his mouth and was too tight to bear. As the wolves approached to bite and tear at his flesh he wanted to scream to ease the pain. His only hope was for someone to come and scare the wolves away, to cut him free of the roots, to heal his wounds. Yet he could not scream, the branches held him too tight and his mind was becoming unable to take the pain.

His eyes searched for help yet he could see his enemy. He poured all the feeling he could into them, even a bitter enemy would not allow him to suffer such pain, yet she stood there smiling as the pain mounted within. He was pleading with her, his onetime enemy, to take away the pain, why was it she would she not help? His world exploded in bright lights, and thoughts no longer passed through his mind.

Pose nodded to Norty, "I have fulfilled my promise to you; I grant his death."

Quickly glancing around the room she saw the fighting was over, the dead and dying all around. Moments later Finglas was at her side, his tunic covered in blood, but none of it his own. With a sigh of relief she checked for her daughter, to see her sat on the table with head tilted slightly to one side. Her sisters and parents were safe and she turned back to Pose, "He was begging for a mercy I could not show."

With her arm around Finglas she beckoned her daughter to her, "Explain yourself."

"I think I need not explain, mother. You see the truth yet fail to accept it."

"I accept the truth before me, I wish an explanation."

"In the battle I found I may use the powers within me together. I may use the mind of an enchantress and cast as a druid."

"Impossible."

"You deny the facts, mother, it is unlike you."

"All efforts must go into controlling the mind, there is nothing left, not enough to cast also."

"Yet you saw me; why deny what is plain for you to see?

"Enough." Whispered Finglas, "We discuss this at a more opportune time; we must be gone from here."

Kare shook his head, "I would know why I must stand in the town square and say such words, Icee. My guild should be at my side and not the enchanters."

"We may trust the enchanters yet it was your guild who came here, yours who fought us. At midday on the third day of the week ring the bell and wedlock will be ours. Pose speaks many enchanters will attend."

With the enchanters close he felt outnumbered, "It will be as you ask."

Standing on the cliffs once more Norty fought down the feelings boiling inside of her. She had hoped time would lessen the hatred; it had not. She wanted to show him the power of the enchanters, the might she now possessed; to make him pay for the effrontery to her. His voice brought back feelings hard to control.

"You believe I owe you and payment may be collected on your whim?"

With difficulty she held down her words; she had mediated for three days without rest to gain contact with them, and this was how he repaid her. Almost shaking with anger as it built up inside of her she kept her voice calm, "I make no demands; I ask only a favour."

His ways were not as she remembered; he had been powerful and strong but there was compassion and care in his heart. Those feelings had ceased to exist in him; in their place was hatred towards her, it was returned tenfold as she fought harder than she had even done before to retain a clam voice. Anger would not get her the wish she wanted for her sister, she would remain calm and not let him goad her as it seemed he tried so hard to do.

"Remain still, elf! One movement from you and I shall have my pleasure as I rip your body to shreds."

Slowly he began to walk round her as he tugged and prodded at her robe, "Your robe is not as it seems; it is made by other than elfin kind."

She stood with teeth clenched as he claw moved over her robe and body, shivering at his touch yet keeping thoughts of retaliation under control, somehow. He had touched her without permission and all her elfin ways were revolted at the thought.

"You have hatred for me, elf. It boils within and consumes you."

"I have."

"Yet still you come with a demand!"

"A favour is all I ask, not for myself but for my sister and the dark elves."

"You are wood elf so your sister is not dark elf. Favour denied, be gone!"

"You have heard not of what I would ask."

"I have no wish to hear it!"

"I would have thought you to listen."

"You think wrong!"

The control over her voice finally broke. She had seen enough of his ways and her anger spilled out in one mad torrent, "*I would ask a favour and you will listen to me or suffer the consequences!*"

"You would dare show anger to me?"

With all her will she hung her head, "Forgive me; I have not the right to speak such to you."

"You have been fruitful and born a child?"

"I have a daughter, yes."

"You named her what?"

"She is named Nortee."

"Where is the girl child now?"

"She is at home in our city."

Without moving his face from hers he called a name and a black dragon appeared from the cave, "Ah, Voldare. Go to wood elf city and kill the child named Nortee."

"No! She has done nothing to you, wished you no harm!"

"No, Voldare, do not kill her, bring her to me. This elf will see what it means to show anger towards her betters. If her father is there bring him also; I will feast on him while they watch."

Never had she felt anger as she did now, desperately she searched for his mind to control him, to stop his desires to kill her daughter and husband, but his mind was closed to her. Her only recourse was to make a direct attack on him, one she knew would work; "My daughter and husband have nothing to do with this!"

There was only one way to save their lives she would use any power available to her. Her staff pointed to him, sending blood red ribbons of light to encircle him, and he writhed in agony. As she watched she found herself saddened for her sister; she had let her down, her wish would remain un-granted and her sister would not join in wedlock in the city of the dark elves. It was the first time in her life she had ever broken a promise, and it was to her sister.

His body danced in slow motion, the mana spinning him round on the spot as it engulfed him, his head bobbing up and down as if in a trance. Willing more mana into the staff she felt hers begin to drain, to enhance the blood red glow of the light flowing to him. Finally he collapsed; the ground shaking as his mighty form slammed into it.

Tears stung her eyes as she shook her head, "I wished only a favour, not your death. You threatened my daughter and none may do so, ever. Do you wish to fight also, Voldare?"

"I do not. You think the fight won?"

"In truth I have lost. I had no wish for him to lose his life yet he pushed me beyond which any should be expected. I am sorry for his death, truly sorry, yet he would not listen to the favour I would ask."

"He will listen now."

The ancient one rose, throwing his head back as he laughed, before swinging it towards her, as huge smile on his lips, "Well, elf. Has the anger for me burned and gone?"

"I.... I am unsure."

His claw touched the end of her staff and the last wisps of mana vanished, "I could not harm your loved ones."

Sinking to her knees she sobbed, "Please, what are you doing to me?"

"I have released the anger buried within you. You have helped me and I had the need to help you also. With such feeling we could never be true friends and I wish this above all. Is the hatred for me gone?"

She looked up at him, "How did you know it was there?"

"You know the hatred left behind when you leave the mind of another, as I also know. Your thoughts of me had changed yet still you sought me out and kept them hidden, an admirable trait."

"Thank you for releasing me, they have been within me too long."

His claw encircled her to bring her up and close to his face, "I would be a friend to you, elf. The favour you would ask, how may I help?"

"My sister would join in wedlock to a dark elf yet there are those who would use the wedlock to their advantage, to start a war. We fought the ones who would openly bring the war, others would find the ceremony an excuse to fight amongst themselves and then with others. Wedlock is a joyous time and should not be marred by fighting and war."

"It would seem you have thought long on this. How may we help?"

Dark Wedding

Leaving her place with the enchanters in the hall of The Great Bell Pose walked towards him, her thoughts of him changing over the last few days. He had shown he was more than ready to fight, and die should it be necessary, for the cause of an elf almost unknown to him, Nortee.

His love for Icee was obvious from her talks with him, but there was more to this elf. His ways had changed from those of distaste for any not of their kind to thoughts helping others. Legend spoke the dark elves were once as other elves, caring and with a deep need to aid. Her need to help had begun to grow within her as she began training at high elf city. At first the feeling had upset her, as if she was acting against the will of her God, but she dismissed it. There were many Gods and she realised she had switched allegiance to a more beneficial one.

With the realisation came a feeling she had to teach those in high elf city the dark elf enchanter ways, and again this was new to her, only mentors of each class in her home city were allowed to teach. Before sunrise, so many years ago, she had dressed and gone to see Caspo Kwil but on reaching his study stopped, unable to enter. She fought within herself to find a reason not to return to her room. Finally she decided, as she turned to leave his voice had startled her.

"Pose, it is not our way to let troubled thoughts haunt the mind. Enter and speak with me."

She remembered it took a great effort of will not to run away, but turned and entered his study.

Sitting in his large chair he motioned to another, "You have been here often, yet this time I feel it is for different reasons."

"I have feelings new to me. I wish to help, not only the elves but all others." Glancing at him she hoped he would ask her to continue, he had only nodded.

"It is strange, the feelings are becoming strong and I worry over them." Once more she noted he nodded; nothing else.

"I have slept little in my thoughts of where these feelings will lead me; it would seem they have led me to your door. I offer training in the ways of my people, the ways I have been trained. This is also new to me. I have a need to help and the way I wish to do so is first by the sharing of knowledge. In my guild it is the mentor of each class only, or someone bid by them, who is allowed to train others. You have not bid me such yet I would offer my services. If this is offensive to you I will leave."

She remembered her feelings; how she had hoped he would accept her proposal and not let her leave, above all she had wanted to stay and learn, and to be a mentor. She knew it was minutes before she dared to look his way; when she finally forced herself he was smiling at her, his head shaking gently.

"Pose, my dear Pose. I had thought this day would never show itself to you, it is here and I am pleased. Others have asked if they might approach you to see if you would be willing to teach, to show them your ways. You have friends here aplenty who would willingly learn from you."

"I have friends here?"

"Many, you are popular amongst those you train with."

"I thought they merely tolerate me."

"Nothing could be further from the truth, you are well liked. I include myself as your friend, if I may call you such. I would wish you to begin mentoring others. You may start this day."

"You know not the honour you place on me."

"It is we who are honoured; we gain a new mentor from our students."

Reaching her room just as the sun rose her morning song had been one of the happiest she had ever sung.

Tapping him on the shoulder she whispered, "You are ready?"

"I am nervous, more so than when I was bid to stand before the elders to demonstrate my abilities."

"A natural state for males I believe. Come, stand with me."

As he reached the enchanters he gave the customary nod in their direction, he was nervous, he still had no idea of his future wife's plans.

Smiling encouragingly to him she turned to those assembled before her, "The call was given for as many as possible to be here on the third day of this week. The day has arrived and I thank all here for their presence. I have spoken of the death of Mel D'elith, of the battle and why our loyalties have once more been returned to the re-unionists."

She paused but there were to be no questions, "Good, you seem satisfied, yet if any here are unhappy then speak, I will try to explain."

Once more no questions were asked.

"There are but six here who know there is more to this day than is obvious, I release them from their oaths of silence and thank them also. I present to you Kare E'Thelt, this day he is to join in wedlock."

"We were called for a union of…. wizards?"

"There should be no disdain in your voice, Grat D'Helyt. It is from such feeling we must be free if civil war is not to be fought. Yes, you were called for the union; he is to join in wedlock to Icee, wizard of the Chosen Ones."

She let them talk amongst themselves for a few moments, before clapping her hands once, "Silence. We are here to help with the union and help we will receive also. At noon this day we assemble outside and form the Arc of Protection around Kare, *each and every one of you*."

She checked again, they were nervous and had a right to be. They knew how near civil war was, and this could well start the war. But she would make them far more nervous than they were now.

"I know your feelings on the war, I have spoken to individuals, yet no war will start this day."

Grat D'Helyt stood, "It is impossible to say when the war may begin yet it is likely, if they join in wedlock, this day it will."

"No war will begin this day, if any move to start one they will be killed!"

"We have no such power. If but one spell is cast, one sword drawn, then each must choose their side."

"We form the Ark of Protection this day and help will be ours. As the bell sounds its last note look to the skies as others listen to the speaker and there you will see our hope, our only hope, of returning this guild to the pride it was once held in. The Arc of Protection is sacred, our promise of security to the one at its center; *none* may move until bid to do so. If any move from their allotted place I will deal with them as Lore demands!"

Kare pulled the rope and the great bell sounded its deep tones; for two minutes he pulled and watched through the window as the crowd grew, anxious to know the reason for the ringing of the bell. Finally he emerged from the tower, three hundred and seventeen enchanters following, to stand on the top step. His hands rose and the gathered crowd fell silent. Slowly his arms lowered before beginning his rehearsed speech.

"This day I am to join in wedlock, my bride is unknown to any yet many know her name. She is Icee, wizard of the Chosen Ones."

A small murmur ran through the gathering and grew in volume, there was mixed feelings in the crowd.

He shouted to continue, "Yes, to an elf. This day we join in wedlock."

As Pose moved her arms upwards and outwards, the enchanters fanned out to either side of her as she remained at his side, "Be it known the enchanters support Kare E'Thelt. To this end we form the Arc of Protection."

The murmurs started again, none had ever offered protection to one of another guild. With the enchanters around him the crowd was unsure of what to do, only the necromancers remained silent, unmoving.

He watched the trolls sitting around the bottom of the steps, some thirty feet below him, indifferent to the mood of the crowd. No one seemed to voice support, although he did not expect any to welcome the news the lack of support saddened him.

As the murmurs subsided he called again, "This day all are welcome to attend the wedlock and to feast afterwards in the hall of the enchanters. Let there be no violence on this joyous occasion."

He wanted Icee with him, he has said the words and she was nowhere to be seen. Even a Chosen One could not reach the steps in time before the crowd erupted into violence.

An ear splitting screech and beating of giant wings made the crowd look up, and fear surged inside of them. In the skies above an enormous black dragon was swooping down, to glide without effort above their heads. Most ran in terror, only the enchanters remained at station, yet even they were nervous. Only Pose, facing them with a look on her face speaking of what would happen should any try to flee, seemed oblivious to the fact a dragon had landed just paces from her.

His head swung round to face the town square, and the few brave enough to have remained, "I am Voldare, here by command of the Chosen Ones."

There was no place in the city, no house or corner, his deep voice did not reach. Slowly the square began to fill as the elves, curious about the dragon and the Chosen Ones.

"I am the emissary of the dragons, friend of the Chosen Ones and all will hear my voice. This day Kare joins in wedlock to Icee and I attend, as do my brethren. There is talk of civil war; to strike others, the elves, the river elves or the dwarves. We do not interfere with this; it is for you alone to decide. Yet no war will begin this day! There will be peace and much happiness."

Standing his head swung round, slight wisps of smoke escaping from his nostrils, "If any wish not this happiness to be I would speak to them!"

Curling his lips back his right leg shot forward to a statue next to him, "If any wish to question me let me show them why they are wrong."

With blinding speed his claw cleaved the statue in two, "Any wish to speak with me?"

Picking up the top half he squeezed and the statue crumbled, "To make myself quite clear; should any cause a fight this day...."

He turned back to Kare, his voice almost a whisper, "I am for this wedlock. Too long have the elves let the differences they thought to exist rule their lives. Live long in happiness."

His head rose to let forth a bellow to the heavens.

The crowd gasped, intent on Voldare they had failed to see the arrival of ten dragons circling the city and beginning a long slow glide down.

Dismounting from the first dragon Norty stood at the side of Kare; a yellow landed and Malinna took her place with her sisters. Juin and Elesee dismounted as the next dragon landed, and an exuberant Sha'Dal was disappointed as he left his mount to join them. Finglas and Flight landed last to take their positions with the family.

Voldare roared above the excited chatter, "Befla J'Orrow, come to me."

Swallowing hard he did was asked, fear showing in every fibre of his being."

"Your promise was to preside over the wedlock if a guarantee of peace met your approval. I guarantee the peace."

"Gladly would I do so yet there is no bride or attendant maid."

Once more he growled at the skies and a dragon, white and majestic, began his slow decent to the city below.

The ancient one landed on the top steps to revel Icee dressed in white from head to soft white shoes. Her back, normally only covered with her robe, was now adorned with a fine transparent silk cloak trailing behind her as she walked. Yet she also wore something no elf had worn to her wedlock in their known history. From head to breast she wore a veil so fine as to be almost invisible, held in place on her head by a thin sliver of mithril.

Kare was in awe, never had he seen her looking so beautiful as she did now. His heart went out to her, captured once more the way it was the first time he had seen her on the mountain pass.

"Icee, second born of Elesee and Juin, my hand is stretched before you. If you would join in wedlock take it to your heart."

The correct reply she knew by heart, Pose had instructed her in the way he must act towards her, and she to him. All her life she had been taught to bow, now she found it hard not to do so as she reached for him, her hand gently taking his to her breast, "For now it is my heart. Soon all of me will be yours to command."

As he reached the lowest of the bow he could see she was impressed, and had not expected it, "Pose has spent days to ensure the bow is correct."

She bowed back, "Pose has been busy. A white elf we make of you yet."

"After you make a husband of me."

Standing before the statue of D'Yelith Befla J'Orrow gave a sharp nod, "Two more come to you this day to join in your presence."

His arms moved backwards and each took a hand, "Icee, second born of Juin and Elesee, asks to join with Kare E'Thelt, first born of Hals and Liss E'Thelt. The wedlock displeases his parents and they wish not to attend."

Slowly he drew his arms back to his sides and they followed, to stand either side of him.

Kare lowered his head, "Lord, this is my wish. I ask for her to be mine, now and for all times."

"I accept him, now and for all times."

Befla J'Orrow placed her hand in the outstretched hand of the statue, "Icee accepts his offer, should this union not be your wish show it to us."

Waiting the customary two minutes before continuing he placed the hand of Kare on the hand of Icee, still resting on the statue, "Lord, accept these, your children, to your love and care. Bless them and keep them in your heart for all times."

His nod to the statue was sharp as he turned to face the people, "These two are joined as is their wish. They join this day and for all the days to come."

Turning back his hand rested on theirs, still on the statue, "Icee and Kare I charge you now by the love within your hearts, to each other be kind and truthful, to be to each as you would be to yourselves. Hold in your hearts the love for each beating there now."

His hand lifted theirs as he turned once more to the assembly, "This union is blessed by D'Yelith as all here witness and will testify should they be called to do so. Leave now for the enchanters' guild; there is food aplenty, all are welcome."

Norty turned, "Trouble may yet come."

He could only squeeze his massive head into the guildhall doors, withdrawing it to speak her, "No trouble will start at this time; we remain until their time."

"Until their time?"

"What happens to them now?"

"They feast and their lives begin together."

He chuckled, "Different thoughts have been suggested."

The feasting lasted for several hours, the enchanters keeping careful watch on all present, but not so as to be noticed. Yet all eyes continually swept towards the three necromancers standing silently close to the doors, watching the proceeding but not mixing with the revellers.

The merriment was cut short by a long low roar of a dragon, "Icee and Kare E'Thelt come to the town square; the time is now."

Malinna turned, "To what time does he refer, sister?"

"He would speak nothing of this. Best we go and all will be revealed."

The assembly followed them out of the guildhall and towards the town square as Norty turned to her daughter.

"You know of this, speak to me."

"It would spoil what is to be. Wait, as do all."

Reaching the town square they found most of the dragons had departed, only two remained.

The ancient one lowered his neck, "Icee and Kare, mount me."

Looking at each other they shook their heads, wondering what was to happen. As they sat astride him he spread his wings, taking to the skies to circling above.

Voldare turned to the crowd, "They are wards of the dragons and under our protection. *If harm befalls them, now or in the future, all here will suffer our wrath!*"

Finally he turned to Norty and Malinna, "They go to our land to rest and be happy. In seven days they will return but let them not enter this place for many days after. It is not safe yet for them, in time it may be so."

"I will be happy when all may walk freely in either city."

"One day it may come to pass. Nortee, your thoughts are good, all should be alone after wedlock to bond."

"Thank you for your promise. If there is anything I may do in return..."

He held out a paw, "A gift for you; make of them what you will."

With a smile he turned to Norty, "Your mind may connect with us again when you will it. The dragons are friends of the Chosen Ones."

Spreading his wings he flew to join his brethren as they headed back to their own land.

"No, Nortee, no. Both arms must fall together or this is the result. We come to the glade so we may not be seen and plans revealed."

Looking down she saw her own legs under those of the dwarf illusion she had tried to cast, and giggled.

"Nortee!"

"I am sorry, mother, it looks so funny."

"Be serious, Nortee. Time presses and you must be perfect or we will fail."

"Illusions are hard; they take all my concentration yet still elude me."

"The reason you must practice hard. We must get this right, Nortee, we must."

"I will continue."

"I would have you cast the illusion of an ogre."

"Mother, they are so hard and ugly, a dwarf is much the easier."

"An ogre you must be and the one I would have you practice."

Trying again she still could not get the illusion correct.

"As the hands come down twist the palms inwards to turn the magic towards you. Try once more."

She tried, and watched as her mother shook her head.

"No, Nortee. Place your left arm in the spells start position, move the hand and arm correctly. No spells, the movement only."

"Mother, I have practiced for over an hour, my arm aches, may I stop?"

"You may rest your arm as you do the same with the other."

"Mother...."

"You will get this right, daughter. Illusions are a spell to save your life and you must ensure they are perfect, yet for once we will have fun with them."

"It is unlike you to use magic for fun, yet this time I gladly join with you."

"The fun will not be known until later."

"I am sure my aunts will play their part."

"I have not spoken to them of this; I will do so when the time is right."

Catching her arm as she left for the glade Finglas swung her round towards him, "You leave early to train each evening, why so?"

"We have work to do, the enchantress must be perfect for some of our spells to work. We will return when the time for training is over."

"It seems you spend so much longer with Nortee. Is there a reason?"

"She must practice hard, her days in your guild leave little time for her to be what she must in mine."

"I feel you try too hard with her."

"We make a game of the training and the time passes quickly. It is hard for her, the reason I train her here so she may concentrate."

"It is mayhap too much for her?"

"This part of training is practiced with the parents. It is difficult and needs so much concentration."

"I would come with you, to watch mother and daughter train together."

"There is much for her to learn and you would be a distraction. In time she will show you her new ways and you will be proud of her."

Once again she cast her illusions, failing on each attempt, "Mother, never will I get this right. When others cast it looks so easy."

"Your arms still move too quickly. There is another way, recite these words in your mind as you start the illusion, when the words are finished your hands should be by your side and resting."

"Yet I must speak the words or the spell will not happen."

"It is a way to ensure your arms fall correctly. I will show you."

Her arms rose above her head and she began the rhyme.

"Illusions I cast for your eyes to see,"
"Illusions I cast so I may fool thee,"
"Whatever I cast you see what I be,"
"Yet who is the fooled, thee or me?"

"Try once again. Cast not the spell and say the rhyme."

For three hours she practiced until her mother called a halt.

"I am sorry, illusions are so much more difficult then I imagined."

"Why are you sorry? You have cast it correctly for the last half hour."

Watching as he lay in their bed she began her singing as the stars first appeared, letting her song drift him gently to sleep. His day had been hectic and his mind troubled, it was so unlike him to worry. He had been chosen to join in the tracking of the young ones, as Nortee had once been tracked. The honour of becoming a member of an elite trackers party had sent him sleepless nights and he had spoken of little else for days, pacing the room, never sitting still for a moment.

'Norty, this is a day I never thought would be; yet it is here. I am the youngest ever to be chosen. I wish not to let them down.'

Finally she had coaxed him to bed, but he would not settle, choosing to talk continually of the tracking and his fears. As she listened she knew he would never sleep and her decision was made. Her song began and she knew he would think little of it as he spoke with her. She was using her enchantress ways with him and it lay heavily on her mind, yet she had no choice. He needed to be fresh for the morning, and would ensure his worries were chased away and his body relaxed for the morrow.

Before sunrise she gently shook him, "Beloved."

Slowly he came awake, "Yes?"

"Today is the day and you must ready yourself."

"You used your ways to have me sleep?"

"I am sorry, husband."

"Do not concern yourself, it was of necessity."

Reaching over he pick up his tunic and trousers neatly placed at his side, "Verin spoke to me of how pleased he was with Nortee and spoke at length of someone who seems not to notice him."

"Rinini is my thought, I have seen the way his eyes always follow her."

"He is afraid to speak to her of his feelings."

"I know of someone else who would speak not of his feeling."

"It would seem she thinks of little but the hunts."

"It must be he who first speaks of love; such is our Lore, yet if another were to make the path easier for him...."

Taking the root he smiled to her, "My thoughts also."

"Three days we chased our young through the forest, none taking over three hours to find, their training somewhat lacking I fear. They were let on the chase too early; to be found so easily may discourage some of them."

"You have spoken to Rinini?"

"I have not, so many were on the chase the time did not allow."

"Tomorrow you track again yet who was the better?"

"Heris. He has a quick mind and knew tricks above his teaching."

Moving the empty plate she sat beside him, "How so?"

"He spoke with others who have attended the test, asking how to avoid capture. They should not have spoken of the ways."

"Not all may be learned by teaching; questions often help where tuition does not."

"Yet we found more than our quarry and the older ones were concerned, they seek the council so it may be reported."

"What did you find?"

"Tracks of many skeletons there for all to see."

"They have not been seen in any land for countless centuries."

"The tracks start and end suddenly; only dust did we see where they ended. No trace of them otherwise and the trackers worry."

"Time will show their meaning."

"Do not brush them aside so easily, they have been the cause of many a war. One thousand years ago they fought man, and the elves lost many to them also."

"I recall the teaching; yet man had allies, gnomes and river elves."

"Halflings also. I fear war with them may return soon."

"Little has been heard of them."

"A thousand years are passed; mayhap they have grown strong in number, enough to wage war once more."

"Where were the tracks?"

"They start at the clearing in Whisper Valley; we followed them down the valley towards high elf city."

"The valley runs through the city!"

"You feel there is more to this?"

"We are ill prepared to defend the city and it is obvious where they would choose to fight, plans must be made or this may be our downfall."

"We would fight all the harder to protect our own lands, and would win."

She decided to change the subject, "With the new moon you begin your travels once again. Where do you go this time?"

"To the land of the trolls, I wish to become known to them, to be a friend."

"They hate us, except for whomever Malinna and Flight take with them. Join them when next they go, become known to them first."

She held her breath, hoping he would refuse.

"I would do it this way for now, to see if they will accept me for who I am and not as someone Flight brings with him."

"With Nortee once more in study I have a way of wishing you farewell."

"I know you, wife, this time you wish me not to leave."

As her robe fell open she laughed, "You may see me the sooner than expected."

"I think not, it will take time for them to accept me."

"Flight spoke he let them see him for over a year. I do not wish you gone so long."

"I shall let them see me for a week or so before I return and try again."

Her plan had worked and she would see Malinna in the morning when he left. Inwardly she breathed a sigh of relief; sometimes his stubbornness could be put to good use.

"Sister, I would borrow your husband for a while, if I may."

Malinna looked sideways at her, "You scheme. What do you wish of him?"

"His powers for Nortee and myself and mayhap a day or two of his time."

"You tease; it is not often this side of you is shown."

"The tease will be enjoyed. I would ask also a favour from you."

"You have but to ask."

"I would wish you to forget your skill in the dwarf's language."

"How may I do such?"

"I ask you repeat not the words I will say in anger. May I borrow your husband?"

Finding the trolls was easy and he had followed them for several days as they wandered around the land, letting them see him several times, usually in a sitting position, to show no aggression towards them. At first they had rushed at him but when he did not move or show retaliation they returned to their group. He smiled to himself as he thought of his long talks with Flight, of how to be and what to do when he saw the trolls. He now realised how hard it was for Flight to get them used to him. It was hard work but he was enjoying himself.

He let them see him again as they awoke and broke camp, yet noted there was always one of them watching him. He would not move an inch or follow them as they moved out; it was disquieting to them. He would wait half a morning and then get ahead of them, waiting for them to pass once more and see him sat near the edge of the path they followed.

They were almost out of sight when movement caught his eyes, instinctively he leaned against the tree and became one with it, almost invisible to the untrained eye; his eyes searched for the movement which had drawn his attention, it had disappeared.

Long minutes passed before he saw it again. Sharp and darting; almost impossible to see in the tall grass. A female gnome had appeared on the hill at the other side of the lake, watching the trolls as they disappeared over the slight rise of the land, before running down to the lake to wash and sit on a fallen tree, her feet dangling in the water.

His head shook as he wondered what she was doing, trolls were not friendly to the gnomes but would not harm her unless provoked, and his curiosity became aroused. As she sat he noticed she fidgeted, constantly looking around as if expecting someone. He began to wonder who she was waiting for so far from her lands. Even at this distance he could see she was singing, once in a while the odd word could be heard as the gentle breeze changed direction. He decided to get closer, it would be easy to catch up with the trolls later; he had an idea where they were headed.

It had taken him most of the morning and cautious manoeuvring to get near and her singing had stopped, but not the constant watchfulness. He was thankful for his druid abilities to hide; it had served in getting him this close to her, only forty paces separated them.

As he lay in the top of the tree in a position to hear and see everything she did he noted her robe and profession, the green and blue of her robe denoting her as a mage, and it puzzled him; it was unusual for a gnome, they tended to be wizards above all others. Mages were rare, even amongst other races.

Yet her hair intrigued him the most, shoulder length and black as midnight. It was different; most gnomes were bald and what little hair they had was white, but he had never met a gnome mage, never been introduced to the mage Elesee knew, and oft wondered why. When he had mentioned them to Xandorian he had become agitated and would not speak about them. Pushing the subject as far as Xandorian would let him he had been given a curt reply, 'They are from a past I will not speak of.'

The more he watched the more fascinated he became. Her movements were sharp; always the way with gnomes, her eyes darting all over, missing nothing. He nodded to himself; it was the way he had always known Xandorian to be. Suddenly she stiffened, her back straightening, eyes ceasing their constant movement to fix on a point left of her as she jumped off the tree to crouch behind it, catlike in the way she moved.

Cautiously he changed to a sitting position on the branch, lifting his head to look around, wondering what it was she had seen or heard to startle her, a gnome's hearing was as acute as any elf's. It took only moments before he saw the ogre as she lumbered down to the lake, stopping at the edge before glancing round and scooping up some water in her hands to drink. In horror he saw the gnome creep along the branch leading up and past the ogre, she was going to attack; yet the only weapon he could see was the small dagger at her side. He shook his head; mage spells were for use at long-range and had great force. Used to almost cripple an enemy, to slow them down, then run away, stopping once in a while to cast again. In this way they usually managed to keep ahead of their enemy, and for a gnome it was life itself, their short legs did not offer them a great turn of speed.

She should have used her spells on the ogre the moment she saw her, not wait and attack with only a dagger to protect herself. The ogre would have the advantage and the gnome would be committing suicide. With the dagger still sheathed, and no sign of glowing fingers donating a spell was ready to be cast the gnome looked as if she would rely on surprise. Thoughts of Xandorian once more entered his head and he moved to cast a spell to help the gnome but stopped mid cast, blending once more with the branches. He could almost hear Xandorian 'what must be must be; let it come to pass.'

He saw the ogre stretch and sit clumsily down before lying on her back; she must see the gnome as she stood on the branch above her. The thoughts on what would happen sent his heart racing as he leaned closer. The gnome jumped, landing on the ogre in a tangled heap of arms and legs. Shrieks and moans assaulted his ears as they fought and rolled towards the river's edge, the splash of water almost reaching him as they sank beneath the surface. Standing to gain a better view of the river he waited to see which of the two would break the surface and live.

His first thought was the ogre; she was almost five times the gnome's height and by far the stronger. Although the gnome had the element of surprise on her side the moment it was lost she would die to the ogre's great strength.

The waiting was almost agony as he watched for them to surface, and realised there was blood in his mouth; he was biting hard on his bottom lip.

The surface of the water erupted as the ogre broke free from its grasp, to hold the gnome high in her arms. He was surprised, the gnome would live a few more minutes, but he doubted she would get the better of the fight. He froze as the ogre lowered the gnome and began to laugh, the gnome giggling almost hysterically as she was thrown backwards into the lake.

He was in awe of the scene, they should fight until one was dead, yet these were friends, and had been so for a long time by the looks of the way they were playing, splashing about in the lake, laughing and enjoying the water.

"This time I fooled you." He heard the gnome say, "If you had not laid back you would not have seen me."

"You good. Better now than first time. Then you easy to see."

"You teach well, my friend, but today I have sad news."

"Tell news."

"I must to leave for home; I will not see you for a long time."

"How long time?"

"Maybe after the festival I will try to come back them."

"Me miss friend."

"I will miss you too, but I must be home for the festival. You know I must return for all to see I still live. It is part of the festivals, when families know all is well."

"When you leave?"

"Friends will be near the caves soon, an hour, maybe more."

"Take long time to get to caves. You go."

"I know, and I will miss you. But I will see you here again soon."

The ogre laughed, "Not long, or me get you. Smash you."

"Till we meet again, friend, be sure you stay safe."

Watching the ogre as she lumbered back up the hill his eyes returned to the gnome as she began removing her shoes; suddenly his interest in her grew.

"Waters of life. Thank you for your love and take me with you once more."

He cursed himself for not knowing exactly what she had said; her tones were unusual for a gnome. He spoke gnomish well from his days travelling with Xandorian, but he made a mental note to get Norty to teach him more of their language, especially the way the mages seemed to alter words, to almost chant rather than speak. He wanted to return and see how this friendship had started and how it would fare.

With a last look around her robe dropped to the ground and she stood there as she was on the day her mother gave her life.

Somehow the gnomes had always held an attraction to him, but this was the first time he had seen one as he did now, and he was impressed.

With great care she stepped into the water and sank up to her neck, a moment later her head went under, and she vanished.

'Xandorian, now I see why you always spoke in reverence of your females.'

".... The last I saw she was heading for the caves."

Juin nodded, "It would seem the ogre and the gnome was friends."

"Friends for some while." Added Elesee.

"I saw it as such. When the festival is over I will return to see if the friendship is renewed. I would like to see more of her."

Standing her foot stamped on the ground, "Have you not seen enough of her? Ig thar grut, Finglas? Id greer heth ut jusp veer nicht grenst! Whej jur grut gret gnome Id brunk der riber!"

Turning she walked quickly from them, never once looking back.

Taken aback by words he turned to Malinna, "I speak dwarf but not as she does, what did she say?"

Malinna suppressed he smile as she remembered her sisters words of earlier, "There are words used by others for which we have no equal, sometimes it is best they are spoken in another language. She chose dwarf and I see why, yet some of them I would never speak, even in anger."

"It would seem I have trouble to come."

"Mother is by the river, she chooses the place you fish. It would seem a good idea to speak with her, yet your words must be soft."

They let him get out of hearing before bursting into laughter.

Juin eyed them suspiciously, "You tease, all of you. I know enough dwarf to understand she spoke of love and the river."

"It would seem my teachings of ambassador ways were not as entirely dismissed as I had thought. She asked Finglas to meet her by the river if he loved her."

"She did not swear?"

"Many of the dwarfs' words sound as such, if enough emphasis is placed on them."

As he approached he noticed the way her back arched a little and her form become stiffer, he would have to be very gentle, to act as if he understood her words, "I am here."

"Do you come with words of gnomes or words of elves?"

Kneeling behind her he let his voice become little more than a whisper in her ear, "I come with words for you, for you alone."

"You think words may smooth your passage to me?"

"Words are all I have."

"It would seem as she disrobed you did not avert your eyes."

At last he knew. The thought he had seen the gnome in such a way upset her. His hands rested on her waist as his lips strayed close to her ear, "Somehow, I know not how, it seemed impossible to look away."

"Impossible, Finglas?"

He stiffened a little, hoping no answer was the right way to play his part.

Her smile was unseen by him, "A question requires an answer, Finglas."

"I will answer when I have thought on this."

Forcing the smile from her face she turned to him, feigning hurt feelings, "When you think of an excuse?"

"I could not look away, I know not why."

Her head tilted upwards, "Huh! You were pleased with what you saw?"

"Such is no question to ask."

"Do not try to find a way to free yourself; there is none as well you know."

He nodded; trying to place is arms around her, "There is but one female in my life."

"You think your arms may mend this?"

"They can, and this is where they belong."

"Ha!"

He was confused, he had watched and listened as she had taught some of the ways a body moves to Nortee, and thought he had understood also. She was different, her voice and words were wrong for her actions, and he was unsure how to act. One thought kept running through his mind, he never wanted to argue as they had done when their daughter was so young. He would make amends no matter what the price was to be.

"My arms belong around you as yours belong around me. I see them not as the problem but the cure."

Unable to control herself she turned, giggling as her hand covered her mouth trying to stop the laugh rising within her.

"Always you have confused me, yet this time more so."

She could not stop herself, the more she thought of the look on his face the more she giggled, "Till we meet again, friend, be sure you stay safe."

His eyes narrowed, a smile starting on his face as he spoke her name slowly, "Norty..."

Backing away from him, unable to control herself any longer, the giggle turned to a laugh.

"Norty, if you have done what I think...."

Continuing to back away her laughter changed back to giggling as she entered the water.

"Damn you, you did it..."

With her head just above the water she stopped.

"Norty, you...."

The water turned grey as bubbles broke the surface, and a gnome with hair as black as midnight walked out towards him.

"Waters of life thank you for your love and take me with you once more."

Running to her he picked her up in his arms, "Who was the ogre, surely you had little time to befriend one?"

"Nortee learns well the ways of the enchanters."

"So this is what you do so long into the evening."

"Her training was hard yet she learned well the ways of illusion."

"As you also learn well the traits of others. Perfect beloved, perfect; you fooled me."

Dragon Tears

"Malinna?"

Looking up from the scroll in the dwarf's city she smiled at her niece, "Yes, Nortee."

"I would ask from you a favour."

"You have but to ask."

"The dwarves are masters of craftwork, better than the elves?"

"In some work they are known to be the masters, on what do you wish."

"Who is the better?"

Placing the scroll back in its place she looked at her niece as she fidgeted, "You feign an excuse to be here and watch as I work yet there are thoughts in your mind, speak to me of them. I will say nothing to your mother if such a fear is in your head."

"No fear, Malinna. I wish for a gift for my mother and her sisters."

"A gift? Of what form should this gift take, or is it the favour you ask?"

"There is no question of the form of the gift. My mother and her sisters are special; the gift must also be special. I would see the finest craftsman the dwarves have in the skill of a ring maker."

"Why so?"

Withdrawing a piece of mithril from her pocket she placed it on the table, "I asked Pose to enchant this before I left the city and speak not to mother."

"Enchanted mithril makes a special ring, Nortee."

"There is enough for four rings, one each for my mother and her sisters, and one for me."

"A nice thought, your love is plain to see."

Opening her hand to show blue pieces of tear shaped stones she asked, "Are these the stones they call dragon tears?"

"They are, Nortee. I have only heard of them and never have I seen one. You have four, where did you get them?"

"Voldare gave them to me as he left the wedlock. I have wondered for days on what to do with them and it is the reason I came here, to ask a dwarf to make rings from them."

"Icee and I cannot accept such a gift yet your mother will be pleased if you were to offer one to her."

"You may not refuse the ring as Icee may not. Voldare gave me four tears and long have I thought on why. Then it seemed so obvious, one each for the Chosen Ones and one for myself."

"Artir Golnmas is the one we need to speak with, he is by far the craftsman with rings. He will not make the rings for you, he works only for the dwarves, yet I think he may do so if I ask him."

"How so?"

"I healed his son years ago, Graforge."

"Your self-styled protector. I like him, he has a ready wit."

Taking her arm she guided her from the study room, "Artir works each day down the sixth tunnel. It is unused for most of the time."

"He wishes to be constantly alone?"

"He says he is not to be disturbed when working."

"His work is so delicate?"

"I think not, he likes the solitude."

"Most odd for a dwarf, they like to be with others."

"As does he, when the time to drink ale arrives."

Taking the stones and mithril he examined them carefully before handing them back to her, "I cannot do it."

"Please sir, I beg you to make them for me. I will pay any price you ask, apprentice myself to you for a year if you would but make them."

"You are kin of Malinna and if I could make such rings I would, there would be no price set for the task."

"They why do you refuse to make the rings?"

"I've never made a ring of dragon tears, I may ruin the stones."

"Have little fear, Malinna speaks you are the best in the making of rings."

"Malinna sings my praises when she should whisper. If I were to fail...."

"I absolve you of any mishap yet you will make them as you have never made a ring before. This I know, you will make all four rings."

"I'll try for a promise. You speak nothing of my work for you; I have a reputation to uphold."

Sat in her mother's house she placed the rings in front of her, watching their faces as they gazed on them, feeling humble as she spoke, "There is one for each, take the one you would like."

In turn they took one each.

She placed the last one on her own finger. "This one is for me."

"This is the gift Voldare gave you?"

"Yes, Icee."

Malinna placed the ring on her finger, "The mithril is enchanted, and within the week none but the owner may wear the ring."

She took her daughters hand, "Voldare has a heart to match his size."

"I like Voldare he and I seemed to enjoy the company of each other."

"Ah, then he did not tell you he was ordered to bring you before the ancient one, so he may eat you?"

Her eyes widened, "He wanted me dead?"

She laughed, "A short tale I may now tire you with."

They talked for hours before she finally left the house and stood to watch the sunset, contentment deep inside her.

"They sit and speak as they have not done for many a summer."

"Father, are you disappointed you have not a ring?"

"Dragon tears are not for me, they are given only to deserving females."

"I sat in thought of what to do for days. Caspo Kwil came to see me thinking I was ill for not attending training. I spoke to him of the tears and he agreed, making rings of them was best."

"A wise elf. He guided your mother from the first day of her training."

"He guides me also, yet he is old in years and wonders who he must choose as his successor, I feel mother will be chosen. Do you know the honour leadership would bestow on her?"

"I know the honour which would be mine were I chosen as guild elder."

"Yet mother is wood elf, never has one been an enchantress and now she may lead the guild. My heart is bursting with pride for her."

"She may not be chosen."

"She will be chosen by him I see it in his every move."

"I hear you train in private with him, as your mother before you."

"He takes it to himself to ensure I am trained as hard as he trained mother."

"She had no training during childhood and I had thought she would never make an enchantress. I am happy to be wrong."

"I know how hard it was for her. I feel the work she had to do to be accepted as an enchantress. Has she not spoken of this to you?"

"I have asked, always she changes the subject to other matters."

"She turns the subject when she likes not to speak of it, her way to defend herself. Those days still pain her, best you speak of it with her. Now is a good time, she has the mood to talk."

The shrill cry of a hawk made her look up, excitement touching her heart, "He comes back to see me, father, may I go to him?"

His thoughts turned to the troubles his wife had when she was first accepted into the enchanters' guild. He had wanted her to talk to him so often of those days but each time she had evaded the question. Now he knew why, but this time she would not evade him so easily. He would ensure she told him all, when her sisters left.

She sighed, "You are persistent."

"I would know of those days and this time I will not be dissuaded. I once told you 'answer my questions as I asked them, it would be a starting point I believe'."

"I remember those words; it is where I will start."

She had been cornered, but she had wanted to be, and this time she wished to answer his questions. She had wondered how long it would be before he would be persistent enough not to be veered onto another subject, "On the third week from my birth mother sat me on the floor and offered me a root, one poisonous to me."

"She wished you not to take it, if you did not it would show you had druid ways."

"I knew her mind, and of the test."

"Impossible, none of such age may know. The reason it is taken so young."

"I knew, as did my sisters. Mother took the root before I placed it in my mouth. She knew I was no druid, as she knew my sisters were not."

"She tested them also?"

"She had to be sure she knew what profession they would be. Yet she could not be sure of me. I was to follow you for you are a druid as my sisters were to follow Xandorian and Keitun to their guilds. She knew they would take the root yet I should not have done so. I confused her so much; she has spoken often to me of it."

"Your ways always confuse others, and I know you remember everything ever spoken to you."

"I confused my mother for a while, until near my eighth year I believe."

"This I know, it is your training with your guild I wish to hear."

"Caspo Kwil took to my training in private at all times. It was not until the end of my eighth month did I meet the others I was to train with."

"Why so?"

"It was his wish. He had fears for me and what may happen were I to join the guild too soon. He trained me hard from first light until almost midnight. He taught me well and I became good enough to join the guild. Until then he had spoken to none of me, although many were curious as to why he did not attend training."

"Why train you so long into the night?"

"I had had no formal teaching before I left for the guild, being none to train me in the forest. I had so many years to catch up, and still he fought to keep the secret. He had me dress in clothes of one not yet of guild so none should see me and realise. Then came the day I must enter the guild and stand before them, it was the worst day of my life, as it still remains."

"I would have thought it to be a happy one."

"The others hated me, never has another but high elf been an enchantress. They would not speak with me or help me, I was shunned and it hurt so much. For many weeks they would not accept me and I trained before the guild always with Caspo Kwil, which served to annoy them more. He would train any he found lacking in a skill yet he had not done so for months. He trained me in singing, and did so in front of all. Always did he speak singing was my weakness."

"I love to hear you sing."

"You say so out of wedlock, yet I mind it not. My voice is poor when you listen how sweet Nortee sings."

"Think not to sway me away from which I seek, I would know all this night."

"One day he stood before the guild and offered the challenge to all there."

"What challenge?"

"The challenge of the enchanters. He asked if any would enter my mind and have me leave, never to return, I would be barred from the guild."

"I thought him your friend."

"I could not believe his words, you know not how I felt when all stood to offer the challenge. Caspo Kwil called the highest amongst them to the challenge and we sat in the arena."

"I knew not there was an arena. Of what level was this enchanter?"

"It is a close secret, the high elves have no wish to be seen to have flaws and such would show they have one. He called forth Jenay, an enchantress of the twenty-first understanding, mentor to the class."

"You could not hope to beat a mentor, and I would have thought the females would be more the likely to protect you."

"They were the worst of all, females can be..." She searched for the right word, "whistern's at times."

"I know not the word, speak it in wood elf."

She felt her face flush, "I cannot say the word."

"I think I know."

"I was terrified, thinking I had somehow failed him and this was his way to be rid of me from the guild and still keep the respect of all there. We sat with our backs to each other and he gave the command to start. I was determined I would not be beaten. The Gods had decreed what I was to be and I would serve their wishes. "

"I begin to see why he had you sit back to back."

"An enchantress must see the one whose mind they have need to enter, Jenay could not see me and, therefore, not my mind. Yet I entered hers and commanded she leave the arena. She rose and left."

"It would seem Caspo Kwil knew you need not see the person."

"He knew yet I did not. He is wise in ways beyond which I could ever be."

"From this time the others respected you?"

"On the contrary, they hated me more and tried so many ways to make me leave the guild."

"I knew not you were so unhappy."

"I was unhappy yes, so I looked on them as a test and then I did not mind their silly games. All changed for me when you became known to them."

"How did I change matters?"

"They hated me more, calling me a swik. You know the word?"

"I have an idea as to its meaning. I heard you use the word to Veldeth."

"They tormented me to the limits over you; it was when they threatened to charm you and make you attack the guards I became mad, the guards would kill you with ease. I was furious with them, swearing all the words I knew in high elf to them. Ones they had used to me so often."

"I see now why you knew so many words when I was injured."

"I used more than words; I cast spells and hurt so many. I fought all present in my class, fifteen in all."

"An impossible fight."

"It was hard, yet I was beyond reason. The battle was noisy and the council heard the commotion and came to see what it was. I was so scared they would bar or even imprison me. They demanded an explanation and Caspo Kwil came forth to answer yet the others would not let him explain telling them it was a free for all practice somehow out of hand."

"They protected you?"

"They wished me to fight and prove my worth, yet I did not see it. You know why I took to learning how to read the bodies of each I meet? To me it is a form of protection."

"Pose had the same problems?"

"Yes, yet the mould had been broken. They were used to the idea of change and she was accepted quickly. She is a firm friend to many of the guild. The new ones adore her and her ways; I have heard them as they speak of the games she lets them play when she is not around. The highest levels train her and give voice to their thoughts. Few are so popular yet she seemed as if she knew it not for many months."

"Now I see why you use not magic until you must. You have never liked to hurt; it must have been hard for you."

"To harm so many enchanters was pain to me. They were right, at the time I did become a swik."

"Caspo Kwil nears the end of his years, who does he choose to lead the guild when he sits with the Gods?"

"Have you not guessed the answer?"

"I have spoken to Nortee. I have an idea as to who it may be."

"Caspo Kwil has no heir to his position yet voiced to Ilsto Ventrel his thoughts I should follow in his stead."

"How would the enchanters feel for you to lead them?"

"Pose spoke with me a short while ago; Jenay also wishes me to be the leader and spoke to others of her thoughts, all are of the same mind yet the council will disagree with Caspo Kwil and with the guild."

"Then a fight must ensue."

"More so than you may realise."

"I know your ways, wife, plans are forming in your mind."

"Since I knew of his thoughts I have pondered the consequences."

"You have done more, such is obvious."

It was time to deflect him, her plans were not yet fixed and she needed her sisters to help in them, "Do you realise how proud I am? Never before has a guild asked for one to be their leader, it has always been the decision of the council. On the death of Caspo Kwil the guild will be called forth on the following new moon to hear who it is to be. I must be with them. If they will listen not then fighting will ensue; you know well the result."

"Lore says should the guilds fight then all elfin kind will perish."

"I agree, yet it is why the guilds *must* fight."

Next. Guild Wars

214